THROW OFF SPARKS

A RILEY REEVES MYSTERY

Michael Pool

P.I. Tales
Denver, Colorado
www.pitales.com

Book and Cover design by P.I. Tales
Edited by Chris Rhatigan

First Edition: May 2020

ISBN: 978-1-7345495-0-8

But I can hardly sit still. I keep fidgeting, crossing one leg and then the other. I feel like I could throw off sparks, or break a window – maybe rearrange all the furniture.

-Raymond Carver, *Where I'm Calling From*

PROLOGUE

The rain cleared out and left the streets feeling like a steam shower as I crept south on Harry Hines in the right lane, stopping every so often to check the street girls' faces against pictures on my phone, hoping in equal parts that I both did and did not find a match for the petite brunette with innocent green eyes in the picture.

My clients' words replayed in my mind every time a girl's face came close to a match. *We don't care where she is or what she's been doing, we just want Kaylee home.*

It wasn't the first time I'd heard that sentiment from a girl's parents. Often, they had a hard time making good on their promises when the details came clear, and the girls would end up back in the same situation, only more hurt than before.

With luck, the experience only left them a little worse off. Without it, they often overdosed or disappeared, or their parents were right back in my office the next week, begging me to find their daughter again.

I finally picked out Kaylee Richardson coming out of a convenience store two blocks south of Royal.

The green eyes gave her away. They were still big and round like in the pictures, but with a reptilian glare replacing the innocence. If such a thing as innocence existed to begin with. I had my doubts about that.

I drove down the block and parked in an old hotel's parking lot. It had been a Holiday Inn at some point in the past, but time had stripped it of its corporate franchise and left it dilapidated and forgotten. Now a half-lit sign with a hole the shape of a rock labeled it The Jupiter Inn.

I backed my grey Honda Pilot into a spot by the sidewalk and got out to lean against the back bumper.

Times like these I regretted quitting smoking, though my heart had never really been in it. I'd mostly done it for an excuse to spend time with my ex-husband while he drank himself into a coma on the back porch at night. When we split, I quit, no longer requiring the connection.

Kaylee stopped a hundred feet from me when a late-model Ford Taurus pulled into the driveway in front of her and tooted its horn.

The Taurus' driver said something to her through the open passenger window that I was too far away to hear, but I had a good idea about the subject matter.

Kaylee looked down the street in my direction and up the other. She gestured toward the hotel behind me and said something to the driver, then headed off toward the hotel's side door. The Taurus made a U-turn at the next block and came back toward us. It turned into the hotel and pulled in up against the building.

"Kaylee," I called out as she made her way over to the car. She stopped at the mention of her name, her head already turning in my direction out of habit. I hoped I didn't look like police in my battered grey Asics, torn jeans, and blue three-quarter-sleeve ringer t-shirt. I almost always kept my curly black hair pulled back, which didn't help matters.

"I know you?" she asked, pulling on a thin cigarette I'd watched her light outside the gas station.

I shook my head. "Not yet. My name is Riley Reeves, your parents sent me to make sure you're okay."

Electricity washed over her at the mention of her folks. No doubt shame had run her out of Tyler, Texas, a socialite gossip mill where everyone knew everyone's business and no one tried to hide that. But only desperation could have landed her in a place like this, where anonymity might shield her from judgment, but her addiction could only mute the danger to a dull throb in thirty-minute bursts.

"Tell them to leave me alone," she said, flipping away the cigarette as if to shake off an insect, then turning to walk away.

"Kaylee, wait," I said.

The Taurus' driver froze halfway out of the car when he noticed us talking.

Kaylee's eyes tracked him as she spoke. "They wanted me out, so I've been out. Nothing else to say. Now kick rocks, you're cramping my style."

"Kaylee," I said again. She shot me the finger and beamed a fake smile across the lot to the driver.

"Everything good to go?" he asked, glaring at me from behind the safety of the car's open door. I made note of his appearance, about six foot with a paunch belly and balding head, Lou Case shirt half unbuttoned above jeans that had to be two decades old.

"Everything's fine," Kaylee said to him. "This lady's on a mission from God, but she decided to go to hell instead."

I memorized the Taurus' plate as I walked across the lot and around the other side of the building. When I rounded the corner I started to run, hoping to make it into the door on the other side of the building in time to see which room she went into.

I caught sight of the far stairwell door slamming shut as I stepped inside.

The place smelled like a mixture of cat piss and vomit. In some places, the carpet had peeled back from the pocked walls, which I assumed were full of mice. I'd been in this same hotel the day before, where a disinterested Indian clerk assured me he'd never seen the Kaylee in my picture before.

Maybe he hadn't, given recent changes.

I took off down the hall and opened the stairwell just in time to see the door a floor up close. My footfalls echoed as I took the first set of VCT tile stairs. I dodged a puddle of what looked to be urine on the landing before taking the second set two at a time.

It opened to an empty hallway that smelled as bad as the first, with a lingering smell of burned marijuana.

I wanted to figure out which room was hers, see if I could get her to talk to me after her date left. Nothing I could do about what happened between now and then. Or so I thought.

I made my way down the hall and back, listening closely at each door for voices. Some rooms had televisions playing. Others had no sounds at all. A few had the unmistakable anonymous grunting that accompanies sex work.

I stopped again at the closest door to the stairwell, which I figured was hers, and put my ear up to the yellowed, cracking paint.

"I told you I don't do weirdo fetish stuff," a voice I made out as Kaylee's said.

"I'm not asking," a male voice replied. There was a hollow smack and Kaylee moaned.

I tried the handle but it held, as expected, so I banged on the door and called out her name. The room fell silent for a moment, then the male voice spoke again.

"You setting me up, is that it?" he said.

Kaylee whimpered but didn't respond. I reared up like a horse and kicked the door above the handle.

It didn't give, so I kicked again. And again.

I stumbled and fell sideways on the fourth kick, saving my own life. Two shots from inside the room sent door fragments spraying out into the hall. The bullets struck the wall beyond where I'd been not two breaths before.

I hit the floor and rolled right in the direction I'd fallen. I had to fight the urge to get up and run.

Kaylee screamed from inside the room.

"Open your mouth," the man's strained voice said. "Now. And you, out in the hall," he continued, "I'll blow her brains all over this room if you don't back off."

I took a deep breath to calm my nerves.

"Don't do anything drastic," I said. "We both know that the cops are on the way, the entire building probably heard the shots. My guess, they'll be here in a few minutes, maybe less. But you can still get out of this unharmed if you'll listen to me." I paused to give him a chance to digest my words, then added, "Now. How much money do you need?"

"What?" the man said, his voice shaky now, probably from the adrenaline.

"How much did you pay her?" I asked.

"Seventy-five." His voice sounded far off now, hollow.

"Okay," I said. "I'm going to drop two one-hundred-dollar bills right here outside the door, for your trouble. Then I'm going to go back to my room and let you leave in peace. All you have to do is grab the cash on your way out the door, get in your car, and drive away. No one will ever bother you about this again afterward, I guarantee it. Everybody goes their separate ways, you with an extra $125 in your pocket."

He didn't respond. I tried again.

"Look, we're running out of time," I said. "I'm going to slide the money under the door so you can see it. Please don't shoot me. Then I'm going back to my room so you can be on your way. Here." I crawled over and slid the money under the door, doing my best to stay low and out of the line of fire.

"There it is," I said. "Do you see it under the door?"

"I see it," he said. His voice sounded hoarse like his mouth had gone slack and dry.

"Okay, good. I'm gone now. I was you, I'd go too. Cops could be here any second."

I backed down the hall and ducked into an unlocked linen closet that had garbage in it instead of supplies. The smell would normally have made me wretch, but with my adrenaline so high, I barely took note of it.

I pulled the pulse Taser in my back waist holster out and peeked through the cracked closet door to watch.

The handle clicked and the door swung open. The man I'd seen in the parking lot stuck his head out and looked both ways down the hall. He knelt down and picked up the cash while he scanned with a chrome revolver, what looked to be a .38, in his right hand. He backed toward the stairs sweeping the hall with the .38, then turned and pushed through the stairwell door in a hurry.

I stepped out into the hall with the targeting laser already on his left kidney and popped him with fifty-thousand volts that sent him vaulting into space above the stairs.

The momentum sent the pistol over the rail as the door swung shut between us, severing the Taser's line. I heard him hit the landing with a muted thud.

I found him collapsed there in the piss puddle on the landing, took the stairs two at a time and hit him with the Taser's contact stun for good measure. That put him down for a while.

I retrieved the .38 and ran back up the stairs, stopping to grab as many of the identification tags from the Taser as I could see from the hall carpet. No use leaving unnecessary tracks, though I doubted anyone would notice them.

The door to Kaylee's room hadn't shut all the way. Kaylee, naked from the waist down, was curled up into a ball on the bed, hugging her knees. She had a split lip, bruised cheek, and wild, almost catatonic eyes.

"We need to go," I said. She looked at me from a thousand miles away and I worried she'd gone into shock. "Kaylee, did you hear me?" I said.

Again she didn't respond. I pulled her up by the arm and guided her toward the door anyway.

Her eyes came into focus at my touch, but she made no move to resist.

"Where are you taking me?" she finally stammered as we stepped into the hallway.

"Home," I said. "But we need to get out of here soon or there will be trouble."

"Okay," she whispered.

We made our way down the stairs. Her attacker had managed to get to his knees on the landing by then. Kaylee stiffened at the sight of him, then pulled away from me and soccer kicked him right between the eyes. His face erupted and dropped into the slurry of urine and blood on the concrete landing. I bent down and snatched the Taser cartridge from his back, then we continued down the stairs.

Sirens radiated in the distance as we got into my Pilot. I put it in drive and used my blinker to make a right onto the street. I had confidence that my surveillance vehicle was unremarkable enough to go unnoticed, but there was no need to draw attention by driving erratically or breaking minor laws. I reached into the go-bag behind Kaylee's seat and pulled out a pair of sweatpants I used as pajamas when files kept me out of town overnight.

"Put these on," I said, handing them to her. She nodded and complied as best she could in the cramped space.

I swung onto I-30 with the Bank of America building's neon green lights reflecting down onto the windshield. Twenty minutes later we were moving out of the city. Kaylee hadn't said another word in that time. She was fast asleep by the time we hit I-20 going east, headed back behind the Pine Curtain of East Texas, where we both belonged.

CHAPTER ONE

I UNLOCKED THE DOOR to my office, tucked into a small building on South Palace Street a few blocks off the square in downtown Tyler, and stepped into the musty hallway. I'd bought out my brother Chip's half three years before, a few years after we'd co-inherited the small, beige-brick building from our father. It had been left to us by our grandfather, who had run a small note car lot out of it in the seventies and eighties. I'd had to mortgage my half to buy Chip out, leaving me with more overhead than I would have liked but enough autonomy to make up for the cost.

I worked as a private investigator to pay the building's mortgage now.

The small blacktop lot still had faded yellow parking spaces around the perimeter where the inventory had once been parked. Legend had it that in the 1970s my grandfather had latched onto an angry customer's open car windowsill and knocked the man unconscious as he recklessly circled the lot trying to escape, eventually slamming into the beige brick on the back of the building.

The brick was a different color where they'd fixed the damage, and the story only sounded crazy if you didn't know the Reeves family's reputation.

My father always said I'd inherited my temper from my grandfather, Ralph Reeves. He'd been hard on my father. So hard that they'd barely spoken for the last ten years of Grandad's life, but that detail never made its way into the family legend, forever buried behind the veil of propriety that masked most Tyler families.

Mail had piled up on the floor beneath the mail slot over the couple of days I spent tracking down Kaylee Richardson. Her family had been ecstatic to see her home, though she'd seemed less happy to see them. Either way, the case was over, for now.

Judging by the bills I found sorting through the mail, I needed to find another case ASAP.

I unlocked the steel door that led to my personal office, the only room in the building with no windows. My grandfather had the steel doorframe installed along with the impact-proof door as a security precaution because they took weekly cash payments from their customers. *We Tote the Note*, the sign out front had once read. For all intents and purposes, the interior office served as my safe room now, though I'd never had to use it as such.

The surrounding area had always been rough at night. I kept an alarm system on the property that I controlled through my smartphone, and cameras I could control the same way.

But it still made sense to protect against smash-and-grab break-ins by locking down the interior office itself. Other than a body found in the abandoned clapboard house behind the lot, I'd never had any trouble. But lately I'd been finding more and more of it in my work, so the security made sense.

The old, worn-out building had a comfort to it borne of my childhood memories washing cars out back.

My older brothers had both done the same, spending summer weekdays shampooing carpets and scrubbing fenders for $5.15 an hour. Watching the same cars recycle through the lot over and over as people inevitably failed to pay them off and had them repossessed instead. The business model always bothered me, though as I grew, I came to see there were two sides to the story.

A framed cross-stitch that my grandad had gotten after finding sobriety in his late fifties still hung on the office wall. It read, *God grant me the serenity to accept the things I cannot change, the courage to change the things I can, and the wisdom to know the difference.* It amounted to a personal prayer for me now, a roadmap to navigate the internal struggle that constantly threatened to tear me apart.

In my heart, there was nothing on earth I could not change. Except for myself, of course. That kind of stubbornness has a danger to it, but no amount of wisdom ever seemed to convince me to behave otherwise. Serenity had never darkened my door, maybe never would. Courage I had in spades, but that brought an entirely new set of problems along with it.

The office phone had one voicemail, from Jerry Richardson, calling to thank me again for finding Kaylee and bringing her home. As glad as I was that she hadn't taken off again, the message also made me stew a little. I'd hoped it might be another case, or at least some insurance work to keep me billing. New work was always a challenge to lock down in the rural East Texas economy. Even something as small as a few days of insurance surveillance would do me right, just then.

My smartphone's screen lit up with my best friend Latonya's smiling face on it, bringing me out of my brooding.

"Hey girl," I said by way of answering.

"Don't hey girl me, Riley," Latonya's big, booming voice said. "Why you ain't been answering my calls and texts?"

I sighed audibly into the phone to let her hear my contrition. I had a habit of not returning calls while working a case. But only in the most stressful times did I dare not answer Latonya's calls. She was the kind of friend who would break her back to keep you from skinning your knee. Not the kind of friend who took kindly to having smoke blown up her ass.

"I'm sorry, L," I said. "Things got a little crazy and I needed some time to sort it out. You know how it is."

"Mmhmm. I know how you is. Just like I know you snuck in the back door last night and went straight to sleep to avoid having to talk about it. Done the same thing this morning, snuck back out. If I knew you was gonna make things so awkward, I'd never have agreed to move in."

"Sorry," I said. "I promise I'll cut it out. What's been up with you?"

"Shoot, workin', like always. You know I'm just messing with ya, right?"

I laughed. "Of course. Hey, what are you up to for lunch?"

L had a way of lightening my dark moods. We'd been friends since the first day of school in the sixth grade when she'd wowed me from the front row in gym class, making up humiliating rhymes about the boys who were trying to flirt with any girls who would look at them. They'd mostly left me alone or ignored me, which I preferred anyway. No one could ignore Latonya, with her powerful laugh and sharp tongue.

After my divorce, when I started really allowing myself to fall into the black holes of my work, L had insisted on moving into my place to keep me company. Or, as I saw it, to keep an eye on me and make sure I didn't get too unmoored from reality.

We lived in the small ranch-style home my brothers and I had grown up in, located five miles out of town down Old Jacksonville Highway at the end of a private caliche rock road, the house at the center of thirty acres that now had a toll road backing up to it.

My father had raised longhorns on the property after his retirement from the sheriff's department, but now the only animals around were the pack of stray dogs and cats I occasionally fed when they showed up hungry. The worn-out white picket fence around the house no longer had any livestock to keep out and wouldn't have accomplished much if it had.

"I was gonna pick up some Earl Campbell's from the hotlink spot on my break, but if you want to go together, I be all right with eating tacos," Latonya said.

"How do you know I want Taqueria?" I grinned into the phone.

"Girl, please. You the most predictable maniac I ever met. If anything, I'm surprised you ain't already been over there this morning."

"They weren't open yet," I said.

That was another thing I liked about L. She knew my habits. Beyond a little teasing, she accepted them. We'd both spent plenty of evenings in high school eating number sixes slathered with enough red and green sauce to make smoke come out of your ears. At least mine had been.

"Meet you there at eleven thirty?" I said.

"Bet. I see you then."

L hung up and I set my smartphone on the desk, went back to sorting the bills. Halfway through the stack, I found a letter from my brother Charlie, who everyone called Chip. Like all his letters, it was marked Charlie Reeves, inmate 11355269, postmarked from the Stevenson Unit, Cuero, Texas.

I was in the process of opening it using a switchblade letter opener Chip had given me for Christmas when the bell on the front door dinged.

"Hello?" a woman's voice called out.

"Back here," I said, setting down the letter. Two sets of footsteps shuffled down the short hallway and stopped at the office's steel doorframe as if it were the entrance to a jail cell. It was a man and a woman, both in their late forties, both with an air of projected wealth.

"Miss Reeves?" the man asked, placing his right hand into the front pocket of a navy-blue sport coat that hung unbuttoned over a white button-up shirt. A snakeskin belt and neatly starched jeans over matching snakeskin boots completed the getup. My father had called that kind of outfit a Texas tuxedo.

The woman wore a black lace blouse divided at the waist from an accented skirt by a white belt with a golden rose for a buckle. She had makeup caked on her face like putty to fill in the wrinkles and a lot of jewelry hanging like Christmas ornaments off her wrists and neck. In spite of the makeup, she had a confident, attractive quality, the kind of woman who must have been very striking in her day.

I nodded. "Yes. Can I help you folks?"

The man started to speak, but the woman cut him off. "You're the detective from the papers, the one who helped catch the serial killer, what was his name, Barlowe?"

Her tone suggested she had a hard time believing the plain, unassuming woman seated in front of her could do such a thing. But I had.

The man she referred to, Carl Vincent Farlow, had been a local storm chaser turned serial murderer. He'd used natural disasters to cover his tracks over the course of a twenty-year killing spree that claimed at least nine victims before I dropped onto his head.

I'd taken an interest in his work as a distraction from my divorce, which was still playing out in those days.

He'd been suspected for years, but no one had been able to link him to the killings.

Eventually, I'd cornered him in Hurricane Harvey's churning surge and helped save the life of a woman he was in the process of mutilating. It was still a touchy subject for me now, in part because it brought up the wounds of my divorce, but also because the coward had committed suicide in custody and never lived to stand trial for his evil.

The families of his victims would never feel the closure they desired and, as a result, neither would I. I had a fixation on justice that L constantly reminded me was more vindictive than fair.

My entire life had pivoted on that experience. Now, thirteen months later, it still felt like unfinished business. The case had launched me into a new version of my career, helping parents and women in crisis, taking risks that often got difficult to justify as anything else but obsession.

"Yes ma'am, I am," I responded.

"Huh." The woman took a fancy pink iPhone out of her purse and clicked it to life. Maybe she wanted to double-check my face against the news broadcast online, or maybe she had something else in mind. Either way, she'd managed in less than one minute to wear on my nerves in a way that only a very specific breed of East Texas women could do.

Her neat, shoulder-length black hair looked like she'd spent hours on it and framed cold blue eyes that found the world around them, my world, lacking in fundamental value. She was the kind of woman who had either come from money or become so good at pretending that you'd have to see her bank statements from the last thirty years to tell for sure.

I wanted to chew her up and spit her back out, but I needed work, so I smiled instead and waited for her to tell me why they'd stopped into my office.

She continued. "I... we... Oh, hell, why don't you take over, Paul, this was all your idea anyway," the woman said. Her husband nodded, probably wondering why she'd interrupted him in the first place. Or maybe he was used to it. He looked used to it, I decided.

"Miss Reeves, we'd like to hire you on a case, if you're interested," he said.

"I could be," I replied, measuring my words to keep from saying too much too fast. I've never cared for pure walk-in clients, they're often more trouble than they're worth. Like most investigators, I prefer to source my work from attorneys, or insurance companies, or at least from walk-in mothers who knew how to introduce themselves without trampling on my last nerves. "Let's start at the beginning. I didn't catch y'all's names."

The man relaxed a little and let out his breath. "I'm sorry, that was rude of us. My name is Paul Wallace. This is my wife, LeeAnne. You come highly recommended from a friend over at the Smith County Sheriff's Office."

"I see," I said, wondering if one of my father's former colleagues had sent them to me. "What's your friend's name? And please, have a seat." I directed them to the two angular Eames armchairs across from my desk. I clicked my phone to life and hit the record button on my voice notes. LeeAnne eyed it as if it were spraying out nerve gas.

The chairs had been in that room since the 1970s but were mid-century in origin. They reminded me of my grandfather, who had always been sweet to me in spite of his reputation. I'd been told they were classics but had no frame of reference. They'd been there for so long now that they managed to look chic in their retro style, I did know that much.

The style must have been lost on the Wallaces because they both hesitated before shuffling into the office and sitting on the orange cushions. If LeeAnne had taken out a sanitary wipe and rubbed hers down first it would not have surprised me in the least. Instead, she sat on the edge as if trying to touch as little of the surface as possible.

Paul Wallace continued. "His name is Deputy David Bell. He's fairly new on the force, couple years, I think. His father works for my company, Wallace Oil. With the problems we've been having, I had him stop by our house to look around and see if he had any advice. We don't want to make a big fuss and embarrass or stress out our daughter any more than she already is, but..."

"Someone is stalking our daughter, Carmen," LeeAnne broke in, cutting him off again. "And not just any someone. I'm sure it's our trashy neighbor boy, Kaleb Parks. He's had a crush on Carmen since we first moved in."

"I see," I said. "So what do you need me for? It sounds like you've got it solved already. I assume the sheriff's department would probably be a better fit to handle the problem, no?"

"You see?" LeeAnne said, gesturing to her husband as if to suggest his density could swallow stars. She looked back at me to be sure I'd caught the gesture, then added, "That's exactly what I told Paul. We know it's him. I have half a mind to go over there with daddy's shotgun and give him two good reasons to back off, but Paul says that will only make things worse."

"The problem is we don't have much evidence to go on," her husband interjected. "But someone is leaving notes on our daughter's car, knocking on her window, stuff like that. Carmen's already had a lot of health issues in recent years. She was just getting back on her feet from her most recent lapse when all this harassment started up.

"Phone calls in the middle of the night, tapping on her upstairs window, drawing lewd stuff on the windows of her car. Whoever it is, the little son of a bitch is sneaky. Other than a few half footprints, we've never even come close to catching them in the act. In fact, the three game cameras I hung up around the house disappeared the first night they were there."

"I see," I said. "That does sound like a problem. So tell me this. How can I help?"

"I thought that would be obvious," Paul said. "You can catch the little goober in the act and give us enough evidence to get a protective order. Or else prove it's someone else. Right now David says we have nothing to go on to get a protective order or have him arrested for harassment and stalking. He did stop over and talk to

Kaleb, but the little punk denies everything. I've seen him out wandering around on the back of their property, right where it butts up to ours. There's nothing but a barbed wire fence separating the properties, so he's got easy enough access. When we first moved in, he came on and off our property like it was part of theirs. His parents run a small horse farm over there. Fine horses, but the rest of the property could use some work, you ask me."

I sat back in my chair and considered what they were saying. I wasn't sure what to make of it.

LeeAnne leaned forward, legs crossed so tight it left creases in her skirt. She seemed like she wanted to say something and was waiting for the right time to land it with maximum effect.

I decided to wait her out.

"So?" she finally asked.

"So, what?"

"So are you going to help us? And so, what is this going to cost? And so, why should we hire you? I can't get a read on what you're up to."

I smiled. Her attitude amused me. She had good social instincts because I was sort of playing a game with her, seeing how she would respond.

"The short answer is I'm not up to anything. Just listening and taking the problem in. And as for why you should hire me, I'm not sure you should. Don't get me wrong, I could use the work. But it seems like a beefed-up security system would probably solve your problem for the most part. Or if not, I'm not sure what services I would actually provide, unless you want a bodyguard for your daughter."

"Absolutely NOT," LeeAnne said. "Under no circumstances do I want you so much as even speaking to Carmen. She's fragile, and she's been through more in the last two years than most girls go through in a lifetime. People in this town talk more than they should. I don't want them talking about this. She was just starting to bloom again after her most recent medical troubles when this happened. You can't imagine the sort of stress that puts on a mother, too."

She was right about that. I'd never wanted kids, had no real sense of motherly instinct. Not that I didn't care. I did. I'd just never been particularly nurturing or girly.

"Maybe to start with, you could come out and give us some security recommendations," Paul said. "I read that private detectives do security consulting, is that something you can handle?"

I figured his wife was probably doubling down on things by being insufferable at home. I could barely tolerate her here in my office and it had only been five minutes, so I felt for him. He wanted a solution today, or at least something that gave his wife enough of a sense of enough control to calm her down.

"I could do that," I said. "But I bet a security specialist would be even more help than me in that regard. I specialize in missing persons and surveillance. I could recommend a better security consultant than me if you want to beef up your home system. Or else I could develop a safe-movement plan and give your daughter a few tips on how to follow it if you don't want full personal protection. But it sounds like you don't want me to do that."

"Maybe there is someone better," LeeAnne said, her milky teeth poking through below pursed red lips. I got the impression they might flee her mouth if she smiled, but she never gave them the opportunity.

"Honey, butt out for a minute and let me talk to the lady," Paul said, cutting off whatever she wanted to say next.

Her face was more dismissive than upset at the comment. She relaxed into her seat and let him talk.

"Maybe you could ask some questions, take a look around the property for evidence Kaleb is coming across the fence line?" he said.

He had his heart set on dealing with the problem today, that much was clear. And I did need the money, this woman's attitude aside. An idea came to me, so I tossed it out.

"I can't make any promises, but here's what I'll do. I'll think it over this afternoon and see if I can find a clear inroad to solving the problem for you beyond security. If I can, I'll speak with you about a retainer this evening. If not... well, we tried. All I'd need from you, in that case, is a small bit of permission."

"Permission?" Paul repeated as if trying to digest the word. "I'm not sure I follow."

"I mean permission to interview your daughter this evening before I decide. I want to see what she has to say first."

"Absolutely not," LeeAnne said. "Are you deaf? Carmen is under enough stress with keeping her grades up for college and hardly sleeping because this psycho won't stop tapping on her window and taping notes to her damn car. No way you're coming in and putting a bunch of new ideas into her head to make it worse. Our household is stressful enough. I can barely sleep either."

Paul crossed his arms. "She's fine, LeeAnne. It's you that's stressing her out by being so worked up about everything. Besides, a little stress is worth trading off in case Miss Reeves can find a solution." He looked from his wife to me. "Miss Reeves, I want you on this because my understanding is that you're a bit of a champion for girls who are in trouble. David assured us your father was a respected deputy at Smith County for many years, too. Carmen needs someone she can trust who understands her position, someone who wants to help her. To me, another woman makes more sense than anyone else. It will keep her calm. You can speak with her tonight around eight, if that suits you?"

LeeAnne scowled.

I nodded in agreement and took out a new client packet from the drawer by my left leg. "That'll hunt," I said, my father's favorite turn of phrase. "In the meantime, fill out the first page of this packet with your info so I know how to get in touch with y'all. The rest we'll leave in the air until after I speak with Carmen this evening."

Paul took the packet from me and started filling it out with a pen from his breast pocket. LeeAnne crossed her arms and acted like she could not care less about any of us. For my part, I wanted to get them on out of the office so I could get to lunch with L on time.

Lord knows I'd worked up an appetite dealing with LeeAnne Wallace, and anyway who knew how much more of my blowoffs L could take. I sure didn't want to find out.

CHAPTER TWO

L WAS ALREADY WAITING when I pulled up to Taqueria El Lugar. The Wallaces had finally left in a fit of reluctance. I promised to meet them around eight at their residence, which was out on the edge of the city limits. That would hopefully give me enough time and daylight to take a quick look around their property before speaking with Carmen. I had no idea what to think of their story. I'd just have to treat it with the usual skepticism until instinct told me otherwise.

"Hey girl," I called out to L as I approached. She made a show of fanning herself against the heat with a real estate catalog taken from a stand against the wall behind her. The small white building had a Mexican pueblo feel, arched brick windowsills lined with red-and-green stripes on the stucco walls. A second story had been added on about ten years earlier to accommodate more seating but looked like it had always been there now.

The building itself was tucked up between a private residence the owners lived in on one side and a Valero gas station on the other. Beckham Street ran past the front, separating it from a Hispanic neighborhood I'd hardly ever ventured into. The entire northeast side of town was considered the Hispanic side, according to the white people living south of Loop 323. Segregation had ended more than fifty years before, but it seemed like most people in East Texas still wanted it on all sides. The restaurant only took cash and had been there for at least thirty years.

"Hey," L said back to me. "What took you so long?"

"Had a walk-in, potential client," I said, pulling open the door and holding it for her. "You could have waited in the AC inside."

"You know I don't like to be sitting around no bunch of people waiting. Shit make me nervous."

"Sunshine makes you sweat."

"Please, girl. I glisten. Anyway, I'm just messing with you. I only been here maybe five minutes."

We moved between the faux wood-grain booths and stood in the line for counter service. It had about ten people in front of us. Waiting was a given. The clerk still used a notepad to write down your order and manually operated an analog cash register to make change. At least with the addition upstairs, it wasn't a problem finding somewhere to sit anymore.

"I guess you ain't gonna say nothing else about the new client?" L said.

I shook my head. "Nothing to say right now, they're not a client yet."

"Yeah yeah, secret P.I. code and all that. I don't even care, anyway."

I smiled. "Yeah, you do. The only way you wouldn't is if I told you. Then you'd roll your eyes and say, 'Can we talk about something else, please?'"

L laughed at my impersonation of her, which was pretty good. I'd been practicing it on her for years. I knew her better than anyone on earth, save my brother Chip. She knew me about as well as I'd ever let anyone, too. I kept my cards close, and it tended to bother L. She wore her heart on her sleeve and dropped opinions on people like rain in a thunderstorm.

"You know I don't like secrets, though. And anyway, lunch be boring with you when you got a new case. You be sitting over there thinking the whole time while you pretend to listen."

"I don't pretend. I just get distracted when I have a lot going on."

"You only be distracted when you awake, is all. When don't you have a lot going on?"

"I could use to have more going on now, I'll tell you that," I said, my way of bringing the conversation back to a neutral place. "Caseload is slow and bills are getting ready to pile up. How are things with you at work?"

"Shoot, good. Somebody always need something, and mama Latonya always the woman to bring it to 'em. My feet gonna be flat by the time we forty at this rate."

I patted her arm and said, "Not so far off these days. But you love it. You'd be madder than a hornet if people weren't depending on you. It's what I love about you."

L laughed. "My heart as big as my booty, which mean it getting bigger all the time."

Latonya was the most comfortable person in her own skin that I'd ever known. Though she only stood about five feet five inches, she had powerful legs and a thick neck, a round shape that hid freakish strength and made her seem much taller. Her eyes could call coyotes, but that was an act. Beneath it all she had a heart so warm it would thaw your icebox. She cried in just about every movie we went to see, a mainstay activity on Friday nights back in high school, and more often at home now, since my divorce. When I didn't flake out.

As for men, L never kept one around long. She didn't seem to want one, either. It used to make me feel sad for her, until my own relationship went belly up and I realized how little I'd figured out on the subject. Lately, I'd started to see she had a point—maybe some people were better off alone.

"What are you gonna eat?" I asked. I already knew, but I liked the look on her face when she talked about it. For all the trouble she liked to give me about it, this was one of her favorite places to eat, too.

"Two number sevens, extra avocado, both dyin' for air under that green sauce. I already know what you gettin'. Two number ones and a number six. I don't know how you be squeezing lemon on yo tacos. That shit is nasty."

Unlike a lot of taquerias, El Lugar didn't have lime slices, only the lemons they used for water glasses and fresh-squeezed lemonade. Over the years I'd come to prefer lemon over lime, a point of contention between me and almost anyone in Texas who liked tacos.

I didn't take the bait. This line of conversation usually ended with agreeing to disagree anyway. And besides, I'd just stumbled across the unopened letter from Chip in my purse while digging for cash.

"When you get that?" L asked, gesturing to the letter.

"It was in my mail pile today at the office," I said.

Chip always sent his letters to my office. The idea of me living in our childhood home must not feel as real if he never sent mail there.

He'd been in prison for three years. Our mother had passed away a year and a half after he went in, which broke my heart in more ways than one. It broke his, too, but he never mentioned or admitted things like that. After my divorce, I'd moved into the house, which was just as it had been my entire life. Even now I had trouble changing anything, not even a decent security system to match the one in my office.

Our mother's will had left the house and the thirty acres surrounding it to the both of us. It was only a matter of time before that turned into a problem, I knew that. Even at the end, mother had never abandoned the hope that something, even just a house, might bring Chip and me back to our childhood closeness.

But I'd long ago learned that getting too close to Chip was like curling up with a rattlesnake. Sooner or later you'd get bit, and it might take months or even years to counteract the poison from that bite.

"Why you ain't opened it yet?" L said.

The construction worker in front of us finished paying for his order and moved to get a drink from the cooler next to the counter, saving me from having to answer.

For now. L would try again once we sat down. She knew what mattered to me almost more than I did. And she knew how much I liked to avoid all things Chip, as well as the guilt it always caused me. I wanted to be mad at her for it sometimes, but it was also the source of my greatest attachment to her. She was the most decent and intuitive person I knew, and she always knew the right thing to say or do.

I'd long thought that she would make a great detective, but anytime I mentioned it she'd clown all over me about not getting down on some Sherlock Holmes BS, so I stopped trying.

After we ordered, we bickered for a moment over who would pay. L won, as usual. I took my fresh-squeezed lemonade in a Styrofoam cup, and L took her bottle of Mexican Coke, to one of the booths upstairs. My butt barely hit the seat before she was on me again about Chip's letter.

"So?" she asked.

"So, what?" I said, which earned me a direct blast of side-eye.

"Girl, you think you complex, but you ain't. Stop playin' around and tell me why you ain't opened that letter from your brother."

I sighed. "Just a lot going on. A potential client stopped in and distracted me. Plus, it came on top of a stack of bills. It just seemed easier to leave the real trouble unopened and focus on the bills."

"Problems can't be contained by no damn envelope, Riley. You need, I give you some money to get straight on the bills at your office. You want you can take it out of the rent."

I shook my head. "That's okay, L, I've got it under control. Besides, since when do you pay rent?" I smiled to show her I was kidding. We both knew that she paid for so much else between us and that was why I always refused her rent check. The Hispanic woman from behind the counter arrived with our food, saving me again from having to say more about Chip.

She set down the two plates, L's wrapped up like burritos, mine laid out flat, the number ones with chopped asada, cabbage, onions, and cilantro, and the number six with the same beef on top of a half-inch of white, gooey cheese. Half a lemon sat in the middle of the plate.

The woman left and returned again with two squeeze bottles, one jalapeno green, and the other chili red. Both were spicy enough to melt a hole in a sheet metal barn.

I put a line of the red sauce down the middle of each taco, then squiggled enough of the green to turn them into soup. I topped it off with as much of the lemon juice as I could squeeze out of the rind and took a big, wet bite. It would have made me sweat through my shirt if not for the combination of the air conditioner blasting from the corner and the super-sweet lemonade, which balanced out the spice.

The rest of the meal left very little room for words between big, sloppy bites.

By the time we finished, L had to get back to work and I felt like I needed a nap. But at least I hadn't had to finish the conversation about Chip. That would have led in short order to a conversation about my ex-husband, Marty. He was Chip's lifelong best friend.

Except things don't ever work out that easy. Not ever. When I arrived back at the office, lo and behold my eyes must have deceived me. There was Chip sitting on the front step, a beige canvas duffle bag that had once been our father's sitting next to him.

He stood up as I pulled into my spot and shut off the engine, held his beat-up Stetson in his hand like an old-time cowboy gentleman, the same way our father always had. He looked so much like our late brother, Benjamin, and our dad, that it made me feel their loss all over again. But, as men, the two could not have been more different than Chip.

Our eyes met as I got out of the car. He grinned like he could sell a ketchup popsicle to a man in white gloves. I frowned, always uncomfortable with surprises.

"I guess y'all didn't get my note in the mail," Chip said, always able to read my reactions.

"Hey, wow," I replied. "I just got it a few minutes ago, actually. I've been out of town. I was waiting to open it until I had the proper time to devote to reading it this afternoon."

"Couple minutes ago, huh? And here I thought I'd been standing in this heat for the better part of an hour."

"You know what I mean," I said. "Now get over here and give me a damn hug. I've been worried about you, big brother."

He stepped up and wrapped me in a hug. At that moment it was easy to remember how much I had always loved him and forget all the things he'd done to erode that love over the years.

I'd followed him around like a shadow as a kid, even wished I could be a boy so that he would allow me to hang around more. That passed as hormones kicked in, but I'd never quite escaped the feeling that I needed something from my brother, and he'd never escaped the feeling that he would never be able to give it to me.

"How are you out of prison?" I said, pushing past him to unlock the office door. "I thought you had another year before they'd even consider parole."

"You sound like you want me to go back in," he said, still grinning. "Anyhow, it's a long story. I don't want to get into it just now. Here I thought you might be happy to see your last living relative."

The words stung. They reminded me that we'd once had another brother, Benjamin. And parents, God rest their souls. Our folks had both been so young when they passed, making Chip and I the last of a bloodline, unless Chip had a few illegitimate children running around somewhere. Which was possible.

All these years later, I still couldn't shake the feeling of being somehow responsible for our brother Ben's death, though he'd died on the other side of the planet at the hands of strangers in a warzone that no one could convince me was a worthwhile expenditure of human life.

The rush of nostalgic feelings for Chip morphed into painful memories of Ben, who we'd both idolized. Our nuclear family had never recovered from his loss, and

Chip had never stayed straight for more than a day afterward.

By the time I reached true adulthood, our father had just sort of faded off into his thoughts and memories, never to return, then died from a heart attack a few years after, like many of the men in our bloodline.

The doctor said it was all the smoked brisket, bacon, and Winston cigarettes that killed him, but I knew the truth. His heart had been attacking him nonstop since the day he found out Benjamin was gone. Heart failure was the only realistic outcome, holding it all in like that.

My mother, for her part, had been too stubborn to succumb to grief. It had taken stomach cancer and long, slow starvation to beat her. It would take more than that to best me, or so I liked to tell myself. My father would have said I sounded just like her talking like that.

The memories blew the last traces of my pleasant feeling out like a candle.

"Let's not do that yet, Chip, okay?" I said, trying to reignite the flame's warmth. "I am happy to see you. If you don't realize I've been worried sick the whole time you were gone, then you ought to have your head examined."

"That why you only came to see me three times in three years," he said, a statement rather than a question.

"I came more than that, didn't I?" I tried to count in my head but honestly couldn't recall.

He followed me into the building and stood behind me while I unlocked the interior door to my office, then dropped into the chair across from my desk like he'd done many times when taking a break from washing cars. I sat down behind the desk.

"Nope, you didn't. Marty did once a month, like clockwork, but not you. Trust me, there ain't a lot to do in there, so you tend to keep track of that kind of thing. I appreciate all the commissary money, though."

"I was happy to give it. I'm sorry I didn't visit more. It's just work gets intense, and with... well, with splitting from Marty, my life's been a little crazy."

"Too crazy for your big brother? There was a time I couldn't shake you off my leg, Rowdy."

My childhood nickname actually got a smile from me. "You wouldn't like trying to shake me off anymore," I said. "I'm pretty good at sticking on people. It's my job."

"Not so good at sticking on Marty, though."

The comment stung, just as he knew it would. I'd figured this discussion had to come sooner or later. Part of me had wanted it to wait. The naïve part. Chip and Marty had ties that ran even deeper than my own ties to either one. They had a redneck bromance that I could neither fathom nor intervene on.

They didn't love each other like brothers, exactly. More like twins. I'd spent half my life feeling like their third wheel, wanting us to be a trio, but it always felt like there was a line between me and them. That line only ran deeper after Chip got arrested and the truth of what they'd been doing to feed their drug and alcohol habits came to light. Chip's absence only served to prove he'd been the last thing holding Marty and me together at all.

"That's not fair, Chip. And you know it. He was out of his mind back then, the same as you. It's like he took over for the both of you when you hit the pokey in his place. He was running over mailboxes and passing out in the yard. Eating Percocet by the handful and running up thirty thousand dollars of debt. Besides. You know damn well I'm not sitting around letting someone put their hands on me. Or did he leave that part out of his version of the story?"

"He did not. I will say he ought to have known better. You're meaner than a coon dog, always have been. When dad was mad at me he used to enjoy pointing out how you'd got all Grandad's strength and all mom's morality. I always felt like that didn't leave much for me to be proud of."

"Please, Chip. Can we not do this? I'm happy to see you home. Let's not spoil it yet," I said.

He sat back in his chair, propped one of his thin-soled boots, which had his worn-down old Wranglers tucked into it, up onto the desk.

"Okay fine, we won't. Speaking of home. You been taking good care of our house while I was away? Must get lonely out there by yourself."

I had to work hard to keep my face neutral. He was poking the bear on purpose by bringing the house up. And doing it for reasons which would only come clear in time. I decided to get out ahead of the conflict.

"L's been living out there with me for the last few months. I gave her mom and dad's old room."

He raised an eyebrow. "Latonya, huh? I guess at least I ought to be happy you ain't moved into the master yet yourself. I'd rather take my old room anyhow, tell the truth."

"It's just as you left it last," I said, then wished I hadn't. Chip's living with our mother had been another deep point of contention between us, especially when the full depth of how much criminal shit he'd brought to her doorstep came to light.

I arranged the stack of mail on my desk to have something to do with my hands instead of my mouth. Something wasn't matching up with his being out of jail, and the detective in me was having a hard time not asking questions. In the end, I lost the internal struggle anyway.

"So you're paroled to mom and dad's house?" I asked, changing the subject away from L, who he'd always disliked. "How's that work? I figured either you'd be in a halfway house or they'd have had to call me to get permission to parole you to me."

The grin he gave me this time was more conniving than an actual smile. "I bet you'd like that, wouldn't you? Me paroled to your care, having to tow whatever line you put in front of me. Nah, I ain't on parole. I'm free as a raccoon on garbage day."

"How's that work?" I asked. "The governor give you a pardon for being clever or something?"

"How bout we don't do this right now like you said." Chip put his hat on his head and tilted it low over his eyes. "Suffice to say, I'm moving back into the house for a while. And don't worry, Latonya can stay. Long as you make her promise to play nice."

"Can't nobody make Latonya do anything, you know that Chip."

He stood up.

"I get it. I share her inclinations in that regard. But hey, listen, it's been great catching up and all, but I've got some celebrating to do. I'm free. Can I catch a ride with you over yonder?"

"You might if you could tell me where over yonder actually is," I said, standing up with him.

Giving him a ride would be the easiest way to get him out from underfoot for a while, keep from having the conflict we both knew was inevitable. I wasn't ready to start looking over his shoulder just yet, though we both knew that day would come.

"Truth is, I don't exactly know. But I figure you do," he said, leading the way down the hall and out the glass door onto the parking lot.

"How's that?" I asked.

"See, despite everything, I'd be surprised if you don't know where Marty's been shacked up." Chip's smile made it clear that everything had just changed in my life, like it or not, and I'd better get on my toes to deal with the inevitable coming storm.

CHAPTER THREE

I DROPPED CHIP OFF at the entrance to the rundown apartment complex off south Broadway that my ex-husband Marty lived in. We'd had to sell our home in the divorce to pay off the various restitutions he and Chip had racked up while facing the music in court. I told him he could walk the rest of the way, having no inclination to see Marty.

"I can probably come to pick you up in an hour or two if you want, but I'm not coming to the door," I said.

Chip showed me his chipped tooth, the source of his nickname, which had long ago gone grey. Somehow it didn't make his smile any less charming. "Don't worry about it, Rowdy. I'll catch a ride with Marty once we get good and finished."

I caught his arm as he opened the door to get out of the Pilot. He snatched it away as if I'd stuck him with a knife. Only then did I remember he'd been in prison this time yesterday and probably wasn't used to being touched unexpectedly. "Hey Chip?" I said, hesitating, but needing to say something.

"What?" he said, looking away to hide the fear my touch had spiked in him. The look in his eyes was the same as every man I'd ever known who'd been incarcerated. A mix of desperation, bravado, and if you looked deep enough, self-loathing.

"Marty's not supposed to be drinking. He's been trying to sober up, or so I've been told."

Chip's face betrayed nothing of what he thought about that. He shook his head and mumbled something about it being hard to see why we got divorced, got out, and closed the door behind him.

Normally a comment like that would have pissed me off. But in truth, I was glad to see my brother, though also worried about what he might do with his newfound freedom.

Chip and Marty may have loved each other like brothers, but they found trouble together like rabid coyotes. I'd have felt better knowing he wasn't on parole if I could shake the feeling that he'd done something stupid to get himself off. That stupid thing might end up at my doorstep someday. Knowing Chip as I did, it would be sooner than later, no doubt.

I hooked a right going south out of town on Highway 69, past the new strip malls and fancy outdoor shopping center that everybody called a mall. I drove beyond it into the countryside with its pine trees and pastures, occasional red clay hills. At least, what passed for hills in East Texas.

The Wallaces didn't live but five or so miles from the family farm Chip, Ben, and I had grown up on. I tried not to let Ben's memory into my consciousness very often, but it showed up anyway, often unannounced.

Chip's arrival seemed to be bringing pieces of the past to the front of the line again. I shook off the feeling and walked myself through the questions I wanted to ask Carmen Wallace instead.

Latonya would have pointed out my tendency to hide from my feelings and problems in my work, but I didn't have time to unravel all that right now.

LeeAnne Wallace had said that Carmen might be sensitive to questions that were too invasive. Not knowing the girl, it would be hard to determine what to say until I was sitting in front of her.

I didn't want to upset anyone, but it came with the territory most of the time. This didn't sound like the kind of case I would normally take, either, but I could already feel the rush of curiosity that always pulls me in over my head.

I made a right on Highway 346 and curved down around a long traverse of highway that afforded a brief but beautiful view of rolling green pastures and stocked private ponds. I made another left down a smaller country road, following my phone's GPS now.

By the time I found the house, a huge two-story with red brick and four box windows on the second floor, the sun and heat had started to ebb.

I put the Pilot into park in front of their house and took out my pocket notebook to jot a few notes about the layout.

The house had a patch of pine woods behind it maybe five or six acres in size. Beyond that patch were more pastures and the house, which must belong to the neighbor in question, a rundown ranch-style with tractor attachments set in the front yard like decorations. A few horses grazed in the pasture behind it, their beautiful brown coats shining in the late afternoon sunlight.

I jotted down the distance to the neighbor's residence. It looked to be maybe five hundred yards, give or take. The distance back to the main road was more like a quarter-mile. Though I wouldn't call the house isolated, it did have a sense of privacy and isolation. There could be no reason to approach it other than business with the owners.

It was the kind of property I hated running surveillance on in insurance work. No way to get up close. Set off a narrow country road where parking on the shoulder would be too out of the ordinary to go unnoticed, with two egress routes to keep an eye on and no way to get a direct view of the residence.

In those cases, I would follow the most likely route into town, park at the first low-key place I could find, and wait for the vehicle associated with the subject to pass by. If they came that way, of course. Being a good investigator is all about understanding human nature and decision making. Over time I'd become an expert at predicting what people were likely to do in a given scenario.

In this case, they'd invited me here for an interview, making all that prediction moot for the moment.

I moved past a lifted F-250 truck, a red BMW 5 series, and white Toyota 4Runner, all parked in the circle driveway, and knocked on the front door.

LeeAnne opened the door almost before my knuckles stopped touching it.

"Miss Reeves," she said, her tone still as curt as if she'd just left my office. "Guess you ought to come in."

I nodded, looking over her shoulder at the Ring doorbell. The house had bone-white travertine in two-foot square tiles throughout the main area. A central limestone fireplace and a few whitetail deer heads mounted above it set the tone in the formal living room, which was two stories high. LeeAnne led me to one of the big, plaid-patterned couches.

"Please, have a seat," she said. "Carmen's finishing up the last of her ACT prep packet. She'll be right in. Can I get you a Coke, or maybe some sweet tea?"

"No, thank you," I said, satisfied with her manners despite the earlier hostility. "You have a beautiful home."

"It needs updating, but we like it all right, I guess." She gestured around her as if to apologize. For what, I didn't know. My guess, she'd been on her husband about redecorating, but as yet had no luck. If so, I would have liked to receive her hand-me-downs.

"Well, anyway, sit tight, Carmen will be down shortly."

"Is your husband home as well, Mrs. Wallace?" I asked. She froze her progress out of the room at his mention. Tension radiated off her like hairspray. I wondered if he had a history of being unfaithful.

"Paul's working back in his office. Why?" she said, not bothering to strip the accusatory tone from her voice. She turned back to look me in the eyes.

"I had a thought that I might want to ask the two of you some more questions after I finish speaking with Carmen. To get a better idea of what the whole family is up against here, that's all."

"I'll tell you exactly what. That boy's slippery as a pocket full of pudding. His parents sent him away to some military school down in Harlingen for a while. Now he's using whatever training he got there to get around all our cameras, steal some of the others, and thwart our best attempts at security. The most we've ever got on him is a dark shape running across the driveway and around the back of the house. The Smith County Sheriff's Office says it's not enough. I guess it will take him hurting or killing Carmen for them to finally take action."

I turned on my recorder, pulled out my notebook, and started taking notes.

"Now what are you writing?" LeeAnne said. "I feel like I'm being interrogated every time I'm around you."

"Not at all. I'm just making note that there's a video of the perp and the details. You said he ran around the house. Was that around the garage side?"

"No, the other. He knows we have a Ring doorbell on the porch, so he comes from the other side, away from his place. That's where we put up the game cameras, but he took them. That tells you how much he's paying attention—he knew right where they were soon as we put them in. So you're on the case now, is that it?"

I stopped writing. "Not necessarily. It sounds like that's not what you want."

"I just don't see what bringing in a private detective will do when the police can't even help. Short of putting Kaleb in a cell, he's not going to stop. And besides, people talk around this town. There's been enough gossip about Carmen without you introducing more into the mix by asking around or blabbing our secrets to everyone."

"That's not the way this works, Mrs. Wallace," I said. "You hire me, I'm like an attorney, what we discuss, or I discover is between us. I won't even say that I work for y'all if asked in court unless you say okay. Confidentiality is currency in my business. And sometimes it pays to have someone not as bound by legal regulations as the police tend to be. Sometimes that's why people hire private investigators."

"Well, that's good to know, at least. Except you don't work for us yet. For all I know, you'll be out telling our problems to everyone in town after my husband smartens up and realizes you're of no use to us."

I let the jab roll over my shoulder because just then, a dark-haired, frail teenage girl came down the stairway.

"I'm finished, Momma," she said. "I don't know why..." Carmen stopped mid-sentence when she noticed me sitting on the couch. She had beautiful, flowing black hair so thick it barely stayed behind her ears. Her pale complexion could be attractive but was on the verge of crossing over into anemic. The sunken green eyes made her look like she was peering out from a cave, and gave her a shy, insecure look.

In a way, her healthy head of hair struck a meaningful contrast to the rest of her tepid appearance.

When I made eye contact with her, she looked away, confirming my suspicion that she might be a bit unsure of herself. She looked lost inside the oversized Baylor sweatshirt that engulfed her.

"Sweetheart, this is Miss Reeves," LeeAnne said. "Daddy asked her to come by and speak with you about the problem we're having with Kaleb."

Carmen's green eyes grew even bigger. "Mom, no," she said, just a hint of real rebellion in her voice. "Can we just please not make a big deal out of this like you always do with everything?"

"A big deal? So you don't think someone tapping on the windows and putting notes on your car and sneaking around all hours of the night is a big deal?"

Carmen sighed. I could see she was tired. Maybe more of her mother than tired in general, but I knew that exhausted look, I saw it on my own face every day back when I was married to Marty. One look at this sad-seeming girl made it easy to see she had frayed nerves as a default setting.

I remembered her parents saying she'd had some medical problems. I jotted a note to ask about it at the right time. Just now I wasn't about to interject the topic into their mother-daughter struggle.

"Hi Carmen," I said, pushing for a casual tone that never seems to suit me, "I'm Riley, nice to meet you."

Her mother's face wrinkled at the interruption, as I'd figured. I think it bothered her that I hadn't provided her with the option to use my first name. I hadn't meant it as a slight so much as a way to keep her at arm's length. Carmen would need to be comfortable with me if I wanted her to open up, which was why I had been less formal.

"Nice to meet you," she said. "And there's no problem. Someone is just playing a joke on me is all."

"What joke are they playing?" I asked.

"Just, like, putting notes on my car saying they can't live without me, or they're going to hurt me the way I'm hurting them, which makes no sense. Someone keeps tapping on my window in the middle of the night, too. It's mostly harmless stuff, you know? It's just a stupid prank."

"Well," I said, "do you know who would want to play that kind of prank on you, then?"

Her face seemed to sink a little at that question. "No," she admitted, "but it's still nothing."

"It's not nothing," LeeAnne broke in. "Everybody knows Kaleb's some sort of pervert. And he's always had a crush on you, since way back when we first moved in. No telling what that boy will do if someone doesn't put a stop to it."

Carmen folded her arms and dropped onto the couch with her ankles tucked up under her. "I haven't even spoken to him since we first moved in," she said, the last traces of energy gone now from her voice. "He was never anything but nice to me anyway."

LeeAnne clicked her tongue. "Those people are trash," she said, turning to me. "I went to high school with Kaleb's father. One of those guys who always came into class smelling like cigarettes or marijuana. When he bothered to show up at all. Most of the time he was looking for younger girls to screw. Apple doesn't fall far from the tree, I guess. He raises Tennessee Walking horses when he's not raising the bottle. Kaleb's always back there feeding them. I think that's how he keeps such a close eye on Carmen. I've been told the wife is a vet tech, but I can't imagine she's all that competent."

I made note of that, as well as a note on the dynamic between mother and daughter.

I'd had plenty of my own mama drama in high school. My mother and I had been too much alike to get along. It's what my father had loved most about me, the combination of her stubbornness and his own father's limitless determination. My mother had liked that combination the least, having always favored Chip's charm to my seriousness.

"Carmen, is your room upstairs?" I asked by way of changing the subject. I didn't want to form too many opinions until I had a chance to see things for myself.

"Yes ma'am," she said.

"It doesn't strike you as odd that someone climbs up on your roof just to play a prank?"

A panicked look flashed in her eyes for a half second. It disappeared just as quick.

"I mean, it's weird, sure. But it's probably just, like... I don't know. It's like someone could just be screwing around, taking it too far. A lot of people think I'm weird because we started doing homeschooling when I got sick."

Her father, Paul, came in from the back of the house. LeeAnne stood up and moved over to guide him in like the usher in a movie theater. "There you are," she said. "I was wondering when you were gonna come in and deal with the woman you invited over against my wishes."

I caught her eye and grinned to show her I knew what she meant. She wasn't all that far from the truth, though—he had invited me against her will. If he hadn't insisted I at least try to help, I probably wouldn't have been there in the first place, considering her attitude in my office. Not to mention the mild nature of the case, so far.

I'd learned over time the risks of taking cases where one or more of the clients didn't want my services. Sooner or later they always won the other one to their cause, too, and occasionally left you holding an unpaid bill.

But now, sitting here speaking with Carmen, whose nerves were so frayed you could almost see them ticking under the surface of her skin, my intuition was starting to burn that the girl might need help on some level other than the problem I'd been brought in to address.

I stood to greet Paul as he entered the room from a door to the rear. "Mr. Wallace," I said.

"Please, keep your seat, Miss Reeves," he said. "Thanks for coming. I see you met Carmen."

"I did, thank you. She and your wife are just catching me up on your case."

LeeAnne smirked at the word "case." I smiled at her to let her know I'd caught it.

"So it's a case now? Does that mean you'll help us out?" Paul said, already pushing for the outcome he'd had in mind since before stepping into my office.

"I'm still not quite sure."

Carmen stood up and said, "Daddy, please. There's no need to turn this into an inquisition. This summer I'll be down at ACC. Then UT by next fall, hopefully. It's not like whoever it is will follow me off to college. It's just a dumb joke."

"Sweetie, you don't know that," Paul said. "Besides, three months is a lot of time for him to harm you if he gets it in mind." Paul shifted his focus back to me. "Miss Reeves, what would you say are your reservations about helping us? I know for a fact you're not afraid, the whole town saw what you did to Carl Farlow on the news. Is this just too small potatoes or something?"

LeeAnne sneered this time. "Do you think our daughter's safety is beneath you?" she asked. I almost pointed out that she was the one who didn't want me, but I held my tongue.

"I wouldn't call them reservations at this point," I said, measuring my words. "I'm trying to get enough preliminary information to see if I can be of help. I don't take on problems unless I know I can solve them.

"Speaking of. Y'all mentioned someone's been leaving notes on Carmen's car. Do you still have the notes?"

LeeAnne gave me a prideful smile. "You must be kidding?" she said. "I can do you better than that. I've got a whole file on this. That's why I don't see how you could be of any help. I've already collected all the evidence and solved the case."

That time I smirked. Back in high school, I'd eaten socialite girls like LeeAnne for snacks. It always surprised them when I met their passive aggression with physical action. They were used to pushing boys around with their looks, and girls with their parents' money. I never let anyone push me around with anything, for any reason.

But we were adults now. The way to beat her was with my mind, and I didn't think I'd have any trouble doing that.

"Could I see the file?" I asked.

"If you can tell me why we should hire you first," LeeAnne replied. "You said you weren't sure we should, and everything you've done so far is evasive, at best. You keep acting like you're interviewing us for a job, but I'm sorry to tell you it's the other way around, and you need to get that straight now."

Carmen rolled her eyes. Paul cleared his throat, which caused some sort of Pavlovian response in both of them. They each put their eyes on him instead of the other.

"We should hire her because I said so," Paul said. "This thing has gone far enough. You've wasted enough time obsessing over it, LeeAnne. It's not healthy. Miss Reeves is a professional and highly recommended. If she finds nothing, she finds nothing. It'll be worth the money to put the problem in someone else's hands in the meantime, so I'm willing to pay. By the way, Miss Reeves, any idea what it will cost me?"

I nodded. "If I take it? A two-thousand-dollar retainer, refundable if I stop working before the end of it. I bill domestic work at fifty an hour, assuming it's billable. I do a lot of research I won't bill for, as well. But I've got a few requirements before I decide."

"Two thousand dollars for forty hours of working on something we already know the result of? That's robbery," LeeAnne said.

I shrugged. "I'm good at what I do. And that's some of the cheapest P.I. work you'll find anywhere for this kind of thing. Besides, I do a lot of research and poking around I don't even bill for, as I said before. That's just my base charge to get to work. It almost certainly will take more to get anything done. That is if I decide to take the job. I'm afraid I still don't see how I can be of help."

"Are we seriously considering this, Paul?" LeeAnne said, her voice showing clear signs of anger now. "The woman can hardly be bothered as is, I don't see why we'd encourage her with money when she's already got our entire relationship ass-backward."

"Enough, LeeAnne." Paul's voice echoed in the tall room. "I get tired of having to point out that you don't know everything. Besides, it's MY money. I'm the one who goes out and earns it while you hang out with the Junior League and get your nails done twice a week. You want to talk obscene? I've seen what that costs, so tone it down a little bit on the financial concerns and let the woman work."

LeeAnne looked like her husband had slapped her. She stood up and walked out of the room without saying another word. I had a feeling he'd hear about that one after I left, but just now her sense of embarrassment had made her flee.

I was glad to have her out of the way.

"So will I be able to see the file?" I asked him. I took note that Carmen had hardly said a word since her father entered the room. That meant he was the dominant force in the home. LeeAnne liked to pretend to be in charge. Where Carmen had argued or acted annoyed with her mother, her reverence for her father was clear. My guess was they were fairly close.

"Does that mean you're taking the case?" he asked.

"I'm leaning toward it now that I've met your daughter. I want to have a look around your property and house first if that would be okay?"

"That's just fine," he replied. "I'll have two thousand dollars in cash waiting here when you get back. And LeeAnne's file. Now if y'all will excuse me, I've got a couple of work issues to finish up in my office." He walked out of the room and I turned to Carmen.

"Think I could take a look at your bedroom?" I asked.

She nodded. "It's kind of a mess, though. Miss Reeves?" she said.

"Yes?"

"Do you think I have anything to be worried about?"

"I don't know," I replied. "Do you feel worried?"

"A little. My medication gives me anxiety anyway. Which is weird, since it's supposed to help with it. My mother gives me the most anxiety, though. She's always smothering me."

"It means she loves you."

"I know. She's always taken good care of me. But I'm not a little girl anymore. I need space."

"I get it," I said. "Now let's go see your room. Do your parents sleep downstairs?"

"My dad does. Mom has slept in the room down the hall from mine for years because my dad snores."

That didn't surprise me. Wealthy Tyler couples often slept in separate bedrooms and always had a similar reason. Over the years I'd noticed the pattern but never knew what it meant, beyond marriages of convenience.

I wanted to talk to Carmen more, but that would have to wait. Right now my instincts said the girl was still closed off with her parents so close by. If she was like other teenage girls, she had another side they'd never even seen. I'd try to catch up with her outside of the household and see if she revealed that side on neutral ground.

I followed her up the stairway across the banister above where we'd been sitting. She moved with the ease of a child in her childhood home. She struck me as someone who wanted to get away so bad that it wouldn't register what she was giving up until it was gone. You can move back in later, but everything that matters changes once you leave home that first time. I could still recall that feeling in my own life as if it had just happened.

The door to her room had a red-and-black homecoming mum hung on the outside that said her name in sparkling silver cursive down one of the ribbons. Someone had mounted a pink card with black stars on it and her name in big block letters above it like an office sign. The room beyond housed a four-post double bed with a pink-and-black quilt and a pink net that draped from the posts over the sides of the bed.

"Sorry about the mess," Carmen said.

It didn't look all that messy to me. There was a small pile of clothes at the foot of the bed and some books scattered on top of the small grey desk in the corner. I took note of a basket of medication and supplements on the desk and jotted down the names on the visible bottles.

"No need to apologize," I said. "It's your space."

"Try telling my mom that." She rolled her eyes again.

I tried not to read too much into it. What teenage girl didn't want to get out from under their mother's thumb?

"Do you always keep the shutters closed?" I asked.

"I used to keep them open. But now with everything going on, I keep them shut." She walked over and unlatched them, swung them open on their hinges to look out at the combination of pine and oak trees on their large, neatly manicured lawn. "What's it like?" she asked.

"What's what like?"

"Being a detective. Is it like in the movies? Like, do you get dragged into murders and cheaters and all kinds of danger?"

I shrugged. "I didn't used to, I don't think. But lately it seems like I have been. The danger, I mean. Believe it or not, it's mostly sitting in a car and filming people for insurance companies or running background checks on people for law firms." I didn't mention that something had snapped in me around the time I split up with Marty. That I'd felt trapped with his addiction, tired of the predictable chaos that came with the territory, so I'd started seeking out the unpredictable kind. That I took risks like taking deep breaths now, as if I needed them to stay conscious. I recognized the yearning for passion in her eyes. I hoped it was healthier than my version.

"You mind if I ask you something kind of personal?" I said.

"I guess not. Unless you're asking for my mother."

"I'm not, at least not directly. And I promise I'll never reveal anything to her that you tell me unless it's what you want. I want you to be able to trust me."

I'd already decided that if I took the case it would be for Carmen's sake, not her parents. It seemed to me she was the one who needed the help. If they were paying the tab it was only on her behalf and I had no problem keeping her confidence, so long as it posed no danger to her.

I had a sense that getting her to open up would be the key to whatever case there was anyway.

The biggest barrier to that with any teenager is the parents.

"Okay," she said, "then go ahead, shoot."

"Have you ever snuck a boy in through your window?"

She blushed at the question, which told me all I needed to know.

"I... yes. But just once. Normally we have the alarm on at night, but for a while, I set up a way to turn it off from my phone. My mom figured it out pretty quick though. They took my phone away for a month afterward."

"How long ago was this?"

"I don't know... a few months ago, maybe?"

"Was it before the trouble started with someone tapping on the window?"

She considered that. "Yeah, it was."

"Any chance it's the same boy you snuck in doing all this?"

"I doubt it."

"Why?"

"Because he lost interest in me and we broke up. My parents hated his guts, but they hate anything that takes me out of their orbit."

"Why didn't they like him?"

"The truth? He's not from the right kind of family. And he's older than me."

I jotted down some notes. I had a hunch there would be more to it than just that. But in Tyler, you never knew.

"What makes the right kind of family?" I figured I probably knew something in the range of the answer. Still, I wanted to hear what she said.

"They have to go to Green Acres and have almost as much money as God. Otherwise, they're all the wrong kind of family."

I chuckled. It made her grin in return. "That's a great answer," I said.

She shrugged, her self-consciousness gone for a second. "It's true, that's why. You might have noticed my mother has a golden scepter stuck up her rear end. It's been there since she was drill team captain in high school, back when the world was black-and-white and nothing bad ever happened to anyone."

I'd had her mother pegged almost to a T. I'd gone to Lee High School myself. I knew plenty of girls like LeeAnne Wallace, though she had maybe a decade on me. I'd even fixed one or two of their attitudes after they'd looked down their nose at me for my tomboy appearance.

I focused on Carmen again. "How did he get up here?"

"What do you mean?"

"On the roof. I noticed there aren't any trees close enough to the house."

"He... you swear you won't tell them?"

"Cross my heart." I made a cross with my finger and thumb and felt old and lame and astonishingly uncool as I did it.

"If you look at the way our brick is done on the front corners of the house, there are bricks that stick out an inch or so, like accents. He climbed right up them. It's not, like, hard to do, I've done it a few times. It's like, maybe the only thing I ever got over on my mom. I used to crawl out my window and sit on the roof sometimes when I had friends spend the night. It's how I had the idea in the first place."

I grinned at her and made a note to check out the brick on the way out. I shifted the subject.

"Do you have any idea why someone would want to harass you like this?"

Her face was solemn, easy to believe. "Not really. Honestly, most people don't even know I exist anymore. Not long after we moved here, I got sick and had to be homeschooled. While I was sick I had nothing better to do and got ahead in school and can graduate early.

"I'm going to ACC in January to get started on gen-eds. I'll most likely get into UT for next fall, but we're waiting to apply until I take the SAT one more time. I scored a thirteen hundred but it might as well be a C. My father's a legacy, so I don't see the point in taking it again. I'm sick of this town, and even sicker of this house."

I resisted the urge to ask about her illness, getting the feeling she didn't want to elaborate on it.

"That sounds like a good plan," I said. "I don't remember my SAT score, but it wasn't thirteen hundred."

School was never my thing. I'd quit college after my freshman year at Tyler Junior College, not because academics were hard, but because I was bored. At the time, I'd told myself it wasn't for me. In truth, I'd wanted more time to spend with Marty and had been anxious to move on to the next stage of life. Marty was already working in the oil fields out near Kilgore by then. It made me glad to see Carmen wasn't making the same mistake with her own older man, who I figured she was still seeing behind her parents' back. One thing didn't totally make sense, so I asked.

"Did your mom teach you in homeschool?"

"No. I have a personal tutor for that, Mr. Carrolton. He's nice, pretty nerdy though. He thinks my mother's as crazy as I do, he just won't say it."

I wrote down his name so I could look him up later and ask him some questions. A long line of experience had taught me to always be cautious of older men with access to teenage girls.

"One more question," I said, closing my notebook.

"Shoot."

"Did you really stop seeing your boyfriend?"

She hesitated. "Yes. It's more accurate to say that he stopped seeing me. My parents wanted to ruin his life."

"Could I get both his phone number and yours?" I asked. "I need to clear him as a suspect, it's just a formality."

She shook her head. "I'd rather not give you his number without talking to him first."

I told her that was okay as she wrote down her number on a pink sticky note. I had every intention of looking into him either way. He might not feel comfortable talking to me, but I wanted to get a sense of him. She might not know the whole story where he was concerned. That's how older boys work. I said my requisite goodbyes to Carmen and made my way back downstairs.

Paul was waiting for me in the kitchen with a bank envelope of money and a beige file folder full of paperwork.

"Here's the cash for the retainer, and also LeeAnne's file, as promised. I'm assuming you'll help us out?"

"I will," I replied. "For now. But if I poke around tomorrow and don't find much else to go on, I'll deduct my hours and give this right back. Those are my terms."

"I can live with that."

"Then we're good to go." I took the cash and the file from him and headed for the front door.

"Miss Reeves?" he said as I pulled the door open.

I turned halfway outside and faced him.

"I don't want to tell you how to do your job, I swear," he said. "But I have a private reason for calling you that I didn't want to mention in front of LeeAnne. If you can do me this favor, I'm happy to let you just keep the retainer either way and maybe double it up even if you don't ultimately want to keep working on the case. How's that sound?"

The hair on the back of my neck pricked up, and I could hear my father's voice the time he'd explained to me the feeling was called piloerection, and it was our genetic response to potential threats. Nothing in life is free, especially when it's a man offering to a woman.

"I can't give you an answer until I know what you want," I said.

"I'd like for you look into a guy named Donovan Mills. He's Carmen's ex-boyfriend. I have a feeling he's not so ex, though, if you catch my drift. He's no good, but I could use some dirt on him to help her see that."

He must have sensed my displeasure at the request, so he added, "She's gotten pretty secretive," by way of explanation. "We used to be close but lately she's shut me out as if to punish me for marrying her mother, who she's really mad at. I've sort of half let the secrecy go because she'll be in Austin soon enough, and that will put real distance between us for the first time, so I don't want to make problems any worse before she's gone. But Donovan is trouble, major trouble in fact. I don't want him to knock her up or something worse before she gets out of here, however unlikely that is."

"Why is that unlikely?"

"The doctors are pretty certain Carmen won't be able to have children because of her condition. It has ravaged her physical health."

"What, exactly, is her condition?" I asked. "I realize I'm being frank, but since we're clearing the air, I might as well join in."

He shook his head. "It's no problem. In fact, I should have mentioned it already. We're just so accustomed to everyone knowing, what with the way people talk and all. Carmen's been diagnosed with acute intermittent porphyria. It's led to a host of other medical issues, too.

But stress can really take her apart and bring out fairly serious psychosis, that's why LeeAnne is so worried."

"And you don't think this Mills is a good guy for her to be hanging around given her condition, does that sound about right?"

"I wouldn't think he was good for her either way, but especially given her condition. She can be impressionable in certain circumstances. I think we shielded her too much, but she was so sick and the other girls were so cruel about her appearance, afterward.

"Besides, I know what older men are about, and I know what they bring with them. She showed up with him for supper one time and her mother about fell out. Diamond earring in his ear and a big flashy watch he certainly can't afford, smelling like the Axe body spray isle at Drug Emporium. Trust me, she can do better. I slipped a snapshot of him from the Ring camera in LeeAnne's file for you."

I wanted to point out how classist and snotty he sounded but I settled for pointing out that LeeAnne didn't much seem to care for me, either. Besides, Chip had worn the Axe spray for years, so I was in no position to argue against his point.

"I know that's how it seems," he said. "LeeAnne means well, she's just… demanding. And uncompromising when it comes to Carmen. She's spent the last few years terrified for our daughter, taking care of her every problem. She devoted her entire life to Carmen after she got sick, gave up her own aspirations in the process. LeeAnne's a singer, she wanted to go on *American Idol* but she chose to focus on Carmen instead. What do you expect but for her to be unreasonable about a thing like this? She's an amazing mother. You need to know that. There's nothing she wouldn't do for Carmen. Donovan Mills ought to know it, too, if they're still sneaking around. LeeAnne is liable to run him over with the truck if he doesn't take a hint and get gone.

"The same goes for whoever is harassing Carmen, though I don't think that's Mills, necessarily. But he's the real reason I personally wanted to hire you. I just couldn't say that to LeeAnne without her having a meltdown.

"That's why she thinks the whole thing is so ridiculous, she's only got part of the story. She'll lose her damn mind if she finds out Mills is still around, I guarantee you that much. For my part, I think that the notes and everything are probably harmless. They smack of immature or jealous girls trying to shine Carmen on, but I don't think they're dangerous. Did you grow up around here?"

I nodded.

"Well then, you know how these kids are. Toilet-papering each other's houses, writing on each other's cars with windshield paint. Half of them are playing social mind games by the time they're ten. The other half are born like that. I want you to take that part of the case serious, don't get me wrong. But Mills, I'd appreciate it if you would look into whether they're running around together and let me know. I have a feeling he's the real danger to our daughter."

"I can do that, but I have another condition," I said.

"Shoot."

"Unless they're up to something harmful to Carmen, I won't tell you if they're together or not. I can provide you with a background check, but if it checks out, I won't be used as a tool to pry into her life outside of your household. She's getting to an age where she ought to have some privacy, so long as it's not concealing something dangerous. I will work to make sure she's safe on all accounts since it sounds like that's what you want more than anything else. Fair?"

He pushed his parted grey hair back with his right hand while considering my offer. "Fair enough, I suppose. I'd like you to let me know if they're together regardless, but her safety is what I want the most, so do what you think is right. Anything else?"

"That's it. Thank you for your time and hospitality, Mr. Wallace."

He held out his hand as a parting gesture. I shook it.

"Thank you. Carmen's a good girl," he said. "She deserves better than Donovan Mills or this harassment. Especially after all that she's been through."

I nodded and headed out to my car. He closed it behind me, leaving me alone with the chirping crickets and sour smell of summer heat. And just like that, I had a new client.

CHAPTER FOUR

SOON AS I PULLED up to the house, I knew there was going to be trouble. It had been a long day, and I'd intended to post up in front of the television with L for the night. I owed it to her, after ignoring her calls all weekend. We'd taken to watching *Fargo*, most recently. L absolutely loved it, and I loved anything that made her that excited.

Most of all I tried to not worry about Chip or what hijinks he might be up to, an impossible feat as it turned out.

Marty's rusted grey F-150 sat in the driveway where I normally parked. The same spot my father had parked his own truck for nearly forty years, ceding the garage to Mom, another of her spaces I still felt uncomfortable inhabiting. I had my suspicions Chip probably told him to pull it there knowing it would bother me.

It made me glad Marty and I had never lived in my parents' house while we were still married. That would have made it feel like living in the bombed-out remains of a war zone.

Technically Chip owned the place and could park where he wanted, the same as me. Not that he'd done much to earn it at the end. I'd been the one to take care of our mother while she shriveled into nothing, coughed and choked and slowly starved as her insides turned on her. Who'd held her hand as the death rattles echoed out of her throat, her last attempt at speech asking about him? I cried with my face buried into her frail chest when she finally slipped away, the both of us having needed Chip more than ever before on that awful day, both let down like always.

For her part, I have no doubt she'd rather it had been Chip there than me. He'd always been her favorite. As a daughter, I always felt like an inconvenience next to two strong sons. Never mind that I'd never had a lick of trouble in my life. And never mind that I would have done almost anything to get even one syllable of affirmation from her lips through the years.

No telling what Chip had been up to in prison. His world had trouble waiting around every corner. Some might say he was the trouble, and I'd have to agree.

I wasn't sure I could forgive him for letting our mother die broken-hearted and desperate to see him one last time. In some ways I still sought her approval, even now.

I pulled my Pilot off into the pasture to avoid blocking Marty's truck in. I didn't want to take L's spot and make her pull her Maxima onto the rough terrain. She took her vehicles seriously. Even the beater Ford Escort she'd driven through high school had been immaculate.

As I got out of the car and stepped across the cattle guard, I told myself that Marty wouldn't be here long, if I had anything to say about it.

I moved between the old riding lawn mower and stacked-up boxes from my divorce in the garage and through the back door.

It opened into a small hallway with the laundry room on the right and master bedroom on the left, kitchen and breakfast room straight ahead. I followed the worn path across dark plank floors toward Chip's voice telling the end of some sort of prison story from one of the chairs at the breakfast table.

Marty shot me a terrified look as I stepped through the doorway, stood up as if to dodge my angry gaze. Chip, feet up on the table where I ate my Honey Nut Cheerios in the mornings, stopped talking and grinned. My loving brother, always happy to sew discomfort anywhere it might take root.

A case of Miller Lite sat on the table next to Chip's feet. He had a matching bottle in his hand.

"Well, hey there, Riley," Marty said, hesitation and longing radiating off his voice. I cut him off before he embarrassed himself.

"Stop talking, Marty," I said. "One of the benefits of being divorced is we don't have to talk to each other anymore. And Chip, can you please get your feet off the table? You know Pop would hate that."

Chip kept right on smiling like I hadn't even spoken to him. I noted the three empty bottles in front of him. It surprised me that Marty had none in front of him. Good for him. But I had no intention of making it my problem. I'd defended him as much as I ever would again by telling Chip he was sober.

"What's got the bug up your bunghole, Rowdy?" Chip said. "This here's a celebration."

I focused my glare on him then. "Not with him here it ain't," I said, gesturing with my thumb at Marty.

"Aw hell, Riley, don't be like that," Marty said.

I squared up to him. "Marty, I remember telling you to stop talking," I said.

I have to admit I winced inside when I saw how much that stung him. Marty still loved me, of that I had no doubt. And I'm not a hard-hearted woman, no matter how tough I talk sometimes. But things had passed between us that I felt like I would never be able to forgive or forget. He wasn't blood, like Chip, so I had no use for him anymore.

Besides, any chance we'd had of remaining friends after our marriage ended the moment he put his hands on me, no matter how out of character it had been. Some lines cannot be uncrossed.

Lighting him up with my Taser hadn't been out of character for me, though I kept telling myself I was working on that.

"Thing is, I invited him," Chip said. "And just now you're being rude to my guest at a party in my honor in a house I own half of."

He pulled out a fresh bottle and twisted the top off, gave it a theatrical pull with his lips for effect.

I set my backpack down on the counter, unstrapped the Taser from my conceal holster, and set it on the table. Marty recoiled at the memory of it. Chip wouldn't have cared if I shot it between his eyes. His indifference started to get the better of me.

"So this is how we're gonna play it, huh Chip?" I said. "I guess I should have known. You've been back five minutes and already here comes trouble. It makes me wonder about things. Like what kind of trouble it took to get you out of prison? And how long it will take before that trouble shows up on my doorstep, as usual? A day? A week? I give it a week, max."

That took the grin off his face. He wasn't the only one who knew how to push all the family buttons. I took a bottle out of his twelve-pack, opened it, and did my best impression of his lip pull with it.

Chip took his feet down off the table.

"Hell, I better just go," Marty stammered, eyeing the space between me and the wall, trying to decide if he could get through it without getting bit. Recovery and shame had left him meek and unsure of himself. I almost felt sorry for him, but my anger always did a good job of drowning that emotion.

"Smartest thing you've said to me in years, Marty," I said.

"Hell naw, man, sit down," Chip replied, shooting me his fake smile again. "You know how Rowdy is. She can't help herself. Let's all try this again. Sis, Marty here's been sober for six months, just like you said. And I know y'all got a lot of bullshit between you. That's fine, and I can't help it if it ain't. But this here night is about me getting out of that unfathomable shitbox down in Cuero, and I ain't asked either of you for a goddamn thing the whole time I was in there. I mean not so much as a dime on the commissary. Rowdy, I know you put money on it anyway, and I appreciate that, don't get me wrong. But hell, y'all, this is the first goddamn time I've felt air conditioning in years, and you both ruining the temperature with this bullshit.

"All I'm asking is if we can avoid going all Shakespeare in here long enough to grill up them filets over on the counter and for me to drink myself into a proper state of inebriation to sleep it off in a real bed, which is kind of freaking me out. So you two shut the fuck up and play nice for a minute. This will all be over in a bit, I promise, then y'all can get back to the Smith County cold war like this never happened."

Nobody said anything for a moment. Finally, I sighed. He had a point. I'd slept next to Marty for ten years. I could put up with him across the table for a few hours if Chip wanted him there, given the circumstances. I wasn't sure how L would feel about Marty being here, but I assumed she'd put up with it so long as I did.

"You got a filet over there for L too?" I asked, as close as I could come to making peace with words. "She'll be home in a minute and I won't leave her out."

Chip shook his head like I'd said something ridiculous. "Do I have a filet for Latonya... Girl I swear to God you've fallen three more branches down the crazy tree since I got sent up. I bet you hit your head on all of 'em, too. Hell yes, I've got one for Latonya. You act like I don't know the way you think. Now cut the attitude. I'm still astounded you can buy beer in Smith County, but also a little annoyed that Marty won't drive me to Coffee City to buy some bourbon. Let's don't spoil anything else."

I said okay, went out the French doors onto the back porch to start up the gas grill, thinking I'd split mine with her if it turned out he really didn't have one. Words meant almost nothing with Chip, it was one of the greatest qualities that separated us. Because they meant everything to me.

I turned on the gas line and lit up the burners. Our father had been so proud the day he'd finally gotten a gas line run to that grill. It became his favorite thing about the entire house, a refuge for a man who'd spent sixty hours a week patrolling the back roads of Smith County for thirty years, which didn't leave a lot of time for grilling out or relaxing. In retirement there was nothing he liked more than hanging out on the back porch with a glass of sweet tea and a grill full of meat, always including a steak cooked well-done, the way Ben liked it, and which was always fed to the dogs afterward.

The back porch had once looked out onto empty pasture with an old-growth pine forest along the backside of the property. Progress had finally encroached along the backside of our land in the form of eminent domain, and now the tollway Loop 49 ran right where thirty-foot pine trees had once been. It reminded me that no place was so sacred that change would not encroach on it.

A loud black Camaro passed a minivan out on the tollway as I watched. It wasn't hard to see why there were so many accidents on it with the way people drove. Tell an East Texan a new route would save them time and you could bet they'd try to see how much. The county had plans to widen it to two lanes in each direction eventually but hadn't in our section yet. When it happened, it would encroach that much more onto what had once been a nice, quiet place to live.

It made me glad my father hadn't lived to see the road's construction. He'd never have said a word, but it would have eaten at him. Ben had died on the other side of the world, and even then our father hadn't said a thing. I couldn't remember ever even speaking to him like two adults having a real conversation, for that matter. He'd been as stoic as Marcus Aurelius, whose writings had been a big part of his life.

I sat down on one of the rusting wire chairs and thought about the last time I'd seen Ben. I'd stood on the porch and watched him drive away in a cloud of dust from the same caliche rock road I now drove every day coming and going from this house.

The memory felt hazy now. Just as many memories, even some from my marriage, did. All I had left of it was the knowledge that Ben hadn't looked back as our father drove him toward the airport in his faded green Z-71, and that none of us had ever seen his smiling face alive again.

Sometimes I wished I could follow his example and stop looking back. At the moment it was impossible when the past invited itself over to dinner.

The sound of Latonya's car bumping down the driveway shook me from my thoughts. I got up and walked around the side of the house to meet her. I didn't want her to think Marty was here on my behalf. That would piss her off.

She didn't even know Chip was out of prison. It amazed me how your entire life could shift in the matter of an afternoon. I'd seen it over and over again in my work, but it surprised me every single time.

I could see L's head already shaking back and forth at the sight of Marty's truck as I rounded the back corner of the house. I shrugged.

"What that boy doing up in our house?" L said as she got out of the car. "You lost yo mind, Riley?"

"Chip's out," I said. That seemed to give her pause, so I added, "He just showed up at my office today after lunch. Marty's here with him. He's apparently totaling all the tea in Smith County, to hear Chip tell it."

"Shit, it don't matter to me if he ain't. But you think I should go? Like, Chip gonna be mad I be staying in your parents' room?"

"He already knows, I told him. He said it was fine, but I bet we'll hear about it at some point. I'd imagine he's more concerned with finding a way to get me to buy him out of the house so he has some running money, but he won't say it yet."

"Figures." L walked around the car and got her purse from the passenger seat. "My folks ain't leavin' me squat when they go. Chip gon pour his inheritance down his throat fast as he can swallow it."

I frowned. "If he doesn't put it up his nose first. But I hope not. Anyway, he brought steaks, I'll split mine with you if there's not enough. Just do me a favor and try not to be too hard on them. I'm not happy about Marty being here but I promised to keep the peace tonight, so I intend to try."

L shrugged. "I ain't never been the one he needed to worry about anyway, *Rowdy*."

L never used my family nickname unless she was teasing me. And she was about the only person who ever got away with that. She was one of the only people I'd ever really trusted, besides my brother Ben.

And Marty, for a short while.

Back inside, I did my best to avoid Marty by grabbing the steaks Chip had just finished salting. I took them straight out to the hot grill and slapped them on. One thing my father had taught me well was how to cook meat. Chip was always more interested in the beer than the food, but I spent those moments glued to my father's side, happy to have his attention for a while.

If I was lucky, cooking would keep me occupied so that Marty wouldn't talk to me about his feelings. L had disappeared into her room without speaking to either of them. Which meant I couldn't make any promises about keeping the peace for long if either of them pulled anything at dinner.

Marty would be off the wagon again in no time now that Chip was back in town. They were about as good for each other as ammonia and bleach. Sometimes life is like that. It binds us to people and things that will destroy us sooner or later.

CHAPTER FIVE

LATE THAT NIGHT, I woke up to my bedroom door handle jiggling like someone was trying to open it. Jolted from sleep, I fumbled around on my nightstand and cursed myself for forgetting my Taser on the kitchen counter. I managed to open the drawer to my nightstand and fumble out the M&P Shield I kept there now. I hadn't carried it in months, not since I'd tried to kill Carl Farlow with it after seeing his handiwork firsthand.

I clicked off the safety just as the person on the other side managed to pop the press-in handle lock from the other side. As the door swung open, I swung my feet to the floor aiming at the doorway. A man's dark shape encased by the dim hallway light came into frame. At the sight of my pistol, the shape dropped to the floor.

"Shit Riley, don't sh-sh-shoot," Marty's slurred voice said. Between the sleep haze and pumping adrenaline, it took me a second to recognize him. When I did my fear turned to anger.

"What in the hell is the matter with you, Marty?" I snapped. "You looking to try on some hollow points?"

Marty, face-down on the floor now, mumbled something I couldn't understand. He was drunk. It figured. Only an alcoholic could make the kind of ridiculous decision that would lead Marty to pick his way into my bedroom. Ignoring him at dinner had apparently not been enough of a sign. That's the problem with a drunk. It drowns their instincts and leaves behind a half-witted monkey where a man once stood.

"What the hell?" I asked, clicking the safety back on, my chest heaving now. I set the pistol on the nightstand.

"I-I'm sorry," he said. "I just... I'm sorry, Riley. For everything. I know I shouldn't be here right now but I can't help it."

"Well, you'd better start trying," I said, "because this is ridiculous. You're lucky I left the Taser in the kitchen, otherwise, you'd be doing the Gainsville flop right now. I don't even have to ask if you're drunk. I can smell it from here."

"I know it. I'm sorry. Chip found a bottle of Turkey in his closet."

"So much for sobriety. It ever occur to you that y'all aren't all that good for each other?" Marty didn't get the chance to answer because Chip's door opened behind him.

"The hell's going on out here?" he said. "I slept through less noise in the pen."

"Your genius friend over here decided it would be a good idea to try and sneak into my room to tell me how sorry he is," I said. "Lucky you're not scraping his brains off the wall. He about scared the daylights out of me."

Chip grinned, like always, and shook his head. "Well shit," was all he said, then turned and closed his door, leaving me to deal with his problem alone.

Marty, sitting on his haunches now, looked at me through squinted eyes. I had no idea what he expected me to say, but I wasn't going to say it.

After a while, I realized he was waiting for me to speak first. I grudgingly obliged him.

"All right, here's the deal, Marty. I wake up at five thirty for work. I better not see you when I do. Set an alarm on your phone if you have to, whatever it takes. I'd like to toss you out now, but it's obvious you can't drive, and I don't think a third DWI would do you any good. Might end up visiting Chip's crew down in Cuero, see if that suits you better. But you'd best be gone in the morning when I come out of this room. After that, forget you ever knew me, and we'll get along just fine. We clear?"

Marty shook his head with a dumb yes. I wondered what I'd ever seen in him. He'd been kind, I guess that was it. And not at all like the pitiful, meek man on the floor in front of me now. He'd been fun once, though whatever magic that held had long faded.

Unlike the men in my family, he hadn't been rough, maybe it was that. Even most of the time when he drank, he was a sweet guy, always smiling. But over time alcohol helped him to take his life apart, and mine with it. Over the years I came to realize I'd married too young, and for reasons that no longer agreed with me. In fact, I'd come to question if I wanted to have a partner at all, given how much energy it took. L was always on my case about taking time away from work to live. I always assumed life was work. Another part of my father in me.

The night I finally told him I wanted a divorce he was so inconsolable that he started to tremble. I realized then that Marty had roughness in him, too. He'd just been keeping it inside, where it slowly poisoned him. Trying to let it out on me had been a mistake, but I understood it, in a way. I ended up breaking his nose with the back of my head and then Tasing him into a puddled mess on the floor. By the time he came back to reality, I was long gone and never looked back.

That he'd gotten his second DWI that night out looking for me to apologize was something I did feel guilty about. I never admitted it to anyone, but it bothered me for reasons I couldn't explain. And now I couldn't imagine his probation officer, Marge Sargent, would be happy to know he'd fallen off the wagon again. He'd been lucky to avoid jail time, unlike Chip, for their orgy of theft and drug binges.

Not that I was going to tell her. We'd gone to high school with Marge, and I knew what she was like. She had never met a man she didn't hate on principle. Working as a probation officer was a perfect fit for her because it put her in control of men's fate. Men who she'd just as soon destroy as reform. Even her own husband's suicide hadn't changed that. Marge was a bad apple, rotten to the core, and no one deserved her wrath.

I shoved Marty with the ball of my foot and he toppled into the hall. I closed the door behind him and locked it again. Then I got an idea and opened it again. I stepped over Marty and made my way into the kitchen.

When I came back through the living room, he was back on the couch. I gave him a low whistle to get his attention. When he looked up, I showed him the Taser.

"You remember this, right?" I said. "Don't come back here again or you'll get reacquainted. Got it?"

Marty nodded. I went back into my room, locked the door, placed the gun in the biometric gun safe under my bed, and tried to find a sleep that I knew probably wouldn't come.

CHAPTER SIX

I WOKE UP AT five thirty and Marty was gone from the couch, as instructed. Chip was nowhere in sight. It didn't surprise me. Prison hours came early, and I'd heard the habit could be difficult to break.

I decided it was good since I'd had enough fussing with him and Marty already, so I pinned my hair up and took a quick shower. I gathered my things and was on the road to the office by six.

I drove down Old Jacksonville Highway, which no longer resembled the rural country thoroughfare I'd grown up with. Now it had shopping centers, restaurants, and grocery stores not three miles from the turnoff to our home.

I arrived at the office around six thirty and parked behind the building, locked the glass doors behind me after going inside, as well as the door to my office.

The small room smelled musty from a combination of time and stale recycled air. Still, it was the one place in the world I could go that no one else could follow.

Being there made me feel like a part of my family history. It reminded me of my grandfather, crazy aggressive coot that he was.

He'd been a stocky, powerful man, like all the others in my family. And though I lacked the size, working here in his shadow made me feel powerful anyway. I had the same spark as he did, like electricity flowing through my veins.

In a world where men try to take from a woman because they assume she's weak, I'd never forgotten what a gift that spark was. Nor did I miss many opportunities to show it to those who came at me wrong.

I opened LeeAnne Wallace's file and looked through it. The woman was organized, I had to give her that much. She'd meticulously arranged everything inside. It had a running log of dates and incidents, notes regarding Kaleb Parks' comings and goings near their property, and a running commentary on how worthless LeeAnne considered him to be as a human being.

At first glance, there didn't seem to be a pattern to the incidents, but I'd only just started looking at them.

Kaleb may have been a bit of a shut-in, but that hadn't stopped LeeAnne from trying to get answers out of him. By my quick perusal, she'd had four different run-ins with him over the last eight weeks. Two on the highway when he came walking by the house, probably headed to the gas station a few miles down the road. Another two where she'd gone straight over and knocked on the door to confront him.

Her notes contained plenty of awful accusations, but nothing to back them up. I didn't figure they'd be as much good to me as I initially hoped.

The file also contained a few pictures of footprints from around the outside of the house, and a few additional matching footprints she'd labeled as being found near the tree line separating their property from the Parks'.

The footprints' thick tread looked like some sort of work boot. Hard to tell the size, except that LeeAnne had apparently measured them. All came in at eleven inches.

In her notes on the back, LeeAnne speculated this was Kaleb's size. No mention of how she might know that.

They'd had nineteen incidents of someone knocking on Carmen's window or writing on her car over several months. Each window incident had the same characteristics—four sharp knuckle raps, then silence, not even the sound of the assailant climbing down off the roof.

Carmen, often too scared to move, usually texted her father instead of looking out the window. In the earlier incidents, he'd come running up the stairs to look out the window. More recently he'd taken to running out the front door with a Ruger .45 in his hand.

In all cases, no one had managed so much as a glance of the perpetrator. Even the footprints appeared in the days following the incidents. Whoever was harassing Carmen seemed to have an almost ghost-like ability to disappear and reappear at will.

The file also contained ten different notes, each printed in block letters, and each smelling faintly of some sort of cologne.

The text in the first few came off harmless enough. Some of them only had a few sentences, said things like "Hey gorgeous, I'd sure love to spend time with you," or "Me again, sexy. Can't wait to see what you do today."

The later notes took a more aggressive tone. "DO NOT IGNORE ME," one wrote in fat red marker, "OR YOU'LL BE SORRY." The lettering took on an almost violent tone in the red ink, though I didn't know how to qualify that observation.

The most recent note gave me chills. "I SEE EVERYTHING," it said. "SOMEDAY YOU'LL SEE, TOO."

The stalker had also begun doing other strange things in recent weeks. One morning Carmen came outside to find dried drops of red paint all over her windshield.

Another all the air had been let out of her tires. That entry had a note about a man's shape caught on their Ring doorbell camera, but if they had a still, it wasn't in the file.

That same night another game camera had disappeared from the side of their house. The third such camera, apparently. It didn't seem to matter where they put them, each disappeared the next night.

I jotted down a reminder to ask about this footage from the Ring camera.

Still, I could see why the police had been somewhat reluctant to act. The whole thing had a juvenile vibe to it, like a jealous teenager playing a prank.

But I always took stalking seriously. The problem with stalking was by the time anyone really knew it to be serious, often someone had either been taken or murdered.

I took it as a good sign that the perpetrator had never tried to enter the residence, and never approached Carmen. At least not yet.

The Wallaces had filed a theft report about the game cameras, but it hadn't done much. I wanted to speak to Kaleb and see if I could get a read on him. The whole thing could be the work of a bored neighbor, but it could also be real, legitimate stalking behavior.

I also needed to speak to Donovan Mills, Carmen's former boyfriend. It was possible this could all be chalked up to his anger at being run off by the parents, assuming he was out of the picture. I had my doubts after talking to Carmen. Something in her eyes made me think there was more to that story.

The thing I most had a hard time figuring was how the person could get up on the roof and knock on the window without detection. It would take some ninja-level sneaking skills.

I took a break after a few hours of looking over the file to send off some checks and respond to a few emails. Around ten, I decided to grab some early lunch at Loggin's a few blocks down the road.

My grandfather and father alike had both loved Loggin's homestyle buffet. It was a smorgasbord of chicken fried steak, gravy, green beans, corn, and mashed potatoes, along with tea so sweet it would coat your teeth for hours after you drank it. The restaurant was a holdout from another time, some fifty-odd years ago. Back before the entire town had gone white flight and shifted south, leaving legacy businesses like Loggin's to fend for themselves.

What remained was mostly a cracked asphalt parking lot and a big marquee sign that said "Loggin's: dining room, fried chicken, seafoods, steaks." It sat tucked up between dilapidated empty storefronts up and down either side of Glenwood Boulevard.

Inside they had Texas A&M memorabilia on the walls and booths lining the front windows. They'd finally updated the place a few years earlier, but it still carried the smell of decades of country cooking. I liked the service. I loved the food.

And although I wasn't much for college football, I loved being around all the Aggie stuff on the walls. It reminded me of my father, who had been in the Corps of Cadets.

The meal was so heavy it would stick to your insides on long days, which I had a feeling this one would be. It cost next to nothing for what you got. That appealed to me more and more lately, a relic of my mother come to bear. It would have embarrassed her to the core to see yet another piece of herself come out in me, for reasons she either didn't understand or at least had never bothered to divulge to me if she did.

After lunch, I shot a text message to the phone number Carmen Wallace had given me. I offered to buy her dinner, hoping to have a more real conversation without the threat of parents overhearing what she said.

After that, I drove south out to the Wallace house, parked in their empty driveway and did another walk around the house. I half expected LeeAnne to come out and run me off, but after a while, it became clear that no one was home.

I made my way behind the house and across a field to the wooded area where LeeAnne's file indicated they'd found footprints moving into the woods.

I didn't find any footprints. I did find a pile of Lone Star bottles near a small bog further into the trees, some of them broken. It looked to me like someone spent a great deal of time out there. That didn't have to mean anything on its own, but it did make me wonder if the police had taken the time to come out to the woods and look around.

I'd just turned to leave when all the hair on my neck stood up. I knew without looking that someone was watching me. I felt in my back waistband to ensure my Taser was still there as I walked back in the direction of the Wallace's house.

When I reached the edge of the clearing I spun on my heels without warning and there he was. Maybe twenty years old, though I wouldn't blame anyone who mistook him for a teenager. He had stringy brown hair pushed behind his ears and the kind of thin face that always looked like it would rather be somewhere else.

A Realtree sweatshirt had helped him blend with the tree line, causing me not to see him at first. I wondered if he'd been watching me the entire time, shuddering at the thought.

Even without a picture, I knew it was Kaleb Parks. Not that I got much chance to stare. Soon as he realized I saw him, he took off in the direction of his home. I gave no indication of wanting to chase him but he ran like he had a pack of wolves on his heels.

"Hey, Kaleb, wait," I called out. Almost as fast as I'd seen him, he disappeared into the trees making very little noise for how fast he moved.

He didn't look like much in the way of threats. But I could hardly deny his stealthiness. Must be one hell of a hunter, I thought. Had I sat there long enough, he might have snuck right up on me without my ever hearing him.

I turned and left the woods the way I'd come. I had it in mind to maybe catch sight of him once I left the trees, but of course, that didn't happen. He might as well have evaporated by then. It spooked me a little. It also lent some credence to LeeAnne's theory. I leaned against my car and waited for my heartbeat to slow down.

When it did, I hopped in and started the engine, drove back up the driveway the way I'd come in. As I turned left and drove past the Parks' house, I could have sworn I felt Kaleb watching me again, but I never saw another trace of him. I shook off the feeling and chalked it up to getting startled, reminded myself that emotional reactions have a way of clouding an investigator's judgment.

I needed to kill some time before Carmen would be home from her tutor, according to her father, so I decided to drive by the house and make sure Chip hadn't burned it down yet.

I stopped at the Dairy Queen in Gresham and got a large Cherry Coke as well as a large Dr. Pepper to take to him as a peace offering. Chip loved his Dr. Pepper. The only time they got it in prison was when visitors came. I'd only been good for two of them in his entire stay, so I owed him this one plus interest.

I loved my brother. I said that to myself a lot, I guess as a reminder to give him the benefit of the doubt. I hated to admit that I bore responsibility for some of the tension between us, but I did. I don't know what I thought a simple gesture like a Dr. Pepper would do to change it, particularly when I knew how little gestures meant to Chip in the first place. He could not care less.

But even that wasn't entirely his fault. Try as I might, I could not remember the last time anyone had made a meaningful gesture on his behalf, other than maybe our mother. Our father had been too hard on him, which had only seemed to make things worse. The truth was, Chip looked more like him than either Ben or I. In my heart I had always felt jealous of Chip's relationship with our father because their shared looks did seem to form a bond between them. As an adult, I came to understand that what I'd perceived as father-son bonding had been my father pulling out the last stops trying to get Chip on a sustainable track through life.

The Dr. Pepper turned out to be a moot gesture either way. When I got home, Chip was nowhere to be found, though I found evidence of the previous night's antics everywhere. I tossed the empty bottles in the recycling bin and wiped the counter down. When I turned my attention to the dishes in the sink, I noticed one of the plates still had white residue cached on it.

Chip was back to his old ways and not even trying to hide it, daring me to say something. I felt sad that he'd dragged Marty back down, too, not that it took much encouragement. Not my problem, I told myself.

I washed the residue off the plate and put it in the dishwasher. I could figure out whether or not to say something to Chip about it later. No question I'd rather he not bring drugs into the house. If something happened, it could cost me my P.I. license.

I decided to hang out and do some work at the dining room table before heading back to the Wallace household. I sat at the head of the table where my father had once sat looking out on the brown, overgrown pasture separating our house from the road.

I'd sat there all of ten minutes when a black four-door Jeep with big shiny rims pulled to the side of the road and stopped in front of our property. It set off buzzers in my head because not many people drove down our road. It had those bizarre oversized rims flashy people love so much.

I sat there like that, looking at the vehicle and wondering who was looking back at me, for close to five minutes. Finally, I said screw it, stood up, and walked out the front door onto the porch to show them someone was home.

Most robberies happen during the day, so they might be casing the place. We didn't have much worth stealing, but when has that ever stopped a thief?

When I stepped onto the porch the Jeep shifted back into gear. It pulled away casual, almost as if to show me it didn't care if I saw it or not. The same kind of thing I would have done on surveillance, though I would never stop directly in front of the subject's rural residence for that long. I watched as the Jeep rolled down the hill and around the bend out of sight. Maybe one of Chip's running buddies coming around to see him now that he was out of the can.

I knew Chip well enough to understand that I couldn't stop him from wading deeper into trouble, whatever it was. But I'd try to protect him anyway, like always.

With Ben gone, Chip on the verge of destruction, and me alone for the foreseeable future, our bloodline looked in danger of dying off unless I stepped in to save it.

Marty and I had never wanted kids, and all my other relatives were dead now. My mother and father had been only children, part of what brought them together to begin with. Sometimes I wondered if I made the right decision not having a child. Then I remembered how things with Marty turned out, and I felt thankful we had no child to put through that mess. I wasn't sure what kind of mother I would make anyway, and I'd long resented questions about it from friends and relatives over the years, the kind that took on an increased urgency every year Marty and I had remained childless. In all the ways that mattered, the women I helped were my children now.

Given those realities, Chip might be all the family I would ever have again. At least as far as blood went. L had always been my real family. Maybe more than my brother. I vowed to spend some time with her that evening when I got back from tracking Carmen's movements.

It would be neither the first nor the last vow I broke to her, spoken or otherwise. Sometimes I wondered why anyone would want to be my friend, a thought made worse when I couldn't come up with many reasons.

CHAPTER SEVEN

CARMEN PULLED OUT OF the driveway in the white Toyota 4Runner I'd seen parked in the driveway the day before. In a place like Tyler, where status reigned supreme, you got used to teenagers driving cars nicer than yours. Many of them had cars much nicer than hers.

I let her get all the way over the small hill to my west and then pulled out to follow, punching it to cover some of the ground between us while she still couldn't see me.

Once I caught up to a reasonable distance, I hung back until we made it onto Broadway where I could blend into traffic. I stayed a car or two back, gliding between lanes without a blinker but mostly staying one lane to her right in case she made any sudden turnoffs. After a few miles, I had a good sense of her mellow driving style, allowing me to shrink the distance near green lights and expand as we came upon reds without too much threat of getting separated. I felt confident she had no idea I was there, having done thousands of hours of mobile surveillance over the years.

She parked in front of a coffee shop on the edge of the downtown square called The Foundry. I'd been in once before and liked the coffee. It had a floral taste I'd once read signified the beans came from the Yirgacheffe region of Ethiopia. Had you asked me I'd have assumed I wouldn't care for it, but it turns out it suited me just fine.

I recognized Donovan Mills standing next to a rusting white Ford F-150 truck right away. Mills waited for her outside the shop, which I found odd given the ninety-degree temperature outside. He leaned on a wall smoking with the sole of one of his Wolverine boots pressed to the wall next to his knee. His posture suggested he might either own the place or be preparing to invade it, the baggy Carhartt jeans tucked into his boots giving off a militant vibe. He had a gold chain around his neck with something hanging off it, making his outfit the perfect blend of country and OG.

His eyes conveyed an angry contempt for whatever they landed on. By his posture and mannerisms, I already took him as an aggressive man on the edge of powerful anger, though I'd been wrong before.

Mills made no move to greet her, instead waiting without affect until she got out and made her way over to him. He gave her a big, open-mouthed kiss, then put a possessive arm around her, using the other arm to hold the door above her head while she walked in.

I parked around the side of the building and waited ten minutes before going in after them, to make it seem coincidental.

Mills and Carmen sat in the back corner, his arm still around her as she sipped some sort of frozen coffee drink. I'd already waited in line and ordered a black iced Americano before Carmen noticed me and nudged him. I let her catch my eye and waved, then signaled to the counter to indicate I was about to order.

Donovan Mills looked at me as if I might need straightening out, shrugging like he could not care less as she appeared to explain to him who I was. Front-running, that's what my dad had called it when men carried themselves like that. It might project tough, but it also betrayed a deep sense of insecurity.

Maybe he felt less than adequate next to a wealthy girl like Carmen. If so, her parents certainly hadn't helped things by forbidding her to see him.

For her part, Carmen carried herself as more grown up than she'd seemed in her parent's home, though still a bit meek. Her shiny black hair hung to her shoulders, and she had on makeup now that covered the anemic qualities in her face. She seemed as much intimidated as enamored by Mills.

The secretive smile that came across her face when he spoke into her ear made her simultaneously look older and more naive.

I paid the cashier and waited where the drinks came out. When the barista handed mine over, I made my way to their table. Carmen took another sip of her frozen drink. Mills gripped a paper cup of basic drip coffee without a lid in his right hand with the bottom resting on the table.

"Hello Carmen," I said, "Good to see you again."

"Hello, Miss Reeves," she said. She turned with some hesitation and gestured to Donovan. "This is my, uh, I mean, this is Donovan."

"Pleased to meet you," I said, extending my hand to him. "My name is Riley Reeves. I'm a friend of Carmen's parents."

"My dad hired her to get my mom off my back about whoever's messing with my car and stuff."

"Okay," he said, his eyes still locked with mine. "Funny running into you like this, I mean, considering the circumstances."

His response made me wonder if he'd noticed me pull up behind Carmen. If he had, he'd done a good job of not letting me see it.

"I work right down the street, so I come over here sometimes for coffee in the afternoon," I explained.

"Really, that's so crazy," Carmen said. "I'm surprised we haven't run into each other before here."

I smiled, said, "Maybe we did, how would we have known?"

Carmen gave a nervous smile back. "I guess that's true," she said.

"You know, while I'm here, do you think I could ask you guys a couple of questions? I've been turning this thing over all day and I think a little more information would really help. It won't take long, and I promise I won't be any trouble."

Mills looked at me like it would be impossible for me to cause him real trouble. I kept smiling and pretended not to notice his hostility. The more he underestimated me, the better. Carmen took a drink and set down her cup. Her eyes pleaded with Donovan to be nice. He exhaled a deep breath and obliged, sort of.

"So?" Mills said.

"So, what?" I asked. It might be counter-productive, but my instincts said getting him worked up a little might inspired emotion-driven responses that revealed more information.

"So what the hell do you want?" he said. "I ain't got all day."

I smiled again to give him mixed signals. "Do you have any idea at all who might want to harass Carmen?" I asked.

He stretched an awkward arm across the space between them and put it around her shoulder, pulled her closer. "Naw," he said. "And if I did I'd have solved this problem a long time ago." He smiled to show me he meant violence as a solution, like it or not.

"Have you ever had any run-ins with her neighbor, Kaleb Parks?" I asked, pretending to ignore the suggestion.

"Naw. The way I heard it, dude some sort of autistic or some shit. Don't hardly talk to people. I cain't even imagine I'd do anything but stomp a dude like that, on the real."

"Do you think anyone in your own life could be responsible for it? No offense, you understand. But you're a smooth guy, I'm sure you've got ex-girlfriends." The compliment seemed to embolden him even more.

"That I do. But I guarantee they don't got nothing to do with whoever's fucking around over at Carmen's house. When she with me, she safe. Motherfuckers don't play around with me like that. Ever. It's her people who can't keep her covered. Won't let me come around the house, nothing I can do for 'em, the dumb fucks. They think she too good for me." He took his arm off Carmen and used his hand on her chin to turn her face toward him. "Sometimes I think the apple ain't fell far from the tree."

Carmen's posture sank but she made no move to take his hand off her chin.

"You know that's not true," she said.

I shook my head as if his words interested me. There was nothing interesting about him, other than his delusion about being interesting.

"How you know what I do or don't know?" Mills said to Carmen. He turned back to me.

"Anything else?" he asked in a tone that said he was about done with my presence.

I didn't respond, wanting to see how he might react to the snub. He didn't like it.

"Yo, you deaf or what?" He leaned forward and put his hands on the table, gave me a hard stare.

"Do you think it's Kaleb who's been harassing me, Miss Reeves?" Carmen broke in, discomfort with the standoff dripping off her tone.

I shifted my attention to her, completely shutting Mills out with my posture. He didn't like that either.

"I don't know yet," I said. "Why, do you?" She shook her head and shrugged.

"Ain't it supposed to be your job to know?" Mills said, reasserting himself into the conversation. "Or did her moms and pops hire you to keep an eye on me and this all a big-ass smoke screen? I seen you pull up right after Carmen."

"It's my job to watch," I said. "And I'm better at it than you might guess. But I don't ask questions unless they're important. And if I were following either of you, you'd never notice me, guaranteed."

Mills sneered at that. "Yeah? I doubt it. Anyhow, I ain't got nothing else to tell you. I don't like this rent-a-cop bullshit, either. You figure out who's messing with my girl, let me know and I'll break 'em off somethin' that solves the problem. Otherwise, I don't see how you and I need to ever meet again."

He stood up to leave. Carmen tried to catch him by the arm, but he shook her off and walked out the front door, leaving his full coffee on the metallic table.

Carmen moved as if to follow, thought better and slunk back into her seat. "I'm sorry," she said. "It's my fault. I shouldn't have mentioned that my parents hired you. He gets really defensive about them. They've been sort of…"

"What?" I asked.

"Shitty to him," she finally replied. "Can I say that in front of you?"

"You can say whatever you like in front of me." I winked for effect. "I'm a big girl too."

Carmen smiled. I smiled back, happy to be building a little rapport with her now that Mills was outside. She seemed like a sweet girl who'd suffered through a lot of problems, not of her own making. But also a girl who'd just found out about rebellion and might take it too far if left unattended.

"I need to catch up with Don if that's okay," she said. "I'm sorry for the dust-up."

"Don't be, it's not your fault. None of this is. But if you feel like opening up to me about anything, I'm here to help you." I took out one of my cards and handed it to her, having forgotten to give her one the night before. "Really, I mean that. This might all be nothing, or it could be more serious than we realize. Until I figure it out, try not to spend too much time alone, and be aware of your surroundings, and who you're hanging out with. Be vigilant getting in and out of your car, especially at home."

"I usually call my dad when I go home and he comes out to walk me in," she said. "As a precaution."

I nodded. "That's good. Keep doing it. By the way, I noticed that everything in the file involved incidents that happened at your house. Have you had any stalking incidents anywhere else?"

She thought about that for a moment. "Just once. I went to a pasture party with some friends, so I left my car parked at the gas station on the corner of Old Jacksonville and Grande, over on the side of the building. When I came back someone had keyed the side of it and written on the windows in red paint."

"What did it say?" I asked.

"I don't fully remember. I think it said slut and some other stuff. We were able to buff the key marks out at the detail shop and get the windshield scraped clean."

"It must have scared you though, no?"

"Yeah, some." She looked around to be sure no one was watching. "I'd had a few wine coolers when my friend dropped me off. I was afraid to drive like that and get pulled over, so I called my mother. She was beyond pissed."

"I bet." I started to say something else but Donovan knocked on the front window, causing everyone in the place to turn and stare at him. He motioned for Carmen to come.

"Guess I better go," she said. Take care, Miss Reeves."

"You too," I said. "And Carmen?" She looked back again. "For the record, you don't have to go anywhere or do anything just because a man tells you to. Just my two cents."

She grinned, then walked out the door. Mills put his arm around her and led her to the 4Runner. I hated it when men acted like that.

CHAPTER EIGHT

I DUCKED OUT THE side door of the coffee shop and made my way to my Pilot to follow them. I hit a quick right then another onto Broadway and picked them up at the stoplight on Broadway and Front Street. They made a right onto Front just as my light went green. It saved me the trouble of having to be obvious about catching up.

I got in the center lane and stayed as far back as I could without risking getting caught at a stoplight. When the 4Runner changed lanes to be right in front of me, I knew they had no idea I was there.

Still, I hung back and didn't change lanes with them the next time, putting me at risk if they made a fast right. I closed the distance between us as necessary, and eventually drifted over to be behind them and one car back. It wasn't perfect, but it provided cover at the risk of hitting a red light if the car in front of me stopped short.

Eventually, the car turned off and left them right in front of me and up about fifty yards.

Mills drove out into the countryside as the road left town and became Highway 31. After we made it through the last stoplight I hung back even more, just barely keeping them in sight enough to see where they turned. Country roads require a wider gap to avoid getting burned. Mobile surveillance is a balancing act that requires as much talent as it does skill or luck, but there are a few hard-and-fast tricks that really help.

They turned North out toward New Harmony. I had a feeling of what they might be up to, driving out on these desolate roads.

I rolled down my window and let the suffocating hot air blow in my face as I turned onto the highway, almost a half-mile behind them. We hadn't gone a mile before I caught the faint smell of burning cigar paper and Mexican schwag weed. I couldn't guarantee it had come from their vehicle, but it seemed likely.

The smell brought back memories. I'd spent a portion of my high school career doing the same thing. We called it going for a country drive. We'd spent hours driving the East Texas countryside getting stoned and talking about a life that, in retrospect, none of us understood yet. It had been an overall positive experience, even as I'd put cannabis down a year or so later due to the anxiety it often gave me.

That didn't mean I thought it was a good idea for Carmen to be driving around smoking. But who was I to judge?

I followed them through miles of green pasture flanked by pine trees, past horses and cows and old barns that hadn't been used in a half century, at least. You could get lost in that big, sprawling country, dotted from time to time with brick ranch-style houses a lot like the one I'd grown up in.

I'd started to get lost in my memories when the 4Runner slowed without warning and turned left down a two-track dirt road that cut through a grove of pine trees like a tunnel. I could just make out a white clapboard house and rotten barn beyond the trees up the hill from them. The house looked like it had been dumped behind the trees to hide it.

As I got closer, the trees blocked the view and all I could see was that the road wound through the small forest, probably to avoid boggy spots.

Mills and Carmen had already disappeared into the center of it. I pulled into the drive enough to back up and turn around, intending to wait for them along their route back into town. My eye caught a symbol carved into one of the trees as I did, three letters linked together and burned like a cattle brand into the bark.

The brand consisted of an N and a B connected in the middle by an H's crossbar, all three in caps. NHB. I snapped a picture with my cell phone so I could look up its origin later. It might be nothing, except that whoever lived on the property must have some level of comfort with a seventeen-year-old girl showing up stoned and smelling like weed. It wasn't Mills' place because I'd already run down his current address at an apartment complex back in Tyler.

The sound of a vehicle coming down the highway caused me to get a move on. As I started to back out, the black four-door Jeep I'd seen stopped on the highway in front of my house earlier that day slowed and made a move to turn in behind me. My heart bucked in my chest, but there was nowhere for my panic to take me.

I tried to back up, but they'd already blocked me in by parking the Jeep across the dirt road's mouth in the middle of the highway. Up close I could see that the Jeep's paint had a texture to it, something like a spray-on bed liner. That distinction alone made me certain it was the same one I'd seen.

The passenger-side door opened and spilled out a barrel-chested man in his mid or maybe late twenties, his hair shaved short with wavy lines cut into the sides. He had on an oversized plain white t-shirt over baggy Nike shorts and what looked to be brand new Air Jordan shoes. His arms looked like pythons with green-inked sleeve tattoos down both that could only have been done in prison.

He looked like trouble on literal steroids. Not the kind of guy I wanted to be trapped on the side of a lonely highway with.

I slid my Taser out of the conceal holster and held it between my legs, opened a guidebook I kept in between the seat and the console to a map of East Texas highways, and set it on top of the Taser to conceal it.

He came right up to the open window and leaned in so close I could smell the Black and Mild tobacco on his breath.

"Yo, what you doing here, lady?" he asked, so casual I might not have noticed him scanning the interior of my car for clues.

"Got lost, trying to turn around and find my way back. Say, if I go up that way will it take me to the Tyler airport?" I said.

He looked down at the open guidebook, then up at me. Then back at whoever was in the vehicle behind him, which had a dark tint that made it hard to see into. He smiled to reveal a silver-capped tooth and looked back at me again.

"Lost, huh?" he said.

"That's right."

"And what you got here?" he asked, reaching inside the window to pick up the atlas. I intercepted his hand and directed it back where it came from. As I did, I noticed that the tattoos on his right arm were arranged around the same brand I'd taken a picture of on the tree. It looked as if it had been burned into his arm, too.

His smile turned into a snarl at my touch.

"I'd appreciate if we kept our hands to ourselves," I said, keeping my voice neutral. "You know how it is, strangers and all that. It's a guidebook of East Texas," I added, gesturing to the book in my lap. I kept it on hand as a pretext for situations just like this one. "I do water rights work for the state, but I'm kind of old school," I added, "I like to use a map to get around instead of one of these crazy phones the kids all use."

His snarl turned into something resembling confusion. The pretext had been designed to throw him off guard, polite but direct.

"That 1998 bullshit might be why you come to end up in the wrong driveway," he said. "And I promise this is the wrong fucking one, you can bet that. This a private road and we appreciate our space, you know what I'm sayin'?"

I frowned and feigned confusion. "I see," I said. "An honest mistake, I'm so sorry."

"Honest, huh?"

"Yes. Honest. So is that the way to the airport?" I tried again.

"So let me get dis straight, so we clear. You don't want my hands up in yo ride, but you using our driveway to turn around. And now you want directions to the only place a blind man could find way out here? That smell like bullshit to me."

"I see your point," I said. "Thing is, I'm not everyone. I can see you don't like the company, so my mistake. It won't happen again, I can assure you. If you'll just back up a few feet I'll get out of your hair and—"

"Whatchu gon give me to move?" he cut me off.

"What do you want?" I asked, still playing the game, but starting to wonder if I ought to just Tase him and be done with it.

They had me blocked in so the only way out was to back through the space the Jeep occupied or risk getting stuck in the ditch. I still needed to talk my way out, if I could.

As I considered my options, I heard a car pull up behind the Jeep on the highway. Relief washed over me.

A state trooper had pulled up behind the Jeep and turned his lights on. In order to block me in, they'd blocked a portion of the highway by default.

The cruiser's door opened and a thin middle-aged trooper got out. He put his Resistol hat on over cliché cop Ray-Bans and took his time about shutting the door.

"Mind if I ask why y'all are stopped out here in the middle of the highway?" he said to the tattooed man at my door. My man said nothing, so the cop made his way toward us. As he walked past the Jeep the passenger window came down, and a black-haired man with a burgeoning beard and squinty brown eyes leaned across the seat.

"Sorry for the trouble, Officer. We come to turn into our driveway and this lady was stopped here or turning around or something, so we stopped to see what we could do to help. We been here like thirty seconds, that's it. I was about to pull down and turn around in the neighbor's driveway so she could back out."

The trooper looked from him to me, then at my tattooed friend, then back to the man in the Jeep window.

"Simms, right?'

"What's that, Officer?" the man said.

"Danny Simms. I know you. Or should I say Danimal? I hear that's what they call you." He turned to the man standing outside my window. "And that makes you TJ Evans, don't it?"

The two men exchanged a look without speaking. The one he'd called TJ let the other, Danny, speak for them.

"You got me," he said. "But I don't think we met before, did we?"

The cop shook his head. "I don't believe we've had the displeasure. But I'll tell you what. Pull forward and park on the side of the highway there over yonder. I'd like to speak to the lady real quick to make sure she's all right.

"If everything checks out, she'll be out of your way in no time, and we won't have to make this a more formal meeting." He turned to face the man at my window. "You, Evans, give that woman some space and go sit in the car with your friend."

The man, Evans by the officer's telling, gave me that same sinister smile as before, and a nod that said we'd talk later. I hoped not. He took his time walking back to the Jeep and got back into the passenger seat. The trooper waited until he shut the door to come over to my window. His eyes registered some recognition when he first saw my face.

"You're the P.I. lady, Reeves, one who took down Carl Farlow."

I nodded.

"That was some good detective work. Crazy son of a bitch. So I guess you realize you've done got yourself cornered up in here by a couple of hostile natives, right?"

"I was starting to get that impression," I said. "But I don't know who they are."

"Call themselves the New Harmony Boys. NHB for short, that's their gang sign over on the tree there yonder. In my line of work, we call 'em redneck gangbangers. Not exactly nice people, you catch my drift. This house is in my notes to keep an eye on when I'm out this way. They usually quiet, but I couldn't resist this opportunity to make contact. You tied up with them on a case or something?"

"I'm running down some leads, but I'm not sure it has anything to do with them. Call it a coincidence, I guess. They just pulled up while I was turning around."

He took off his sunglasses so we could see eye to eye and studied me. "I bet," he said after a moment. "Girl like you ends up around a lot of bad people by coincidence. Folks might start thinking you're looking for trouble. Anyway, look. I got no reason to press the issue, but I was you, I'd steer clear of these boys if you can. The one, Simms, just got out of the pen a few months ago. They's knee-deep in drug trafficking when they ain't pistol-whipping teenagers or robbing keg parties, the way I hear it. I'm gonna wave you on now and make sure they don't follow you. But buyer beware, and all that good stuff."

"Duly noted, Trooper Cantwell," I said, reading his nametag. He took out a business card and handed it to me. "They give you any more trouble, call me." I took his card and exchanged it with one of my own from the console. It seemed like the thing to do. "Now get on back to civilization," Cantwell said.

I didn't make him tell me twice. I wanted to get out of there before Carmen and Mills came back up the road anyway. I could decide whether to tell her parents what kind of people she associated with later. I got the feeling from her father that they already knew to some degree.

I backed out and drove toward town. As I passed the Jeep, the window came down and Danny Simms' reptilian eyes watched me drive past. He winked but I didn't react. I figured Cantwell was right that I ought to steer clear of him if I could. Which made me wonder again why I'd seen them at my home. It couldn't be a coincidence, because I didn't believe in coincidence any more than Trooper Cantwell had.

I watched Cantwell wave them back into their driveway and then flip a U-turn to head back in the opposite direction. I'd never seen a cop so eager to get out of a situation like that. My father would have pulled their entire car apart without a second thought, let them figure out how to complain about it later. If they dared.

To be honest, I'd never cared for that type of authoritarian behavior. Which is why I preferred being a private detective to a police officer. I didn't want to exercise control over anyone else—and I didn't care for others exercising it over me.

At any rate, more and more my instincts told me that Carmen could be into something way over her head. Now I needed to find out what.

CHAPTER NINE

I HAD A DECISION to make. The kind of decision that tended to bother me, too. After my shake-up with Danny Simms and his flunkie, TJ Evans, the first thing I did back in the office was run background reports on both men through my Delvepoint system, as well as the Smith County website.

I did not care for the results. Both Simms and Evans had long intertwined records that combined petty theft with assault, and a few drug charges apiece peppered in for good measure. I had no doubt that a records request at the surrounding counties would reveal additional charges, as well.

As I dug deeper, the news got worse.

Simms, in particular, had a penchant for violence, had just gotten out of the Texas Department of Corrections a few months earlier after an assault on a local attorney named John Webb.

Webb had made the mistake of waving Simms and another man down on the side of Old Jacksonville Highway late one night.

He'd been hoping to get help with a stalled-out Jaguar. Instead, he got pistol-whipped, robbed, and threatened with murder if he reported the crime. Which, of course, he did anyway, being a man of the court. I picked up more details from a series of news stories on the case, which I had a vague memory of, in retrospect. Webb's daughter Darlene had come close to being kidnapped the week before the trial but managed to escape. They'd never identified her attempted abductors, but consensus dictated that Simms had a hand in it somewhere. I wrote a note to look up John Webb and speak to him about the case.

I also made a note to get the case files from the county clerk and keep digging. If need be, I could try to work some of my father's law enforcement contacts, but I'd made a commitment early on in my career to avoid it as much as possible. It put them in an awkward position. Misusing the databases at their disposal could cost them their jobs. And these days every keystroke was monitored. I didn't want to put anyone in that position, so I preferred to do the legwork instead, survive on every investigator's bread and butter: publicly available information and the application of foot to pavement.

No one interviewed in any of the news stories had anything good to say about Simms. He'd come by the nickname Danimal for a reason. His bark had plenty of bite and had been like that since long before he'd dropped out of high school. He was a lifelong criminal and by all accounts a sociopathic bully. If he hadn't killed already he probably would someday.

Which was why I had a tough decision to make. On the one hand, I'd rather not betray Carmen's trust by speaking to her parents. On the other, I had a feeling she might be in way over her head with these kinds of people, and I'd made a commitment to her father to inform him if that was the case.

It seemed plausible that Simms and his cronies might have something to do with her stalking as well, given the kidnapping accusations.

I could not in good professional integrity keep this discovery from her parents, I finally decided, no matter how much I didn't want to betray Carmen's sense of trust in me. I'd taken the case to help Carmen, and so I needed to handle things in a way that wouldn't result in her total lockdown. I needed to find the right way to bring the information to the Wallaces' attention without getting put on the outside with their daughter the same way they had. Try as I might, I could not see a clear solution, so I put the problem down and focused on putting together the file on Simms and Evans. I had every intention of expanding it in the near future.

I also put together a file on Donovan Mills, who had an arrest record of his own. His included petty theft, a few possession charges, and an assault charge that had been dismissed. He also came up on a list of possible relatives that included Simms. More research revealed them to be first cousins. I tucked that piece of information away in my mind until I could ascertain what to do with it and decided to hit the streets.

I drove the half mile to the coffee shop where Mills had left his truck. It was gone now, meaning Carmen had dropped him back off. As I sat there trying to decide what to do next, my phone lit up with Latonya's name and goofy face.

"Hey L," I said.

"Where you at, girl?

"Just finishing up some work. You?"

"Oh, you know, just sittin' here watchin' yo butt from across the street."

I scanned the area around me and, sure enough, there was L's car sitting in the empty parking lot across the street, idling.

"You following me?" I teased.

"I was, you'd be in trouble, I tell you that." I could hear the grin in her voice that said she relished this, beating me at my own game.

"You on surveillance, or what?" I asked.

"Girl, just driving by and saw yo dark-ass tint over there making you look like a grade-A stalker. I don't know how you be following anyone like that. You look like FBI, CIA, and police all rolled up into one soccer mom car."

"I'm too boring to be police," I said, laughing now. "And the soccer mom part is what throws them off." It had been a weird day, but L always cheered me up. "Anyhow, what are you up to now?"

"Thinking 'bout letting you take me over to Sportszone and buy me a couple Crown and gingers. Been one hell of a day on my end."

"Mine too," I said. "And I'd love to. You want to walk over here and ride with me or meet me over there?"

"Girl, you slippin'," she said, tapping on my passenger-side window as an answer. I hung up and hit the unlock button. "Makin' me worry about you out there on surveillance," she said through the open door as she got in.

"Making myself worry, too. You've been hanging out with me too long, getting good at sneaking."

"Girl I been good at sneaking, don't take credit." We both had a laugh about that as I pulled out of the parking lot and drove the block and a half to the Sportszone.

It wasn't much as far as sports bars go, but it sure as hell beat the stuffy environment at Rick's. L and I had never been the fancy types anyway.

I parked in front and we grabbed a couple of seats at the bar. I made good on my commitment to buy her a few Crown and gingers. She'd already made good on a lifetime of cheering me up. It was the least I could do.

I ordered a Shiner Bock and a shot of Wild Turkey, nursed them both until L finished both of her drinks. I tried my best to listen as she told me about her day. Usually, I enjoyed her stories about giving people comfort through her antics, or putting a coworker in their place with a smile.

But my mind kept coming back to the issue with Carmen, and the fact that Danny Simms somehow knew where I lived. I'd just about convinced myself to let it go when Chip and Marty showed up, both shitfaced and stumbling.

"Well shit, Marty, look who we got here," Chip said as they beached themselves on two stools that faced perpendicular to the ones L and I sat on. The other four people in the bar watched Chip and Marty as if watching a play. Drunks have that effect sometimes, they come off like caricatures of real people. Or maybe more like a car accident you can't look away from.

"Y'all look like you can barely drag yourselves in," I said to Chip. Marty kept his eyes on the floor, shame being his new posture in life, along with a healthy dose of fear around me. I guess he still had the memory of my Taser hanging in his head right about then. I'd left it in the car like I always did when I went into a bar, but no need to tell him that.

Chip gave me a sloppy smile as if I'd paid him a compliment. "Don't nobody know how to have a good time no more, that's the problem with the world," he said, nudging Marty. "Asshole bartender over at Rick's included."

"They threw y'all ass out, huh?" L said.

Chip sneered at her, too drunk to even pretend to like her now. "No lip from you, Latonya," he said. "Not tonight. Marty and I are still celebrating. Hell, I might take me a day for every single one I spent in the klink to celebrate getting out, if it's all right with my sponsor over here."

Chip gestured to show he meant me. I guess he didn't catch the irony that Marty actually had a sponsor before he'd shown back up and started helping him fall apart again.

"You damn sure better find a sponsor if you plan to do so," I said. "Because I'm not ponying up the money for food or drinks. You're grown, big brother, you can poison yourself if that's what you've got a mind to do, but you'll do it on your own dime and your own time."

Chip tried to gesture to the bartender, who continued to ignore him, probably hoping he and Marty would leave if she ignored them long enough.

"Yeah," he said. "About that. I been thinkin'. I ain't much for being tied to one place these days. Prison will do that to you. I done decided to let you buy me out of mom and pop's house, make y'all's little roommate experiment official. I know it's what y'all want anyway." He swept his arm to indicate L and I. L clicked her tongue in distaste. "I'mo get me a dually and one o' them fifth-wheel campers for the bed, live like a Pine Curtain gypsy for a while. Skip out on bills and everything else that ain't pure, unadulterated fun."

I sighed. I'd known this conversation was coming. It didn't mean I wanted to have it like this, him drunker than two college kids on a two a.m. run to D's Coffee Shop.

"I'll see about it," I said. "But not right this minute. Right now I think L and I are ready to head home."

"If that's all right with you two pudding pockets," L said.

I leaned over and said, "Try not to make too much noise if you decide to make it home later. I'll see what I can do about the house tomorrow, but you need to act right in the meantime. Money's tight, and I don't imagine any banks are dying to loan me the balance thanks to you and the shy guy over there."

I held up my hands as anger flashed over his face. "We're past that. But not far, so keep it together. In the meantime, for the love of God, y'all don't drive when you leave. Take a cab. Or sober up. Honestly, do both, just to be safe."

L and I turned and walked out into the humid night before Chip could respond, leaving them both slumped over the bar like a couple of wounded jackals. In the entire conversation, Marty hadn't said a word to me, which was how I liked it. I hoped it was the start of a new and meaningful trend.

I drove out to the house in silence with L in her car behind me, a little soured after dealing with Chip. A drunk will do that to you.

I decided that in the morning I'd give Paul Wallace a call and go talk to him in person about the people Carmen seemed to be involved with. Little did I know they'd be calling me to come over long before I even got the chance.

CHAPTER TEN

L AND I HAD just settled in on the couch to watch *Hap and Leonard* when my phone lit up with Paul Wallace's number on the screen.

"Hello?" I said, knowing that a call this late couldn't mean good news.

"Miss Reeves?" It was LeeAnne, not Paul.

"Yes ma'am," I said. "What can I do for you now?"

"Maybe this was a bad idea," she said, irritation building in her voice.

I exhaled, tried again. "No, it's not. I'm sorry, long day. What's going on, Mrs. Wallace?"

"We've got a pretty serious problem over here with Carmen. I wouldn't call you but I don't know who else to call, and I figure we ought to get our money's worth from that retainer you'll probably keep either way."

"What happened?" I asked, ignoring the slight.

"She came home high on some sort of drugs. For sure she's been drinking. I think someone gave her whatever else she took. She's a good girl, she wouldn't do drugs on her own."

"All right," I said. "What can I do to help? This sounds like pretty standard teenage girl stuff, to me."

"Not for Carmen. And anyway, if it were that alone, maybe so."

"So something else happened?" I asked.

"Just, please come over and I'll explain everything. I don't want to talk about it on the phone, these damn cell phones record everything you say. The last thing we need is this getting around town."

I rolled my eyes so hard I'm surprised she didn't hear them hit the socket walls. "Okay," I said, measuring my words. "Give me a half hour and I'll be there. Does that work?"

"It'll have to work, I suppose," she said.

I hung up without responding. I wondered what was going on, whether it had to do with Danny Simms or Donovan Mills. Difficult to say. But I doubted it was much of a coincidence, her being out at Simms' farm and coming home intoxicated and defiant.

That she was putting herself in this kind of position confirmed my need to say something to her parents about who she was consorting with. My hope was to speak with her too, privately, see if I could help her pivot.

"What's going on?" L asked. If it bothered her that I hardly managed to finish an episode of anything uninterrupted, she never mentioned it.

I sighed. "My client. Gotta make a house call."

"Damn," she said. "Ole Leonard was just gettin' warmed up, too."

"You can finish it without me and I'll catch up later," I said.

"Nah, ain't no fun in that. I wanna get to bed before yo crazy brother come home anyhow. Them fools were drunk as hell, boy cain't behave once he be like that."

"I'll be surprised if they can make it all the way out here," I said. "You want, I'll leave the Taser. He talks tough you can put a little spark in his step. He seems pretty determined to fry his own brain either way."

"He sho do. I hate to say it, I feel kinda bad about Marty, though. Every time a person be tryin' to do right, it seem like they past come running up with a crowbar."

"I wouldn't feel too bad," I said, picking up my keys off the counter. "Guy really doesn't want a drink all he's got to do is say no. Nobody can keep Marty sober but Marty. I wasn't buying the emasculated act he put on the other night, or the victim act tonight, either. Marty drinks because he wants to. There's nothing else as important to him. Not me, not even Chip."

L shook her head and waved me off. "You a walking contradiction," she said. "Hardest and softest heart I ever seen in the same person."

I walked out of the door without saying anything. I never could think of a smart-ass response to the truth.

***

I pulled up behind Carmen's 4Runner and parked. Paul opened the front door before I even got out of my car. LeeAnne came out right behind him.

"Miss Reeves, thank you for coming so late," Paul said.

"Is Carmen okay?" I asked.

"Not exactly."

"If she wasn't my daughter, I'd have snatched her up by her hair," LeeAnne broke in.

"I get it," I said. "But don't do that, it won't do you any good. I'm sure you had these same things happen at her age, no? What would you have done if your mother did that?"

I spoke from experience. My own mother had done that. And she'd backhanded me so many times that I liked to joke she had the quickest draw in Texas. Even when I knew it was coming, I could never dodge it.

"I thought detectives weren't supposed to work on assumptions," LeeAnne said. "I would never have pulled the shit she pulled tonight, but you don't have all the information yet, do you now? Some detective."

"Honey, calm down," Paul said. I waved him off.

"Fair enough. But you called me, so how about we go in the house and you can explain what happened. You want, I'll even talk to Carmen after, see if an outsider's perspective will help."

"Good luck with that," LeeAnne said. "She's not here."

"Let's all go inside and we'll explain everything." Paul turned and led the way into the living room with the dead animal heads all over the wall. I declined when he offered me something to drink.

"Can you tell me what happened?" I asked, getting to the point. "And where's Carmen?"

"We have no idea where she is," LeeAnne said. "And that's worse than it sounds, too."

Paul sat down as his face took on a deeper seriousness as if what he was about to tell me was privileged information. "When she came in earlier tonight," he began, "LeeAnne noticed her eyes were goofy, pupils dilated like a couple of black marbles. I was back in my office finishing up some work stuff. LeeAnne called me in and I agreed she was on something."

"It was her voice that caught my attention," LeeAnne added. "I know my daughter too well, and she didn't sound like herself. She kept trying to go up to her room to avoid talking to me, wouldn't put her backpack on the hook in the entry hall where it usually goes. When Paul came in he decided we needed to see what was so important that she was keeping a death grip on it like that."

"And?" I said.

"She had… she had drugs in it, several kinds. At first, I thought it was just a Ball jar with what looked like marijuana in it. Then I found the black plastic container in the bottom. It had little baggies of yellowish powder that had been tied off by crude flaps on the top." She paused and looked at me, her eyes serious. "Do you think that was methamphetamine, something like that?" she asked, fear showing in her eyes for the first time now. It was no wonder she could read her daughter so well. They had the same eyes.

"Maybe," I said. "But I'm leaning toward cocaine as a guess. Depending on the light it can take on a yellowish tint, and if it were ice or something, you'd have described more of a sparkle to it. But honestly, the reason I'm leaning toward cocaine has to do with my investigation today. I'll get to that in a minute. I was going to call you about it in the morning and come over to speak in person, actually, but given the circumstances now is probably better."

"Did you find something out about the case?" Paul asked, giving me a look that said he clearly meant Donovan Mills, not the stalking issue.

"Maybe," I replied. "I'm not sure yet. But what I found definitely has to do with your daughter's well-being. First things first, though. Where are the drugs now, are they in the house?"

"That's just it," LeeAnne said, "I sent her to her room because Paul suggested we call you over and discuss whether to take them to the police. Which, as usual, looks to have been a waste of time and money. Paul wanted to get your advice from a legal perspective. I doubt you have one."

The word advice sounded like she might choke on it. Under normal circumstances, I would have enjoyed watching her spit it out. But right then I was concerned enough about Carmen to swallow her condescension.

"You did the right thing by calling me," I told her. "Police have a funny way with drugs, they need someone to pin them on to get credit, and almost anyone will do. They'd want your daughter to cooperate in apprehending whoever she got them from at a minimum.

And with what I found out today, the drugs might belong to people you don't want to get your daughter crossways with unless you have no other options."

LeeAnne's eyes went wide. "What do you mean?" she said, the fear invading her voice now, too.

"Donovan Mills, I bet," Paul said.

I nodded. "Yes. Well, sort of. Mills is a part of it. But it's more the people he's got your daughter associating with. I did some research after following her and Mills to a farmhouse today."

Paul uncrossed his arms and sat forward with his hands leaning on his knees. LeeAnne's expression went from fear to hostility in a single blink.

"You followed my daughter," she hissed. "What does that have to do with our reasons for hiring you? How dare you invade her privacy that way?"

I almost smirked but managed to rein it in. "You weren't so worried about her privacy an hour ago, were you? And with good reason. I followed Carmen to a meeting with Donovan Mills this afternoon at a coffee shop."

"So she's still seeing that piece of trailer trash and has been lying to me?" LeeAnne snapped. "How did you know about him in the first place? I specifically told Paul not to bring him up to you."

I gave Paul an apologetic look. He nodded. "Your husband mentioned it yesterday after you left. But I'd already gotten it out of Carmen when I was looking at her room anyway."

"And you didn't tell us?" LeeAnne exclaimed. She turned to Paul.

"And you, don't even get me started, you son of a bitch. Why am I the last person in this situation to know about something like this?"

Paul crossed his arms again, sat back in a defensive posture. "Don't do that, LeeAnne. What, did you think she stopped seeing him just because we told her to? That's not how it works with a girl her age, and you know it. Or at least I figured it. I didn't know anything, it was a hunch." He turned to me. "Miss Reeves, why didn't you mention that Carmen had already told you this yesterday?"

"Because I told Carmen I wouldn't. It seemed like you had an idea she'd probably confided in me when we spoke last. The biggest benefit I can offer y'all is gaining your daughter's trust. That way she'll tell me things she might not tell you, as her parents, and one of those things could be the key to getting to the bottom of all this nonsense."

"How dare you," LeeAnne said again, standing up now. She seemed pretty worried about how I dared do almost anything in her presence. "If you're suggesting that my daughter doesn't trust me, you've lost your damned mind."

"Did she tell you she had a bag full of drugs? Or that she was still dating Donovan Mills? You want my opinion, it's this. If your teenager doesn't tell you everything, that makes you a good parent. It means they know there are boundaries in your household. Kids do this stuff. It's not a knock on you."

Paul stood and caught his wife's arm, gently directing her back into her seat. It was clear she did view Carmen's actions as a reflection of herself, a sign of latent narcissism, perhaps.

"Honey, I know you've always been close with Carmen," Paul said. "But Miss Reeves is right. She's growing up, and she's going to make her own choices, a lot of which she will hide just to stave off our influence on them. I'm not happy about it either, but it's normal, to a degree."

"I don't care what you're happy about," LeeAnne snapped back. "I'm the one who spent hundreds of hours in clinics and hospitals when she was sick, trying to figure out what was wrong. Held her hand while they poked and prodded her everywhere, violated her every privacy.

"You were at work, as usual. Carmen and I have a bond you will never understand, so don't you dare try to tell me about it now. If she were in trouble, she'd tell me."

I stood up and walked around behind the couch, hoping the movement would refocus them off each other. It did. They both looked at me like some sort of hydra that had wandered into their house with evil intentions.

"Seventeen-year-olds have a funny sense of denial when it comes to being in trouble," I said. "She could be in denial. But if y'all want to argue this out now, I can go. Otherwise, do you mind if we get back to the task at hand, which was of so much importance that you called me over to your home at almost eleven o'clock at night?

"I'm not trying to offend anyone about anything. What I am trying to do is to help your daughter the best way I know how. Which is the reason I'm wondering why you still haven't told me where she is? I saw her car in the driveway."

"We took her keys away when we found the drugs," Paul said. "Her phone, too. I sent her to her room. At some point, she snuck down here, grabbed the backpack and bolted."

"Which is why I'm ready to pull my hair out," LeeAnne said. "She's out wandering the streets with a backpack full of drugs right now and no phone. She could be in jail already, for all we know, future be damned. We homeschooled her to avoid this kind of thing."

"You can't keep the world out, Mrs. Wallace," I said. "And my guess is whoever gave her the drugs probably communicates with her on a burner, so she's probably got a second phone with her anyway. The good news is, I think I have a good idea of how to find her."

"Great. It's about time you had something to offer," LeeAnne said. "Maybe if you'd bothered to tell us about her being back with that jackass Mills we wouldn't have needed to call you at 'eleven at night,' as you said."

I took the opportunity to explain to them about Danny Simms and the New Harmony Boys, how I'd followed her to Simms' farm with Mills. They both looked green by the end of the explanation.

"I knew the guy was no good," Paul said. "But this is worse than I imagined." He turned to LeeAnne and continued. "I've heard of the guy, Simms, and so have you. He's the one who pistol-whipped John Webb and then tried to kidnap Darlene, you remember that?"

LeeAnne gasped, then her face hardened back into anger again. "I cannot believe you didn't tell me you suspected she was back seeing that boy." She bored a hole in him with her eyes as if to say everything that happened from here was on him. To my surprise, he wilted beneath it, adding a layer of complexity to their relationship in my eyes.

I figured they'd have it out once I was gone. For now, I wanted to keep them on track. I said, "Let me go see what I can do to find her while y'all work this out between you. Assuming she gets the drugs back to where they came from, that might be the best outcome, if you want my honest opinion."

"Opinions are as worthless to me as chewed bubble gum," LeeAnne said. "And your honesty doesn't seem much better. Just find Carmen and bring her back, we can talk about the rest later if there's still something to discuss."

I nodded and left the way I'd come in, without saying anything. There's no talking to some people. Especially when they're angry. Maybe I'd have better luck with Carmen once I found her. I had a good idea where to start, so I made my way to the address for Donovan Mills I'd uncovered in my research.

CHAPTER ELEVEN

I THOUGHT ABOUT WHAT I would say on the drive over. Chances were she wouldn't be in a mood to hear any adult lectures. If she'd already found out about me following her, I imagined there wouldn't be much I could say.

Given that Mills hung out with the New Harmony Boys, things had the potential to get heated. I thought about stopping by the house on the way to grab my M&P Shield, but still didn't trust myself with it.

If Carmen wouldn't come with me voluntarily, I'd made up my mind to bring her against her will, figure everything else out afterward.

Fifteen minutes later I turned into the apartments where Donovan Mills lived, an aging complex off Grande Boulevard that had been run down when I was in high school. It was flat-out sketchy now.

His building sat tucked into the back corner, the farthest building from the street. I drove a lap around the complex to get familiar with the exit routes before backing in across the parking lot with a view of the stairs up to his front door, where I could watch without being noticed. He lived in D-213 if my information was correct, which meant only one way out once I went up those stairs or inside the unit. Unless you counted the back balcony as an egress, but I couldn't see Carmen doing that. I'd go right off it with little thought, especially under duress. Carmen's parents would be furious if I brought her back with a twisted or broken ankle or put her in some other kind of danger unnecessarily. I wanted to protect her in every way possible, and that meant hopefully encountering her outside the apartment. I had a feeling she wouldn't want to come with me willingly, hoped I'd developed enough rapport to convince her anyway.

Girls that age often had no idea about the kind of people they were tangled up with. A wild, sturdy man who could protect and show them a good time could also blind them to his true nature for a while. I felt for her parents. She seemed like a good girl, but good girls get swallowed up by bad men all the time.

The exterior light was on and I noted Mills' truck parked out front. That didn't mean he was home, but I figured waiting a bit to see if they came out made more sense than knocking and trying to barge inside all cowgirl. It would be much easier to separate her from him in the parking lot.

An hour later I'd just started to reconsider my options when heavy bass accompanied by a set of headlights rounded the corner headed toward the building. The Jeep Danny Simms and TJ Evans had used to corner me earlier that afternoon drove past me and rolled to a stop in front of the building.

I couldn't tell if they noticed me as they drove past, but I doubted it. I'd chosen the Honda Pilot for its unremarkable qualities. The metallic blue-grey color never seemed to stick in anyone's mind, and with the black curtain hung up behind the front seats, they couldn't have seen me sitting inside in the dark. The Jeep stopped in front of Mills' apartment stairs.

The back door opened and Mills got out, dressed up as if they'd been to a club or something, maybe one of the local night clubs where you could get stabbed as easy as served a Miller Lite.

I held my position as Carmen eased out the door behind him. If I got lucky, Simms and crew would drive off and leave me with only Mills to deal with. I felt confident he'd be no problem after meeting him, all bark and no bite. Simms and Evans would definitely bite. All three of them together would be too much to take on, Taser or not.

Mills shut the door and leaned into the driver's side window as it rolled down. Evans sat behind the wheel smoking what looked to be a blunt. They exchanged some words with the bass still pumping through the Jeep's subwoofers, which must have been huge.

After that, they slapped hands and Mills made his way around the back of the car toward Carmen, who was waiting at the bottom of the stairs.

She looked comatose, at best a strung-out version of the girl I'd sat across from only a few hours earlier. Her anemic pallor had an almost translucent quality to it now, making this the third version I'd seen of her in two days.

My father used to say that people had more layers than a Noonday onion, and the further you peeled them, the more they smelled. This version of Carmen looked ice-cold and disinterested in everything.

The Jeep shifted into motion and drove down the row of cars in the other direction from me. I wanted to wait for them to get out of sight before approaching, but I couldn't risk Mills taking the high ground on the stairway if it came down to a confrontation. Even worse if they made it into the apartment, which I had no authority to enter. Carmen was seventeen, meaning she could date who she wanted but was not free to just leave her parents' home yet, according to Texas law. The police could come and take her out, but I knew the Wallaces would be furious if I called them after what I'd said about the drugs.

I slipped out the door and made my way across the lot toward them.

"Carmen," I called out as she reached the stairs. Mills spun on his heels as if he'd been waiting for someone to show up. The look on his face said he wasn't happy to see me.

"Lady, you bold, I give you that. Heard you stopped by my cousin's house earlier, too. You fuckin' with the wrong people, and you gon regret it, you keep going."

I followed his gaze to see the Jeep backing in reverse at full speed straight toward me as if they'd set a trap. I didn't have time to think, just react. I stepped backward toward my vehicle, afraid to let Simms and company get between me and my only mode of escape. The Jeep slammed into park. Both Simms and Evans exploded out of the car, already moving toward me.

"You following me, bitch?" Simms said.

"Tune her ass up, Danimal," Mills called from somewhere on the other side of the Jeep. Evans sneered and swung wide to cut off the egress route toward my vehicle.

"I'm here to see Carmen, the rest of you are none of my business," I said.

"Ain't none of this yo business period," Simms said.

"Whatever y'all are up to, I don't care. But she's only seventeen. Her parents are worried, and they can legally make her return. All I want is to take her back home so they know she's all right, doesn't have to be anything about you."

"Who gives a fuck what you want?" Evans said. He'd pretty well flanked me now. In a few seconds, it would be impossible to keep my eyes on both him and Simms at the same time. If Mills moved the other way, I'd lose one of them no matter what I did.

I needed to think on my feet.

"Truth is, cops are already on the way, boys," I said. I turned to Evans and said, "You keep trying to flank me over there and you might not like what comes next."

The bravado caught him off guard and he paused. I stepped back and to my right and shuffled toward my vehicle.

Evans and Simms exchanged a look. They both smiled.

"Bullshit," Simms said, nodding to his boy. Evans moved again to cut me off. I eased back into the space between two cars and slipped the Taser out of my waistband. He stopped again when I squared the sighting laser on his chest.

"You wanna bet?" I said. "I'm figuring five minutes until they arrive. You're welcome to wait here and see for yourself. Or I can teach you how to break dance on asphalt, until then. The girl's coming with me one way or another. The only question is who's going with the police when they get here."

Evans took a few steps back with his hands at shoulder height. I've found that no matter how tough a guy thinks he is, electricity makes everyone pause. Simms grinned bigger and relaxed his posture.

"Yo, D, get over here," Simms called out over his right shoulder. "Bring the bitch with you."

Mills came around the back of the Jeep holding Carmen by the bicep. He looked like a whipped dog. She looked like a wet noodle.

Simms continued. "I don't appreciate the fucking heat, cuz. Who the fuck are you anyway, lady?" He kept his eyes on me as he spoke.

"I'm a private detective," I said. "And I think you know exactly who I am. I know you've been driving by my house. That stops now, too."

Simms chuckled. Evans hadn't moved with the laser still trained on his chest. "Yo, check you out," Simms said. "Batshit crazy. Ain't nobody been driving by your crib, lady. Believe me when I tell you we got better things to do. I don't even know you other than you showing up at MY crib."

He had to be lying. I knew without question the Jeep in front of me was the same I'd seen at my house. This was my second time today being up close to it. I had a keen eye for vehicles, the result of running so much insurance surveillance, where vehicles were the easiest path to picking up your subject.

And yet I got the impression he was telling the truth. I didn't have time to dissect it further. Sociopaths lied as easy as breathing. He could be screwing with me for fun. Or for no reason at all.

"I just want the girl. You stay away from her and there's a better than certain chance we never meet again. I could not care less what you boys are up to, so long as it doesn't concern her."

As I spoke I'd moved back out from between the cars again. I didn't want to move too fast but needed to find a path to my car in case things deteriorated. Either of them might have a weapon. Probably both.

"Tell you what. Ima give you this little bitch," Simms said, gesturing to Carmen.

"For now. But I damn sure plan on seeing you again. You think you the only one can snoop around on motherfuckas? That's a mistake. Don't nobody threaten my people without consequence. D, tell the girl to go with the lady now. We be seeing her later, too."

"Time to go," Mills said to Carmen. She seemed to realize that he was talking to her all at once.

"No. Baby I wanna stay with you," she said to Mills. "Please don't make me go back there, you know how she is."

His face didn't give an inch. "What'd I say? Go home and get your people straight. Tell 'em they keep sending this bitch around we gon have to bury her. Might have to bury them, too."

Simms shot Mills a look that said to shut his mouth sooner than later. I guess he was smart enough to realize I might have a covert camera running. If it bothered Carmen to hear her parents' lives threatened, she didn't show it.

"Go on," Mills said. "You done put on enough bullshit drama today."

He gave her a hard nudge and she stumbled in my direction. I moved to my right again to lead her toward the vehicle without closing the distance with Evans. He winked and blew me a kiss. "Be seeing you soon, detective."

"Let's roll, homie," Simms ordered.

"You say so," Evans replied.

"I do, and that's that. D, we holla at you tomorrow, straight?"

"Straight," Mills said. The look in his eyes said he would be happy to put a bullet between mine. I hated all three of them.

Evans got back in the open driver's door of the Jeep as Simms went around to the other side and did the same. I kept my eyes on Mills now. He'd made no move to retreat. I lowered the Taser and backed up with Carmen next to me, headed for my Pilot.

"Get in the passenger side," I said to Carmen.

"You have no idea how much trouble you just stirred up," she replied. "And I can't believe you fucking followed me from the coffee shop earlier. You're as bad as my mother."

"Plenty of time to discuss that and everything else later," I said. "Right now my job is to get you home. Your parents are worried sick."

She opened the passenger door and climbed inside. "That's what they want you to think," she replied, crossing her arms over her chest. "They're just worried about what people will say."

I left it at that. I had concerns that Evans might block my Pilot in with the Jeep, but he cranked the speakers back to full volume and drove out as if nothing had happened. Mills shot me the finger and went up the stairs.

I waited thirty seconds before pulling out and heading for the exit, satisfied I'd earned my keep enough for one evening. Mills stopped again at the top of the stairs and watched us until we rounded the corner and lost sight of him.

I dropped Carmen off at her front door and left without speaking to the Wallaces. LeeAnne would probably take it as disrespect, but I was too tired to care.

She hadn't had to face down a couple of sociopaths to get her daughter back, so what could she say?

I figured they'd work it out and things would look different in the morning. I got back home about two a.m. and slipped into the house doing my best not to wake L up.

I found Chip asleep sitting straight up on the couch, a half-empty Miller Lite can balanced on his knee. I took the can away and left him where he was. No telling how he'd gotten home. Another DWI for either him or Marty would certainly spell more prison time.

I had the thought that it would save me a lot of trouble, then went to bed feeling guilty for thinking it. Prison was no place for people like Chip or Marty. It was the Danimal Simms and TJ Evans and Donovan Mills of the world who belonged there, but we never quite seemed to be able to keep them incarcerated.

CHAPTER TWELVE

I ENDURED A RESTLESS imitation of sleep until five-thirty, then dragged myself back out of bed. Chip was still on the couch, though slumped over onto his side now. L had already left for her shift at the hospital. I brewed a French press of coffee and poured it into a travel mug, took it with me on my way out the door.

The morning landscape had dew on every inch. It reminded me of when I used to get up at five a.m. and go running with Ben while the rest of our family slept in on weekends. We'd do calisthenics and then run up the driveway, go a couple of miles down the quiet country road with crickets and birds chirping all around us, an out-and-back route Ben had selected in advance.

Afterward, sweaty and with a burn in our stomachs, we'd come inside and sit at the same kitchen table that was still in the breakfast room to cool off. The smell of coffee always made me sick with sweat dripping down my back and the heat already gathering outside the windows. Even now the memory of it took away my appetite for the fresh cup in my hand.

I stopped at Shipley Donuts on the way to the office and grabbed a couple of kolaches for breakfast. I managed to eat them both before I arrived at the office a few blocks away, a habit developed from so many mornings on surveillance.

Back in those days, it was usually taquitos from Whataburger, the only place open to get breakfast at four thirty a.m. The hardest part of insurance work was always the early mornings, which often turned into late nights and twenty-hour shifts. At least on most of them, you went unnoticed. The kind of work I'd been doing over the last year seemed to constantly put me in high-profile, life-or-death scenarios.

L insisted that I enjoyed it, that I had an obsession bordering on a death wish. Maybe she was right. But I'd also started to scare myself, at times. I could never decide if I worried more about someone hurting me, or me hurting someone else. It was that thought which reminded me why I still didn't feel comfortable carrying my pistol anymore. It made me nervous.

I ran a couple more searches on Kaleb Parks but came up with nothing new. His background was clean, he had no social media presence, and Boolean logic can only take you so far before you're forced to admit that a person just doesn't have much of a digital footprint. However rare that can be.

I decided to get in touch with Deputy Bell, the officer the Wallaces had tried to bring in. He might not speak to me, or he might not have anything to tell. But I'd been hired to find out who was stalking Carmen, and I needed to get back to the task at hand for my clients' sake.

I found a number for him without too much trouble, a landline. LeeAnne had mentioned he was new. Maybe he worked nights like a lot of rookies. My own father had done that for many years.

He answered on the third ring with sleep in his voice.

"I'm looking for Deputy David Bell," I said.

"Not interested," he replied, still half asleep.

"Mr. Bell, please don't hang up. My name is Riley Reeves, I'm a private investigator. I got your number from my client, Paul Wallace." The last part was a lie, but sometimes it took a lie to open up a source. I chose to look at it as a generous pretext.

He sighed audibly into the phone. "I see," he said after a moment. "What can I do for you?"

"My understanding is that you spoke with the Wallaces about some stalking behavior concerning their daughter, Carmen?"

"I'm not sure that's exactly the way I'd phrase it, but I spoke with them, yes."

"How would you phrase it?"

"I'm not sure I should answer that. Just professionally speaking, you understand. What did you say your name was, Reeves?"

"Yes sir, Riley Reeves. I can give you my P.I. license number if you would feel more comfortable that way. Or meet you in person to show you my ID directly."

"Not necessary, I know who you are. Your dad had a pretty big reputation here at the department. Lot of people wonder why you're not following in his footsteps."

I shrugged, even though we were talking on the phone. "No good with authority, I guess," I said.

"I get it. Regarding the Wallaces, I didn't even file a report, to tell you the truth. It just seemed like kids' stuff to me. Maybe some mean girls playing a prank, but not dangerous."

"If you were a seventeen-year-old girl, you might feel different," I said.

"Maybe. But that's the thing. Carmen didn't seem to be worried. LeeAnne seemed to have the greatest concern."

"You know teenagers, they don't always take things as serious as they should. LeeAnne strikes me as a mama bear."

"She is. Sort of. The Wallaces are friends with my parents. I've known them most of my life. I've watched Carmen grow up, seen her struggle with her health, offered up prayers for her at Green Acres Baptist and all that. It just didn't strike me as a serious problem, or at least not as serious as LeeAnne was making it out to be. She keeps Carmen pretty shielded, and she has... a penchant for the dramatic, you might say."

I thought that over for a moment, turned over my response carefully before saying what was on my mind. "Are you saying LeeAnne is over-reactive, or insincere?"

He breathed into the receiver. Just when I figured he wasn't going to touch that one, he did. "Would I want you to quote me on this to her? No. Is it something people say about her when she's not around? I wouldn't deny it. She likes to play things up for attention, always has."

"What you say here will stay between you and me, I give you my word," I said. "Paul and LeeAnne hired me, but Carmen is my concern. I'm hoping you'll be frank with me."

"All right, I'll do my best. I don't know you personally, but I know about what you did with Carl Farlow. And I respect it. I have no doubt you care, a person, and especially a woman, doesn't do something like that unless she really cares."

I resisted the urge to explain to him that women are persons, and there need not be any further distinction. That we were each as individuals motivated by all kinds of different things, man or woman. Maybe he already knew that. He continued.

"I'm sure you know about Carmen's health problems. Poor kid. I guess the best way I can put it is that there were people who thought LeeAnne made the illness more about herself than Carmen at times. Get up in front of the church dressed like it was a movie premiere, make a big show about lifting Carmen up to the Lord, Carmen not even there.

"I can't really explain it. It just rubbed people the wrong way. But she loves Carmen. It wouldn't surprise me at all if she's just being overprotective."

"Makes sense," I said. I left off my personal opinion, that women like LeeAnne were a dime a dozen in Tyler. That treating church like a pageant show was the norm, not the exception. It didn't strike me as odd, and it didn't mean she wasn't really seeking spiritual help for her daughter, either. LeeAnne did strike me as the type of person who thrives on stress, if not outright conflict.

"Is there anything else I can tell you, Miss Reeves?" he said, interrupting my thoughts. "It was a long night on shift, I could really use to get some sleep."

"I apologize again for waking you, Deputy. My dad worked that shift for years, I know it's tough. And I'm very grateful to you for your candor. One last question and I'll let you be, I promise."

"It's no problem. Shoot."

"Did you look into the neighbor, Kaleb Parks?"

"I did. In fact, I went straight over and knocked on his door. I spoke to his parents, and to him. I figured me showing up would be enough to get him to cut out the hijinks if he was involved."

"And?"

"And nothing. His parents had no idea what I was talking about. Beyond some hostility LeeAnne had tossed their way back in high school, and a couple of awkward interactions with her knocking on the door and chewing them out, I got absolutely no indication they gave the Wallaces a second thought. LeeAnne had characterized Kaleb as some sort of weirdo outcast, but he just struck me as introverted, maybe even has Aspergers or something. I got no sense from talking to him that he would be climbing on roofs and knocking on windows, drawing on cars and leaving notes. I can guarantee you he's not the military-grade genius villain LeeAnne makes him out to be."

"What makes you think he's not the type?"

"It's just, I don't know. He doesn't have the personality for it. He strikes me as too indifferent, for one thing. I was a lost kid at his age too. I remember what it felt like. I saw so much of it in his eyes. Would a kid like that love to date a girl like Carmen? I don't doubt it. Would he believe that the way to do it was to knock on her window and all that nonsense? I don't think so, but you never know, I guess.

"Maybe he's bad at social cues. It certainly seemed that way. But Carmen didn't have anything bad to say about him either. He's just an awkward young guy, in my opinion. The whole thing is a non-issue that will go away when she graduates and heads off to school."

I wasn't so sure. I thanked him for his time.

The conversation hadn't given me much more to go on than I already knew. But I found it interesting that Bell didn't take Kaleb for the harasser. LeeAnne had put up a convincing show about it. I got the impression that Bell had some sort of disregard for LeeAnne, too. It could either be nothing, or a minor annoyance due to the sustained pressure she was putting on him.

Either way, I decided it was time to meet Kaleb face to face and see for myself.

I drove across town under a heavy blanket of humidity and a pulsing midday sun. Whenever I started to feel like life was hard, I liked to remind myself that a generation ago men and women had endured that harsh Texas sun with no air conditioning. They'd also done my job with no technology to back them up, working on instinct and canvassing.

Having learned so little about Kaleb through my online searches, I didn't miss the irony that even in this interconnected, oversharing social media world, a face-to-face conversation often revealed the best information.

A good detective can read a person like reading the paper. My father had always trusted his instincts for people. I'd developed the same instincts in part through his guidance, and the rest through his genes.

I noted Carmen's car still hadn't moved from the Wallaces' driveway as I pulled into the Parks' drive. LeeAnne's car was parked behind it as if to block her in. I figured this latest development with the drugs had temporarily distracted her away from giving me guff. Which was good. It gave me time to do a little actual detective work and see what I could come up with.

My first round of knocks on the door went unanswered, so I knocked again, louder this time. There were no cars in the driveway. I'd been told Kaleb was all but a shut-in. After my experience with him running from me in the woods, I had no doubt he was the kind of kid who didn't answer doors to strangers. Especially not strangers he'd encountered in the woods.

I'd just made up my mind to step around the back of the house and head down to the woods to find him when the lock turned, and the door fell open a crack.

A single eye encased by dark backlight peered out at me. The person behind it made no move to either open or close the door. We stood there, literally eye-to-eye, for a moment before I spoke.

"Are you Kaleb?" I asked, taking special care to use my most neutral tone. "My name is Riley Reeves. I was hoping you might speak with me regarding some trouble your neighbors are having."

The eye disappeared, then reappeared. The door swung open to reveal the same gangly boy I'd seen in the woods the day before. Up close, his cheeks looked more sunken, his eyes more fearful than menacing. He had on mesh Dallas Mavericks basketball shorts and a white t-shirt with the sleeves cut off.

"They think it's me, but it's not," he said in a quiet voice.

"Think what's you?" I asked. It's always better to play dumb when conducting an interview. You'd be surprised how much more information a person will give you if they think they're smarter than you.

"Whatever's going on, the painting on the car, notes, and all that mess. Carmen's mom has been over here a couple of times yelling at me and my parents or whoever opens the door. It's why I almost didn't open it for you."

I put my hands in my pockets to look less assuming. "Well, I'm glad you did open it because I'm the person who can get them off your back. Do you mind if we continue this conversation inside? It's hotter than a rattlesnake's belly out here."

Kaleb shrugged and stepped out of the way, opening the door wider. I moved past him into a small entry hall with outdated beige tile and a few knickknacks arranged on a credenza against the wall next to where the door opened.

The house was old but neat, with worn carpet and floral-patterned couches like those my mother had favored in my childhood. The décor stood in stark contrast to the lavish contemporary farmhouse style of the Wallace home.

Having known so many girls like LeeAnne, it made me wonder if she hated these people simply because they had less than her, had probably always had less. Maybe it offended her sensibilities to have people she viewed as beneath her living next door like they were out of place and needed a good tongue lashing to get them in line.

"Why did you run away from me the other day in the woods?" I asked. I figured it was good to go ahead and get it out of the way.

"I just… You startled me. And I didn't think you could see me, so I guess I was a little embarrassed. I didn't want you to think I was out there stalking you or anyone else. I was practicing my movements for bow season."

"I figured I'd stumbled onto your drinking spot, where all those bottles are."

He shook his head. "Not mine. Them's Carmen's. Her parents accused me of that, too."

I made a mental note to ask Carmen later. If she'd even talk to me again after last night.

"How long have you and your family lived next to the Wallaces?" I asked Kaleb.

"Been in this house almost my whole life. It was my grandpa's, but he died when I was a young kid. I don't even remember him. The Wallaces moved in about four years ago, I guess. I ain't tryin' to sound paranoid, but that woman has had it in for us ever since."

"When you say had it in for you, how do you mean?"

"Just… look. I don't like to talk bad about people. I keep to myself, but that doesn't mean I hate anyone. And Carmen, she's nice. I can admit that I had my share of problems in middle and early high school. I done a bunch of dumb stuff and even caught part of the woods on fire onetime playing with fireworks. Mrs. Wallace acted like I tried to burn their house down. My folks finally got so sick of both my antics and her harassment that they sent me away to Harlingen, to Marine Military Academy. That's where I graduated from. And the reason I got almost no friends."

The kid seemed almost eager to talk to someone, which surprised me. Whether it was the subject matter or just loneliness, I couldn't tell.

"So you got sent away to school for almost burning down the woods?"

"I mean, yes and no. It was like half an acre, is all. Truth is, I started skipping class a bunch. Couple old boys up there liked to kick the crap out of me whenever no one else was looking. Plenty of them down at MMA, too, but never mind that. I preferred hunting or fishing to getting my ass kicked all the time in front of everyone.

"Before the Wallaces bought that house and remodeled it, the Martins lived there. Their son Ron was my best friend, but he died."

"I'm sorry to hear that," I said.

"So was I. But anyway, they used to let me come over and fish in the pond whenever I wanted. Ronnie was there with me most of the time anyway.

"Mrs. Wallace told me in no uncertain terms that I was no longer welcome the first time I did it after they moved in. I get it, that's their right. But the way she did it, she practically threatened me. I'd made a little memorial out of rocks and concrete on the shore and written RIP Ronnie in the center of it, so that's where I was fishing, made me feel close to him. I could tell from the road the next day she'd yanked it out of the dirt and destroyed it."

I nodded. No use denying it. She gave me a less-than-friendly vibe too. "That's rough, I'm sorry to hear it." I paused, out of respect for his loss, then continued. "But tell me this. Why, in your estimation, do they think you're the one harassing Carmen?"

"I guess because of all the stuff I mentioned. I get the impression that they think I have a grudge or something about the pond and the memorial. I ain't like that at all. I ain't sure I know how to be anything else but kind and gentle. As I said, Carmen is nice, I've got no ill feelings toward her or anybody else."

"Do you have any romantic feelings for her?" I asked. "Mrs. Wallace mentioned something about that. No judgment, you understand."

"I get it. She ain't wrong. I used to have a crush on Carmen. That's true. I'm over it now. I know I'm not much to look at anyway. Truth is, she's not really what I'd be looking for these days anyhow."

"How's that?"

"Look around. I look like the kind of guy who can corral a fancy girl like that? I live with my parents and wander the woods alone all day. I don't need anyone to tell me I'm no catch."

"Some people might say that's why you're putting on with the notes and everything, right? Out of frustration, or unrequited love. What would you say if someone said that to you?"

His whole posture sank. "You pretty well just did. Miss Reeves, I can hardly hold down a job that isn't changing oil or hauling junk. I've got no grand ideas about who or what I am. Mostly I want to be left alone to hunt and tend to our horses. Why would I go harassing the people who are the most likely not to leave me alone in my own home afterward? You think about it, what I'm saying makes a lot of sense."

His responses struck me as sincere and truthful. He didn't seem to have either the confidence or the personality to write the notes I'd read. I had no doubt he could sneak around and even climb up on their roof if he wanted. But the more he talked, the less likely I found that.

"You have any idea who might be harassing her?" I asked. "Like, have you ever seen anyone come or go at weird hours?"

"I seen her boyfriend park his truck up at the road once or twice and sneak down the driveway because he come across our property. Never even noticed me on the porch, neither. But I don't think he's up to anything other than looking for a little action. I've never seen anything else though, and that's weird to me, considering all the drama."

"Why's that?"

"Because I do sit out on our porch at night a lot. I like to drink beer and look at the stars. And I keep a good eye on things for my folks. Plus, I've got a game camera facing out across the rear pastures and I've never seen anything but animals on it. Whoever's messing with her, they're sneaky, because I've not seen so much as a trace of them coming and going from the property. No footprints, disturbed brush, nothing."

I stood back up, satisfied with his answers. "Anything else you think I need to know?" I asked, moving in the direction of the front door.

"Just, you know, please ask them to leave me alone. My mamma's going through chemo right now. She can't even work. Our horse business is barely holding on. She loves those horses, I think that is killing her as much as cancer. She don't like folks to know about that, but if it will get the Wallaces to ease up, feel free to tell them that we're full up on trouble over here, no way I'd bring more."

I thanked Kaleb and stepped out the front door into the oppressive heat, squinting against the harsh afternoon light after being in the dark home. Whatever was going on over at the Wallaces' place, I couldn't help but feel that Deputy Bell had been right in his judgment of Kaleb. He seemed like a sincere, if broken, young man.

But where Bell had the luxury of chalking the whole thing up to teenage hijinks, I couldn't afford to dismiss anything outright. One way or another I would get to the bottom of things by finding the culprit. And it's that mentality that always seems to get me in the most trouble.

I decided to look up John Webb and see what else he could tell me about when Danny Simms pistol-whipped him. It might have nothing or everything to do with Carmen's harassment.

If it were Simms or one of his cronies doing the work, I'd have to figure out a way to protect the Wallaces from them. No telling what they might do to Carmen when they tired of playing around with her.

I found an associated address for Webb off Chilton Street over in the Azalea District, as well as an address for his law practice on South Broadway, a few blocks from his home. I figured work would be a good place to start at this time of day unless he happened to be in court.

I drove to the address, a small brick building painted white with blue shutters so dark they could almost be mistaken for black. The building had probably once been a residence before being rezoned commercial. It still had the small front porch common to houses in that area. Fuchsia azalea bushes flanked it, with red roses in pots on either side of the doorway and a plastic sign that said "Open."

I entered a small entry hall that opened into what had once been a living room but was now a lobby of sorts, with various bits of military memorabilia such as model helicopters set on end tables and shelves. A desk sat toward the back with a framed re-creation of the US Constitution mounted just behind it. A middle-aged woman with greying hair pulled back into a bun looked up from a stack of papers on the desk when I entered.

"May I help you?" she asked in a polite but stern tone.

"Yes, ma'am. My name is Riley Reeves, I'm a private investigator. I was hoping I might speak with Mr. Webb if he's in?"

"I'm so sorry, but he's in court today," she said. "He may be in later this afternoon, but a lot of times he doesn't come back to the office if it's a long day. Can I leave him a note with your contact information and what your visit is concerning? I have to be honest, we mostly do contract law and corporate litigation. We don't have a whole lot of use for private investigators unless you're a forensic accountant."

"I'm not, actually. But I'm not here to look for work. I was hoping to speak to him about the incident when he was assaulted by Danny Simms, and what happened to his daughter after."

"I see," she said. "Again, I'll be honest, we're very happy to have that business behind us. We had to keep the doors locked and walk to our cars in groups around all that mess. Had death threats and everything. Mr. Webb even hired a security detail out of Dallas for a few months. I'll be happy to give him your information, but I can't promise he'll be champing at the bit to discuss it with you."

I took a card out of my pocket, handed it to her across the desk. She looked it over and set it down in front of her.

"I can understand that. I'd feel the same way," I said. "My problem is, I've got a client who may be tangled up with Simms, and I was hoping Mr. Webb might be able to provide me some insight on his psychology and how big of a threat he might be to her."

She frowned and crossed her arms at the wrists over her stack of papers, perhaps an unintentionally defensive posture, then uncrossed them and took off her glasses.

"I know he got out of prison a few months ago. We all expected things to ramp back up again at that time, but we've not heard from him. His psychology is more like psychosis. Everything we found out about him says he's at least a serious bully, and probably a psychopath. He finds violence amusing and doesn't suffer much from what you or I might call a conscience. If your client is tangled up with him, God bless them. I don't know how we got out of that mess without anyone getting their throat slit. He certainly threatened worse than that."

"I read that Mr. Webb's daughter Darlene was almost kidnapped. Did y'all think it was Simms who tried to do it?"

She sighed. "We knew it was him. But knowing and proving are two different things, as I'm sure you realize. We never could prove it, not that Tyler PD didn't try. We had to settle for simple assault on the attack, too.

'They never found the pistol, and though John testified he'd been pistol-whipped, Simms and one of his cronies both testified it had been a punch in response to John pushing him. I don't think anyone who's ever even met John would believe that. But anyhow, in the dark John couldn't identify the kind of gun, not to mention his eye was half hanging out afterward. He's still got a serious scar from the surgery. DA eventually had to plead it out to get anything at all. That's why Simms did so little time. If he'd had a clean record, he might not have gone up at all."

"I wondered why the charge was simple assault rather than assault with a deadly weapon," I said. "I found it on his background check, along with all his other shenanigans. If you don't mind saying, who was his defense attorney?"

"I'd rather not say. The guy was from out of town, up in Dallas. I'm sure you can find it on your own if you want. But the last thing we want on our end is to stir him up again, and if you go over there talking to people on a lead from us, even if you say you're not with us, people might get the wrong idea. That's why I'm sure John probably won't talk to you. We've been on edge waiting for the fallout. Danny Simms is not the kind of guy to let things go if you know what I mean. We have a protective order against him for John's whole family, and John keeps tight tabs on Darlene. That girl barely goes to the potty without John or Kathleen knowing about it, though of course she's got a mind of her own so she tries to go around them whenever she can."

That sounded a lot like Carmen and her mother. And made me wonder if the two girls knew each other. They were about the same age.

I made a note to ask her about it the next time I spoke with her. That is, if I got another chance. So far I hadn't heard back from the Wallaces since bringing Carmen home. And speaking of home, I'd spent about as much of their retainer as I felt comfortable spending until we decided how to move forward, so I decided to head home and catch up with L, who ought to be getting off work pretty soon. I thanked the woman and went on my merry way. If you could call it merry.

CHAPTER THIRTEEN

L AND I WERE about halfway through a chicken adobo dinner that evening when Chip stumbled in the door in his usual state of inebriation. I was frustrated at feeling obligated to pull back on investigating the case, but I had a rule about uncooperative clients: never force them. Still, I took on a sour mood when I got like that.

For Chip's part, his sour moods came when he'd ingested enough drinks to bring on the anger and resentment I'd come to recognize as hallmarks of addiction.

The first thing he said when he walked in the door was "Smells like y'all been frying fresh slabs of dog shit in here."

L put down her fork and gave him the stink eye because she'd been the cook.

"At least we saved you a plate," I responded before she could jump down his throat.

"I doubt that. But if so, you can feed it to a dumpster," he said, "cause I don't eat shit."

The shit-eating grin he tossed out after he said it gave me serious doubts as to the veracity of his statement.

I could smell the whiskey on him from across the room. Even if he hadn't reeked, the look in his eyes and slur in his words would have given him away. It was the same look Marty had the night I had to light him up with the Taser. I call it alcoholic desperation. Whatever had him so worked up would surface sooner than later, most likely.

Which it did.

"So listen, Rowdy," Chip slurred. "About you buying me out of the house. How quick are we gon make that happen?"

I put my fork down this time. "Last time I checked they're not handing out overnight loans down at Southside Bank," I responded. "And besides, I've been working all day, not much time to do anything else. I told you I'd look into it and you know I will, but these things take time."

"Time," he repeated like the word meant nothing to him. I suppose after two years down in Cuero and several more unemployed before that, it probably did.

He opened the fridge looking for a beer that wasn't there. L and I had taken the last two he'd left behind. He closed the door hard enough to rattle the condiment bottles inside. "How much time we talking about?" he said as he sat down next to me and took a drink of my beer on the coffee table. I'd barely touched it anyway.

"Keep it," I said as he moved to put the beer back. "Seems like you need it more than me."

I knew the comment would piss him off. I said it anyway. I didn't like people touching my things without asking, and I've never liked drinking after other people. Especially Chip. Who knew where his mouth had been?

He downed the whole beer and dropped the bottle on the table, where it rolled off onto the wood floor but somehow didn't break.

"What the hell, Chip?" L said, standing up off her recliner and moving the TV tray away from her knees.

"Latonya, I got no tolerance for you right now," Chip said. "So be warned. This is a family conversation, and this here's my house on top of that. How 'bout you take your ass out to the porch while I talk with my sister? I heard your kind likes you some porches anyhow." L's face turned to pure rage, as I'm sure did my own.

"How 'bout I bust you upside your thick-ass head?" L said.

"Or how bout I do it for her?" I broke in.

Chip kept staring Latonya down without looking at me. "Girl, I wasn't asking," he said. "Don't think I can't move you if I decide to, either."

"Neither was I," L said. "And I bet you can't move me, come on over and try, we see who end up on the porch."

Chip started to stand up, but I stood faster. That's the advantage of not being a drunk. Your body does what you tell it to. Most of the time. I caught Chip in the chest, shoved him back into his chair before he got all the way up.

"Just calm down, all right?" I said to him. "I told you I would work on this, and I will. It's only been two days. I'll go down first thing in the morning and get the loan application, do everything I can to speed things along. How's that?"

He thought that over, but I could see he was itching for a shot at L. No surprise. He'd come in looking for a fight and come close to getting it. Drunks never like it when you spoil their idiotic plans.

"Fine," he said after a tense moment. "But one thing in the meantime." He pointed the crooked finger he'd broken playing rodeo cowboy in his teens at L. "You pay your rent to me from now on," he said. "Not Riley. You gonna live in my house and talk shit to me, that's MY money."

"The hell I ain't," L said. "I made my deal with Riley. I ain't trying to get in the middle of y'all family drama. I give her the money and y'all two figure out the breakdown for yourselves. Keep this shit up I find somewhere else to live anyway."

Chip's snarl morphed into an angry smile. "Works just fine for me," he said. "But if you stay, I expect cash in hand tomorrow for next month's room and board."

"Our," I said. The comment caught him off guard.

"Our what?" he asked.

"Our house. Not yours. And you get half the rent. If it makes you feel better, she can give it to us together and we'll split it on the spot."

I'd give her my half back after he left, but I didn't say that to him right then.

"Yeah? Well, how many months she been here? Cause I ain't seen a dime of that money. Which means I'm owed back rent."

"I don't even charge her most months," I said. "I just let her pay the utilities and call it good."

Chip's eyes widened like repelling magnets. "Say what?" he said, getting angrier now that he could smell his fight coming to fruition after all. "So she been living here in Momma and Pop's house for free this whole time?"

I was starting to lose my own temper now. "I thought you said it was your house," I said. "And anyway, not free. She pays the utilities as I said. Far as I'm concerned, she's been living in my half of the house." I couldn't resist the snarky comment now that I figured we were gonna fight either way.

"You never did know when to shut your mouth," Chip snarled. "Always some smart-ass comment to show me how much better than me you think you are. Even as kids you was like that. But you got two choices on this issue. Buy me out, or sell the house and we split the proceeds. But one or the other is gonna happen, and the sooner the better."

I felt myself begin to shake. "Sell the house, just like that?" I stammered. "Unless you're suffering from wet brain, you might remember that this is the house we grew up in, Chip. That Ben grew up in. It's all we have left of him and of Mom and Pop too. Doesn't that mean anything to you?"

Chip shot me a look that I recognized as pure alcoholic idiocy. I'd seen it many times on Marty's face over the years. At least he'd been smart enough to leave Marty at home for this one.

"Money talks," he said. "The past has passed, and it ain't coming back. I ain't sitting around waiting on time to rewind. I need money. I look around here and all I see is a check waiting to be cashed."

"You could get a job," I said. "I know you can still work on cars just fine."

Our father had taught Chip almost everything about fixing a variety of small engines and gadgets, hoping to help him find a career, some sense of a future. Pop had been an avid tinkerer, and good at it. Not that Chip appreciated the training, but he'd been good at it, too. All I'd ever heard him do was complain about grease and heat and everything else associated with making an honest living, so a lot of good it ever did him.

"I'm warning you, Rowdy." Chip pointed his crooked finger at me now, instead of L. "One more smart-ass comment comes out of that mouth and I'm gonna shut it, one way or another. We ain't kids no more, and I bet you ten to one you don't try any of that Taser bullshit on me."

I laughed, angry now. "You think I need a Taser to handle you, Chip? Better check your tooth."

It was a low blow, made worse because I'd always felt bad for chipping his tooth as kids. It had happened in a tackle football game. I'd always wanted to play, but the boys wouldn't let me join in. Or if they did, they tossed me around like it was nothing. Until my father pulled me aside one day and told me that the key to being included was to hit everyone out there as hard as I could on every play, so that they learned to respect me. On the very next play I'd driven Chip face-first into a tree, and he'd come up less half a tooth.

One of the worst aspects of family is knowing all the right buttons to push in each other.

Chip didn't give me long to think about that. He flipped my plate at me and followed it up with a hard, open-handed sucker slap that made me see stars on the way to the floor. Chip was on top of me with his hands wrapped around my throat by the time I cleared the cobwebs.

"I told you to shut your goddamn smart mouth, didn't I?" he screamed, the alcohol on his breath burning my eyes. "All my life I've taken your shit because Momma and Pop loved you more than me. Loved Ben more, too. I get it. I'm the fuck up and y'all are a couple of puritans. But they dead now and if you think—" A loud clang cut him off and the pressure came off my throat all at once. Chip slumped to the side and sat dazed on the linoleum.

L's big, round shape filled the space where his angry eyes had been. She had the small cast-iron frying pan from the stove in her left hand.

"You okay?" she asked.

I sat up as Chip tried to get to his feet, then fell back on his haunches.

"I'm fine," I said. My hoarse voice betrayed the truth, but we both pretended not to hear it. L knew me well enough to hear the lie without acknowledging it.

"What the hell the matter with y'all?" she asked, complete disgust in her voice now.

I didn't respond. L turned back to Chip.

"You all right, Chip?" She asked. "Had that coming, can't be putting yo hands on yo sister, you know better."

"You kidding? I'm fine," Chip mumbled. "My head's so hard it's a wonder it didn't dent the pan."

Her face shifted from disgusted to incredulous at having not knocked any better sense into him.

"He'll be fine, trust me," I mumbled, clearing my throat. Chip was my brother. Though I couldn't remember the last time he'd tried to get physical with me, this was hardly the first. I'd learned by dealing with Marty that being angry with a drunk for the things they do is a waste of time. But that didn't mean I intended to tolerate him attacking me.

"Are you serious with this bullshit, Chip?" I asked. "What, you don't have enough enemies, got to alienate your family too, is that it?"

Chip rubbed the back of his head and didn't respond.

"What the hell?" L asked after a moment. "I ain't seen y'all act like this since y'all was kids. Y'all both slipped a gear or something?"

"This family's nothing but slipped gears. Always has been," Chip said. He stumbled to his feet and out the front door into the night without another word. I made no move to go after him, nor did L. No point in trying to talk it out when he was like that.

I went to my room and changed out of my soiled clothing. When I got back, L had already cleaned up the mess from where Chip had dumped my plate.

"Don't worry about what he said about the rent," I told her. "Just keep doing what you're doing, let me handle Chip."

L frowned. "I hear you, girl, really. Thing is, it don't sit right with me. He do got a point."

"I know it," I said.

Funny thing about Chip. He might be two screws short of a box set, but he did occasionally seem to have some sense. Before alcohol and drugs took over his life, we'd been close. That he'd wasted his charm and potential on substance abuse felt like my own greatest failure, for reasons I could never explain. Maybe it was knowing that Ben would have been such an effective mentor for him, not like me. I had no doubt that Chip's life would have turned out differently had we not lost Ben. And that Ben would have certainly continued our bloodline, as where Chip and I had not.

I trusted Chip's instincts, even if he used them for all the wrong reasons. Family is complicated like that.

Chip might act like an idiot and a liability, not to mention an abusive asshole, but he was the only family I had left. I knew it counted for something, for everything, maybe. I didn't want to lose him. I couldn't just give up on him the way I had Marty. And he was right about the Taser. It never even occurred to me to try and use it on him, even with it driving into my back on the floor. He was my brother, and I never had been able to hurt him.

I couldn't save him, either. That much seemed beyond question. It felt more and more like I couldn't save anyone else, either.

CHAPTER FOURTEEN

THE CALL CAME ABOUT four a.m., the first of two calls that would change my life that morning. When Chip disappeared into the night, I figured Marty had come out to get him, being that Marty was the only friend he really had left in the world.

I went to sleep that night worrying about what Chip might do regarding his half of the equity. Alcoholics are nothing if not irrational. No way he could get a job in his current condition, and no telling what kind of trouble he might bring around if we kept cohabitating under the same roof. I'd grown tired enough of that type of trouble living with Marty.

When my cell rang, it felt as if I was already awake. I'd spent half the night in a sort of waking dream state, my body unable to commit to conscious or unconscious completely.

"Hello?" I said into the phone, eyes still too blurry to read the time then.

"Is this Ms. Reeves?" a woman asked.

"Who's calling, please?" I responded, never comfortable confirming or denying anything to a stranger. I didn't even put my name on my voicemail greeting.

"This is Trooper Thelma Rawlins, Highway Patrol. Am I speaking to Riley Reeves?"

I took a deep breath as nerves stirred in my stomach. "This is she," I said finally.

"I'm sorry to wake you, ma'am. We got your number from a cell phone belonging to a Chip Reeves and matched up the last names. Is he your husband?"

I would have laughed if the sinking in my stomach didn't already have me ready to throw up. I knew what kind of calls came at that hour from state troopers. My first thought was about how we'd let Chip wander off into the night dazed and drunk. Shame washed over my entire body, made it hard to respond for a moment. Finally, I managed.

"No, he's my brother. Chip's not married."

Trooper Rawlins sighed, seemed to be collecting her words.

"Is he dead?" I blurted out. "What happened, did something happen?"

"He..." she trailed off. "There's been an accident. I don't have any details at the moment other than your brother is in the hospital ICU. They'd like for you to come down here if you can."

"So he's alive?" I asked.

"Yes ma'am, he is, to my knowledge."

I sensed she wasn't telling me everything. For now, all I wanted was to show up for my brother and figure out the rest once I got there.

"Which hospital?" I asked.

"East Texas Medical Center," she replied.

"I'll be right there. Where should I come when I arrive?"

"Come to the desk at the emergency trauma center. I'll tell them to expect you and they can direct you to me from there."

"Okay," I said, "I'm on my way. One quick question, though."

"We can handle all the questions when you get here. I've got a few of my own."

"Was he hit by a car or something?" I asked.

"No, ma'am. He was a passenger in a vehicle that ran off the road and hit a tree. I'll explain the rest when you get here."

I thanked her and hung up the phone. I put on the same clothes I'd worn the night before out of the hamper, was almost out the door when I decided to wake L. She worked at ETMC and might be of use once we got there. I hated to put her in that position, but she would understand.

Her ebony face went pale when I told her what I knew. In an instant, she was wide awake. She dressed and we headed downtown toward the hospital off Beckham Street, L muttering over and over how much she regretted hitting Chip with the pan.

I wanted to comfort her, but my own guilt had me on the ropes the same way. Anger had clouded my judgment. It might not have mattered. But at that moment it felt like I'd all but run the car into the tree myself.

I blew every empty red light on the way there. I felt angry at myself for getting L caught up in my family drama. I hadn't been helping L by having her move in. She, in her compassionate, intuitive way, had sensed my deep loneliness and isolation. L had seen how much isolation the job created in my marriage, and how much more dangerous that feeling became in the absence of a husband to return to at night. Even a drunk one.

I'd never told anyone about the distance I'd allowed to build between Marty and me, even as I knew it caused a deeper hurt in him, led him to drink more, not less. My obsessive focus on work had helped kill our connection as much as anything else.

L had moved into my parents' house because the two of us were family. That's the reason why I never wanted to charge her rent, no matter how much she insisted. I'd repaid her by dragging her into the nonsensical chaos that had always existed around me and Chip. The thought of her feeling guilty made me feel so much sicker that I almost had to pull over and spill it on the side of Old Jacksonville Highway.

Even then she reached over and took my hand to comfort me. I hated feeling weak like that. Like the person who always needed something from everyone and never had much to give back.

Like the selfish, self-centered girl my mother had often accused me of being. I heard her words every time I went out in search of a missing girl. If I could just save all of them, I might one day make it up to the world for having put up with my selfishness for so long.

We drove in silence the rest of the way to the hospital. The car was full to the brim with tense energy. When we arrived, I parked in the first spot I saw and we hustled into the building. L moved off behind the scenes to see what she could find out. I headed straight for the desk.

I found Trooper Rawlins waiting there when I arrived.

"Miss Reeves, we spoke on the phone," she said before I'd even had a chance to introduce myself. I didn't ask. More and more people seemed to recognize me because of the Farlow case.

"Can I see my brother?" I asked.

"I'll have the nurses come speak with you as soon as they can. They think he's gonna be all right, though."

"Can you tell me more about what happened?" I asked.

"I'm afraid we don't really know all that much. We're hoping that when your brother regains consciousness, he'll be able to tell us more. Do you know where he was coming from tonight?"

I hesitated, not knowing if Chip was in trouble. Or anything else, for that matter. "I assume he was coming home. He's staying with me out at our—" I paused, unsure how to phrase it. She probably knew he just got out of prison. I got stuck on how to refer to the house. Mine? Ours? "Our parents' house. Our mother passed away not too long ago. And I'm sure you know that Chip is fresh out of prison. She died while he was inside."

"I'm sorry for your loss. I appreciate you bringing your brother's... past up, makes me feel like you're being straight with me. He's not under arrest at this time. As I said, he was a passenger. But I want to be straight with you, too. If he's turning over a new leaf, his blood alcohol content sure didn't say so. I also saw he's had three DWIs. And the other fellow, the driver..."

I winced and cut her off, afraid of what she might say. "I was so worried about Chip I hadn't even thought of anyone else. I've got a feeling I don't want to know, but... Was it a single-car accident?"

"It was. The driver... He didn't make it."

The life drained right out of my body right then. She didn't even have to say. I already knew what would come out of her mouth next, so I beat her to the punch.

"It was Marty, wasn't it?" I said.

Her eyebrows raised and she adjusted her utility belt, I guess out of habit. "The driver was named Martin Armstrong, according to his ID. Did you know him?"

I took a step back and sat down without even looking for a chair. All the hair on my body stood on end. My heart pumped like an oil derrick working overtime to make some debutant richer.

All it made me was sad. I felt the tears come like a wave. Goddamn if I could stop them. I hated letting anyone see me cry, for any reason. Even death. It made me feel weak and tired and afraid of the world.

"He was my husband," I mumbled, wiping away tears. "I mean, my ex-husband." The look on Trooper Rawlins' face reflected my poor, pitiful state at that moment. I felt sorry for her, having to tell people things like this. I never could have made it as a cop if that's what it took.

"I'm sorry for your loss," Rawlins said. "Truly." She reached out to put a hand on my shoulder, but I leaned away from it. L came out from two swinging doors behind her and our eyes met. I could tell by the look on her face that she'd heard the same news. She stepped around Rawlins and wrapped her big arms around me.

"I'm so sorry, Riley," she said. "I thank God Chip is all right, but damn I'm sorry about Marty."

"I'll give you two a moment alone," Rawlins said, sensing her opportunity to exit the tragic scene. "Come find me when things calm down, please, Miss Reeves. I've got a few more questions I'd like to ask."

I coughed up something resembling a thank you and turned back to L. "It's like I've spent years wondering when something like this would happen, and now that it has, it feels like my fault. I thought I'd feel indignant, or righteous, not pitiful like this."

"I know, I know, girl. But look, right now we need to be strong. Chip gon be okay, that's what Doctor Nobles say. He broke his arm in two places, and his left femur, and he got a concussion, but he come from a long line of hardheads, just like you."

I sniffled. "I hope so," was all I could say. I wanted to reach out to my friend, but for the second time that night, I didn't have it in me.

My insides felt turned out, barren like a West Texas landscape. Somewhere deep inside me, the girl I'd been years ago had decided to square a fundamental truth with my stubborn adult self. In my heart, I still felt love for my ex-husband. And for the first time, I realized that I'd let him down, too, let my anger cloud my judgment about what he'd needed, in our marriage and beyond. A lot of good that did either of us now.

CHAPTER FIFTEEN

THINGS ARE NEVER SO bad that they won't get worse. It had been my father's greatest saying, and I heard it in my head the second my phone displayed Paul Wallace's number at seven that morning.

I'd been waiting to speak to Chip, but he hadn't regained consciousness yet. Having spent another half hour answering Trooper Rawlins' follow up questions, fatigue had replaced my adrenaline and left me both reflective and exhausted.

"Mr. Wallace," I said in a flat tone.

"She's gone," Paul said. I sat up straight as the words registered.

"Who, Carmen?" I asked.

"Of course, who else? She wasn't in her room when LeeAnne went to get her up this morning, and we've searched all over the property. LeeAnne's over here in hysterics now. We're worried she's been taken. We need

176

you to come over right now, please."

"I'm sorry to hear that, Mr. Wallace," I said. "Unfortunately, I'm dealing with a family emergency, so I'm not sure I can get there right away. Have you called the police?"

"Of course we called the police. They just left. I haven't gotten the chance to tell you that we had another incident last night with the neighbor kid. This time he knocked on Carmen's window and taped a threatening note to it."

"What did the note say?" I asked.

"It said, 'I see you, and it's only a matter of time until you see me.'"

"What did the police say?"

"That she probably snuck off to meet her boyfriend. No sign of forced entry, the alarm wasn't triggered. Damned if I can figure out how anyone got in or out. Only LeeAnne and I have access to the application that controls it."

"She could have guessed your password."

"That's true. And it's why we need your help, Miss Reeves. We can't file a missing person's report until it's been forty-eight hours. We're both worried sick that Carmen might be in danger. Even if it turns out she left on her own as the cops say, we still feel she could be in danger considering what you told us about Donovan Mills."

I couldn't argue with that logic. But I also had my own family problems to deal with at the moment.

"I understand your concerns, Paul. Really. And they're valid, no question. But my brother was in a near-fatal car accident last night, and my ex-husband is dead as a result. I need to be here when my brother wakes up, he's hurt pretty bad. He almost died too. That could be ten minutes from now, ten hours, or ten days, but I need to be here for him. Can you understand that in return?"

The line went silent for a full minute. I could feel Paul measuring out what he needed to say next.

"I'm sorry about your brother, truly," he began, before pausing again. "It's just that we don't have anyone else to turn to, Miss Reeves. Carmen's sickness has been flaring back up the last few days since you brought her home. She's not well, emotionally or physically. She's not thinking straight, at a minimum.

"If she's somewhere and they're continuing to give her drugs or alcohol it could have potentially fatal consequences due to her medication. I can't imagine what your family is going through. And I hate to ask, but I have no other choice. If there's any way you could help us find Carmen, well... I'll make it worth your trouble. In fact, I'll pay you five thousand dollars in cash if you bring her back to us safely. Surely there's someone who can stay with your brother until he wakes up, and then call you?"

I hesitated, unsure how to proceed. I agreed with the assessment that Carmen might be in real, immediate danger. No telling what the NHB might do to her in retaliation for the troubles I'd helped her bring to their door. Worse if she'd been kidnapped by whoever had been harassing her, which I couldn't rule out.

"Can I call you back in ten minutes?" I asked.

"Sure," Paul replied, his voice hesitant. "Just please, help us. We're worried sick."

I promised to call him back and hung up the phone. I went through the mental process of trying to figure out what to do, though my heart had already made up its mind, as it often does. I tried to lay it off on the money, which I could use as a down payment on the loan to buy Chip out of the house, assuming he was okay like the doctors projected he would be.

I even told myself that would be the best thing for Chip. Deep down I knew it was my obsession with work, with helping women who could not or would not help themselves, that made me want to leave my brother lying there with tubes running in and out of his body to go find a rebellious teenage girl who had probably only run off with her asshole older boyfriend.

I found L down the hall and explained the situation to her. She shook her head. "He yo brother, Riley. And he lucky to be alive. Girl, you can't leave when he like this."

I gave her all the same reasons I'd given myself, but L saw right through them and told me so. She agreed out of reluctance to wait with Chip in my stead, to stay at her work on her only day off. I promised to make it up to her, but she just shook her head in a way that said she'd never been more disappointed in me than this.

I'd been having trouble keeping my promises lately, to others and to myself. I couldn't blame her.

I called Paul Wallace back.

"This is Paul," he answered the line.

"Okay, Mr. Wallace, get a pen. I've got a few things I need you to do."

"Already got one right here. Shoot," he said.

"Did she take or leave her phone?"

"It's here. I think you're right that she might have a separate one she uses. Or else someone grabbed her without it, one or the other."

"I need you to send me the last twenty numbers she either called or texted or who called or texted her. Also, gather up the names, phone numbers, and addresses of Carmen's five best friends, and email everything to me."

"Of course. What else?"

"I need you to have five thousand dollars in cash waiting for me when I arrive with Carmen in tow. I don't want to sound opportunistic, but I'm making some big sacrifices here."

I hated to hold them hostage over money but given that they hadn't hesitated to ask me to abandon Chip, I figured it was tit for tat.

"That's fine. Whatever it takes," Paul said after the moment of hesitation. Just please, bring her back to us safe."

"I'll call you when I know more. Go ahead and send me that information so I can hit the ground running," I said, then hung up.

I left the hospital with the bitter taste of self-justification in my mouth and drove to Donovan Mills' apartment, where I felt sure there wouldn't be so much as a trace of Carmen Wallace. At least it would be a starting point until I received the information from her father. I had it as a better than even chance she might be lying low, maybe at a friend's house if not at Mills. But I had a feeling she would be with Mills, one way or another. The "where" might be the most complex detail, considering I'd picked her up at his place once already. I couldn't rule out the harassment, but my gut said it might be a ruse, though I couldn't explain why. My money was on her running away in this case, and when a woman runs, it's almost always into the waiting arms of a man.

True to form, Mills' truck was nowhere to be found. I beat on the door anyway, hoping Carmen might be sleeping inside and open it up. No one answered.

I knocked on the downstairs neighbor's door, where a sleepy, heavy-set woman finally answered after the second round of knocking.

"Can I help you?" she asked, rubbing her eyes.

"I'm not sure I'm in the right spot," I began. "Is Donovan home?"

"Donovan?" she said. "Nah. Ain't no Donovan here. I think the guy upstairs might be named Don if that helps. I don't know him but I heard someone call him that the other day when I went out to my car."

"Did that someone happen to be a youngish brunette girl?" I tried. It never hurt to take a shot.

"Nah. I know the one you mean, though. I normally don't notice people, but she just seemed too young for the crowd that normally hangs around up there. Anyway, I bet you're looking for the guy upstairs, Don."

"My mistake, thanks," I said. As she started to shut the door I added, "One more thing if I could, miss." She paused, the door half shut now. "You didn't happen to see that girl around last night or this morning, did you?"

The look on her face said I was wearing out my welcome. She sighed. "Shit, I was asleep this morning, right up until you knocked. I didn't get home from work until about two forty-five last night. I don't remember seeing anyone around then. Why, you the police or something?"

"No. Just a friend. Thanks for your time," I said.

"Don't mention it," she replied, then closed the door.

I got back in the Pilot and cranked the air conditioner against the mounting heat.

I spent the next half hour driving through various hotel parking lots around town, looking for Mills' truck. I decided it was time to consider going out to New Harmony to look for Carmen. It made sense that Mills might take her out to his cousin's farm to hide. If they were still in town at all. It wouldn't surprise me if they'd taken off for a few days.

Carmen didn't strike me as the runaway-for-good type, but she'd already proven she was willing to run in the short term. I figured this as a power play to punish her parents for meddling in her life. A move to show them she was independent now, like it or not. The business with her harassment had never seemed to be much of a concern to her. And even if it was, she probably thought that Mills could protect her, never once stopping to think he might actually be the danger she needed protecting from.

Whether I liked it or not, it was time to go out to New Harmony and see what I could see. If I could pick up Mills out there and tail him into town, I'd have a better chance of wrestling the girl from his control once they were somewhere neutral.

Of course, she might not come along willingly this time. I understood her parents' concerns. She'd fallen in with some rotten people, and she seemed naïve about it and indignant to outside influence.

I had mixed feelings about telling anyone what they should or shouldn't want from their peers. Personal accountability has always been one of my strongest values. In my line of work, you learned pretty fast the danger in trying to save people from themselves. But Carmen was still just a kid. And like most seventeen-year-olds, she thought of herself as all grown up. That made her vulnerable to real grownups.

The best I could do was talk to her once I found her. She didn't have to listen. But if she didn't want to come home? I'd cross that bridge when we got to it.

For now, I needed to find somewhere to park and wait outside the New Harmony Boys' farm without getting made. I had to switch vehicles if I wanted to stay off their radar.

I drove to my office and parked the Pilot in one of the empty bays behind the building, which I mostly used for storage. I closed and locked that bay and rolled up the one next to it.

My Indian kicked to life on the first try. Marty and I had gotten into bikes for a little while a few years ago before he realized how hard it was to ride one after you drank. He eventually sold his. I'd kept mine, greyed out with low-profile handlebars, for occasions just like this one.

As for Marty, he would never need anything again. That thought tore into my heart. I buried the feeling into the deepest, hardest recess of my soul, hid my tears behind a jet-black helmet visor, and zipped off toward New Harmony and whatever danger Danny Simms and the rest of the NHB might have waiting for me there.

CHAPTER SIXTEEN

MY HELMET MIGHT AS well have been an oven in the Texas heat. Sweat soaked into my hair as I weaved in and out of traffic. At the edge of town, I cranked it up to eighty and lost myself in the freedom of the open road for a moment.

It took thirty minutes to make my way out to Danny Simms' place. I zipped past it the first time, unable to see if Donovan Mills' truck was there thanks to the dense pine forest around the property. I turned around a half mile down the highway to avoid drawing any attention. Just because I couldn't see them didn't mean they couldn't see me.

On the return pass I slowed down and tried to get a better look but couldn't. I rode down the highway in the direction I'd come from, found a big enough pull off and parked the bike on it. I stashed my helmet in the tall grass beside it and walked back up the highway to the edge of the pine forest, where I ducked off into the trees.

As I walked, I felt every single pine needle that crunched beneath my steps. At least I didn't have on that oppressive helmet anymore.

I kept a sharp eye out for copperheads and rattlers cooling themselves along the forest floor as I cut a diagonal line toward the approximate location where the farmhouse ought to be.

It was slow progress through a dense thicket. The smell of pine trees reminded me of playing in the woods around my own home as a little girl. Chip and I had made forts out of the junk we found dumped along the road and out in the woods. We dug big, round holes and thatched pine boughs over the top of them to make domed hideouts. And we shot each other with BB guns, both lucky to make it out of that time with eyes intact.

We'd been so close. Now there was so much distance between us that I was working a case while he laid in the hospital three shakes of a stick from death. Time robbed everyone of everything, eventually. Other people's problems always seemed to matter more to me than my own. L said it was how I avoided them. Maybe she was right.

The one thing Carmen Wallace still had was time to make the right decisions and build a life she could find happiness within. I doubled down on my resolve and picked up my pace through the woods.

It felt like I came upon the farmhouse all at once. I had to change direction to approach from the back corner rather than the front. I found a good vantage point and settled in to survey the property.

Simms' registered black Jeep was parked behind the house on a caliche rock turnaround that served as a driveway, with a white Toyota Tercel on big chrome rims parked next to it. It matched up with the vehicle my reports had associated with TJ Evans, though I couldn't see the plates. A large, rusting sheet metal barn sat beyond the turnaround, and more pine forest beyond it.

From my vantage point, it looked like the passenger side of the Jeep had been torn up by something, though it could have just been reflected light.

With no sign of Mills, I was preparing to sneak over and have a look in the barn when the back door opened. Danny Simms and TJ Evans walked outside. Simms was shirtless. Green jail tattoos covered with a sweat sheen crisscrossed his torso and powerful biceps. He had on baggy jeans sagging down to reveal striped boxer shorts.

They walked over and unlocked the barn's door, went inside. I knew I should hang back for safety, but curiosity pushed me forward.

I stayed tight to the barn's exterior walls as I inched up the far side from the house, careful to step around the various pieces of scrap metal and old appliances discarded there. I held my nose against the acrid smell of rust and decay.

As I reached it the barn door opened again. I laid down flat next to the wall to avoid being seen, watched as they went back into the house without locking the barn behind them. So, of course, I made my way inside, blood pumping in my temples like a migraine. Inside it took a moment for my eyes to adjust.

The barn housed an assortment of four-wheelers and dirt bikes, a backhoe, and a big, double-axel flatbed trailer. Mills' truck was nowhere to be found; in fact, it wouldn't even fit inside the barn, given the circumstances. That should have been enough to get me headed back to my bike. And maybe it would have been, had I not heard the back door to the house open and shut again.

I dropped flat to the ground next to the trailer as the barn door swung open. I managed to squirm underneath without making too much noise, praying there were no snakes or spiders in there.

"D been busy snatching all kinds of shit, too," Simms said. "We gon get a grip off all this combined with it." I kept my eyes shut as if that would make it harder for them to see me.

"Right," Evans replied. "But where do you want to send it all to?"

"Call the homie Rick up in Dallas, see if he interested. If not we might have to send them down to Austin, but it be better to travel up the interstate instead. I been thinking we ought to use the backhoe to bury a shipping container out here before we sell it. Make a good stash spot for cash and merchandise, you know?"

"Sound good to me. I'll make some calls and we can go from there. Do you think D know how to use a backhoe? I ain't got a clue."

I realized I was holding my breath when I almost blacked out. I let it out as easy as I could, hoped these two sociopaths didn't hear me as I inhaled a lung full of dust and heat. I had to suppress the overwhelming urge to cough. If they found me here no one would ever see me again, of that, I felt certain. Every exhale felt like blowing into a trumpet. Fear crept up from my toes to my shoulders. It seemed like a wave of sweat had swallowed me.

And then my phone started vibrating in my pocket. It felt like I'd Tased myself at first until I realized what it was. I moved my arm down to my pocket and fumbled with it through my jeans, trying to hit the silence button. Time slowed down to tiny, terrifying milliseconds. The phone's vibrations sounded like a bell ringing in my ears.

No sooner did I silence it than Simms said, "You hear that?"

My heart was just about beating its way out of my chest then. I wanted to reach for my Taser but couldn't because of the cramped space. The two men were silent for the longest twenty or five thousand seconds of my life. I'd lost all ability to gauge time in that space.

"Hear what?" Evans finally replied.

"Shit, I don't know. I'm trippin'. Must be that chronic D brought back from Austin. I'm high as a motherfucker."

They laughed and headed back out the barn's door.

I let out a big exhale when the barn door swung shut, then got another shot of adrenaline when I realized they might lock it from the outside. I waited five minutes, then slid out from underneath the trailer. My clothes were soaked through with sweat, had dirt caked on them from the moisture.

Better than blood, I told myself.

I let myself breathe again once I confirmed that the barn door hadn't been locked.

I peeked out the opening and let my eyes adjust to the sunlight. Heat waves rose up off the hoods of the Jeep and Tercel. I could see that the Jeep was damaged for sure now, had scratches on the front right panel as well as down the passenger-side door. No telling what these crazy assholes had been up to.

I didn't have time to look it over further. It had to be a hundred-plus degrees in that barn, and I wanted nothing more than to get out of there and back on Donovan Mills and Carmen Wallace. I'd had enough playing snoop in business that wasn't mine for one day. Especially this day. I needed to get back to the hospital at some point to check on Chip, too.

I eased the swinging door open and crept out into the light. I stayed close to the barn's wall as I made my way across the yard to make a break for the woods beyond. Just as I turned the corner, I heard Simms' voice.

"Hey, bitch," he yelled, "Hell naw, you dead as fuck." I looked over my shoulder to find both men coming behind me at a full sprint. Simms had a pistol in his right hand. I took off across the open field headed for the tree line.

I had a good forty-yard lead, but with every step I expected a bullet to drill into my spine. I've never been fast, and both men moved like linebackers as they closed the gap at an alarming pace.

I just ran after that, afraid to look back. Shots popped off like black cat firecrackers as bullets dug into the ground around my feet. I needed twenty more yards to get behind whatever cover the tree line could provide. It didn't seem possible that I could make it.

I zigged and zagged to make a harder target, clenching my jaw and digging my feet harder into the ground with each pivot. Fifteen feet. More shots. It sounded like both of them were shooting now, which meant they weren't focusing on catching up with me anymore, hopefully.

Ten feet. Almost there. Five feet. Still alive. Two. As I broke the tree line, a bullet sent pine bark spraying into my eyes from one of the trees. I ignored the sting and ran with everything I had in me. A moment later I heard them come crashing into the woods behind me, but I had a good start now and knew where I was headed.

If the bike stalled out or didn't start up on the first try, I might be in serious trouble. I couldn't risk trying to snag the helmet from its hiding spot in the tall grass.

The next round of shots made me fight the urge to drop to the ground, but still, nothing hit me. I could see the break in the woods now where the highway's shoulder started. Ten more seconds and I'd be there. At any moment I expected to feel bullets rip into my back.

But no more shots came. As I broke out of the woods onto the highway, I found another gear in my legs. I hopped onto the bike like a horse, fumbled the key into the ignition and gave thanks to the benevolent universe when the bike started on the first try.

I kicked it into gear and launched out of there like a rocket ship just as Evans broke through the trees to my right. In five seconds I'd already hit sixty miles per hour, then eighty. No more shots popped off. I could barely see in front of me as I rode because of the wind.

My eyes strained to see the road, but still, I pushed the bike harder.

After a while, I stopped looking in the mirror and focused on leaning into the turns, keeping the throttle up as high as I could handle.

I rode like that all the way back into town, then across it. I'm not sure I would have stopped had the police tried to pull me over, but they didn't.

I pulled the bike up into the garage behind my office, shut and locked the door behind me. Then I sat on it for what felt like hours, shaking and sobbing like a child. The full weight of everything that had happened that day came down on me then.

In a single twenty-four-hour cycle, Marty had died while Chip and I had both come inches from the same fate. The line between life and death felt almost nonexistent, and I wondered then if maybe I'd died without realizing it. I thought about Tasing myself to see what might happen but shook it off and tried instead to ground myself in reality.

The pain and loss hit me in waves. I felt helpless and alone. I'd felt the same way the day Ben died, and again when my father went ten years later. With my mother, I'd only felt relief that her suffering had finally ended.

The adrenaline dump and the raw emotion shredded my insides, so I puked them up. It took me another thirty minutes after the crying ended to stop shaking and walk out of that tin oven.

I'd spent the afternoon sticking my nose in some dangerous places, only to end up no closer to finding Carmen than when I started. Even I was starting to question my own judgment then. What I needed to do was to go back to the hospital and be with my brother.

The Wallaces would have to wait. At least for a few hours. The stubborn side of me would come sniffing around by then. I knew I wouldn't stay afraid for long. In the meantime, I needed to be around people who loved me. Even if that love was hard to accept, as it had always been.

I parked a block from the hospital and walked the rest of the way to clear my head, realizing only then that I was a dirty, sweaty mess. As I walked, the thunderheads that had been building on the horizon since that morning broke open into a torrential downpour.

The metallic smell of road dust and rain rose up from the asphalt around me as the rain soaked into my clothing and hair. By the time I reached the lobby my soggy blouse hung off me like wet fur on a rat, and water slid off the tips of my hair in globs.

The sterile lobby held a single man sleeping with his head back against the cold wall. I called L to see if she'd gone home.

"Girl, where have you been?" she said.

"You really don't want to know," I replied, my voice still shaky. "Are you still at the hospital, or did you go home?"

"Still at the hospital. I been trying to call you for an hour. Chip been awake."

"Really?" I said. A quick check of my missed calls revealed it had been L who called while I was in the barn at Simms' farm. Along with ten missed calls from LeeAnne Wallace, which I did not regret missing. "I'm sorry," I said to L. "I was in a kind of sticky situation. Is he okay?"

"Don't be sorry, ain't no point. Just get up here and see him, he was asking where you were earlier and I ain't know what to tell him. He asleep again now, but you know that ain't right to do to him."

"I'm here, actually... and I know. I'm sorry, like I said. What's the room number?"

"I got them to move him to room 215 out of ICU. Now get up here."

I told L I'd be there in a minute and hung up. I stopped at a vending machine and grabbed a Dr. Pepper for Chip, as well as a bag of Goldfish. I knew it was a cheap gesture, but I hated the idea of showing up wet, late, and empty-handed. Chip would say something about it either way.

I found the room with little trouble. L sat in a leather chair against the far wall reading *People*. She looked up at me and put the magazine down when I came into the room.

"You get pushed into a deep puddle, or what?" she said.

I could tell she was close to ripping into me, only holding back out of respect for the situation.

"Got caught in a thunderstorm on the way over."

"You look like a ghost swallowed you and crapped you back out. What the hell going on with you these days?"

L's best quality wasn't just her own conscience, but her ability to loan that conscience out to the people she cared for. I wanted to apologize to her again but knew I should wait until things calmed down. If I said it again now she would lose the last of her patience and drop a brutal truth bomb on my head.

Chip had on a hospital gown, and they'd put an IV into his arm. His eyes had deep purple wells behind the sockets and his left leg was in a cast up to the hip, propped up by traction. His left arm was pinned up in a sling, and he had a bandage wrapped around his forehead.

I stood there, L staring at me while I stared at Chip, for a full minute. When I looked back at L, her eyes took on a softer tone, as if she could sense the breakdown I'd had not twenty minutes earlier.

"He were up for an hour, but he ain't all the way with it. Nurse come in and talked to him a little, tried to get him to eat something but he ain't want to. He ask me about you and I said you on your way and he went back to sleep. That was little over an hour ago."

"Did he... did he ask about Marty?"

"Nah. I think he too drugged up to remember, or else he can't on account of the concussion. Last thing that boy need is more head trauma."

"True," I said, moving over next to the bed. I set the Dr. Pepper and bag of Goldfish on the table next to my big brother. "I think I should be the one to tell him about Marty."

"You think right, then," L replied.

I wanted to say something else but tears came out instead of words. I leaned on the bed and sobbed again like before. Except this time I hated myself for doing it in front of L. She came over and wrapped her arms around my soaked body.

"Everything gonna be okay, Riley," she said. "I know it seem bad now, but we gonna get through all this mess."

I tried again to speak but couldn't at first. I wanted to tell her it was about so much more than Chip, or Marty, or Carmen Wallace. I wanted to tell her how profoundly disconnected I'd felt from everything and everyone for the last year. How I'd lost my faith in goodness, and my trust in myself to do what's right. I wanted to tell her how profoundly I felt like a failure no matter how much I managed to accomplish.

Every emotion I'd ever stowed away from my divorce came tumbling out at once, and I realized I'd been drowning in it all for as long as I could remember. I held the best friend I've ever had as tight as I could and wept for all the things that would never be right in the world, and for my inability to make them right.

It hurt worse knowing the tears would not help. That I was shedding these useless things that made me feel weak in front of people I desperately wanted to see me as strong. But I couldn't help it.

"I need to talk to you about something serious," I said to L.

L held me by the shoulders and looked me square in the eyes. "Well, go on then," she said.

I wanted to keep talking, but my insides seized up and no words would come out. I hated the broken, emotionally stunted person I'd always been, maybe would always be.

My crying must have stirred something in Chip because when I glanced over, he was awake and watching us.

"Y'all always do lesbo shit when you think nobody's lookin'?" he asked in a hoarse, weak voice.

I let go of L and turned to face him. "Are you okay?" I asked, tears still pouring off my face.

"Seems like I might ask you that," he said. "What are y'all two blubbering about?"

L's face turned to stone. "I got to go, Riley," she said. "Hit me up later on if you find the time."

"L please don't leave yet," I said. "Just wait for me outside for a minute, I need to talk to you about something urgent. I appreciate you being here and I know I've asked a lot, just please wait for me and I'll explain everything."

"Aight," she said. "But make it soon, please, Riley. I'm worn out."

I wiped the tears from my cheeks. "Thanks, L," I mumbled, then turned back to Chip. "We were worried about you, asshole," I said. "That's why I'm crying. Not that you deserve it."

Chip managed something resembling his smirk. Half dead and his default facial expression was still a smirk. I could have killed him if he weren't already almost dead.

"You always did think you knew what I deserved," he said. "Maybe you can start with how I got here because I'm a bit confused just now."

Chip looked like he might slip into a coma at any moment. His voice came in just above a whisper by the end of each sentence. Even so, his words had the same bite as always.

"I was hoping you might be able to tell me," I said. "Do you remember anything?"

Chip tried to sit up, but I stopped him with my hand and eased him back into the bed.

"Just relax," I said. "You got in a car accident last night."

His eyes lost focus and then focused again. He stared a hole through the wall now, though I was certain he couldn't see that far in his state. "A what?" he asked.

"A car accident. You and Marty. He's..." I trailed off, not knowing how to finish the sentence.

"He's what?" Chip asked, something in the tone suggesting he already knew the answer.

"Don't worry about that right now," I said. "The important thing is that you're okay. Is there anything I can do for you?"

"Not unless you've got a pint of whiskey in your back pocket," Chip rasped. "I'd imagine you've got strong words for that sentiment, but it is what it is."

"It doesn't have to be," I said, "and I don't. You look like it would kill you if I did."

He shifted as best he could and turned away from me, closed his eyes. Our greatest trait in common was our inability to show weakness in front of others. Our mother had been the same way.

Finally, he opened his eyes again.

"When I woke up earlier you weren't here, Riley," he said. "Why?"

I stood up straight and wrung my hands together. It was my personal tell, and I knew he would see my guilt in it right away. I just couldn't help doing it.

"I was, for a while," I said. "I had to go to work once I saw you would be okay. I've been trying to get the money together to buy you out of the house."

Chip thought that over. "I'd definitely need a drink," he said, "if I were going to swallow a line like that. Tell me why you really wasn't here. I know it was work, but not like you just told it. You weren't doing it on account of me."

"Chip, please, let's not do this now," I said.

Chip opened his eyes wider and locked them on me. He opened his mouth to say something but my phone ringing cut him off. I motioned with one finger and stepped out into the hall to answer it, more seeking relief from his eyes than privacy for the call. L wasn't there, so I assumed she must have gone for a soda.

"Where have you been? We've been calling you for hours," LeeAnne snarled into my ear.

"What?" I replied, still caught up with the scene in the room behind me.

"What do you mean, 'What?'" she snapped. "I'm telling you this woman is worthless to us," she added to someone in the room on her end. "Have you found Carmen? I'm betting not."

That just straight up pissed me off. "Try this on for size," I snapped. "I was busy almost getting my ass shot off looking for your daughter when you called. Now I'm checking in on my brother at the ICU, where he's laid up half dead and lucky for the half that's living. You want to show someone disrespect, find someone else, because I'm not your girl." Silence radiated through the line.

She exhaled into the receiver. "Did you find Carmen or not?" she asked, her voice softer but not contrite.

"Not," I replied. I left it at that. Let her dig for the information if she wanted to demand it. It took all my strength not to lay into her with so much emotion pulsing through every cell in my body.

But even as I told myself that, the obsessed part of me started to pull me back toward the case. Even with chaos closing in, and my inner walls crumbling by the second, the work came first. It had been Marty's greatest complaint in our marriage. He'd used his loneliness in my absence as an excuse to drink. In the end, he'd even tried to take the frustration out on me physically. I'd never been able to forgive him for that until it was too late. I realized how much of everything that happened between us had been my fault, too. I had profound emotional issues, there was no more doubting that.

"Has she called or shown up on your end?" I asked.

"If she had I wouldn't be calling, guaranteed. If we weren't desperate I'd end this call and forget your name, in fact. It will cost us an absurd amount of money if you do find her. I don't know how you can sleep after working that kind of deal with my husband, taking advantage of his worry. Where do you get off railroading us that way?"

"That's a bad question," I said. "Where will you be if I don't find her, that's a better one. Have you thought that through yet? You need my help or you wouldn't be on this phone right now, you said so yourself. Whether you believe that or not, it's true. And I'm done taking abuse from you over it, so get that settled in your head. Did you not hear me twenty seconds ago when I told you I almost got shot looking for Carmen this morning? Or that my brother almost died last night? You want my help when it comes to these kinds of risks, that's what the risk is worth."

"Do you really expect me to believe that?" LeeAnne scoffed.

I sighed and resisted the urge to throw my phone down the hall. "Listen, lady. Your daughter is mixed up with some dangerous people. She's not the innocent angel you make her out to be, either. You know it and I know it, so cut the bullshit.

"The same reason you're desperate to find her is the same reason I get off charging what I charge. Now unless you've got something meaningful to add to the search, how 'bout I hop off this call, tend to my brother for a couple more minutes, and then get back out chasing down leads so we can get her home to you safe?"

"Fine," LeeAnne said, suddenly a fountain of composure. "Do what you have to do and call me back if you find her."

I hung up without responding and turned to go back into Chip's room. A foot inside the door I realized he had gone back to sleep. I looked at the chair beside his bed and then back at him. I knew what I should do, as sure as I knew I wouldn't do it. Instead, I turned around and headed out the door toward the lobby.

L had her head leaned back against the wall like a clone of the other man I'd seen there on the way in. She opened her eyes all at once as I approached, then sat up rubbing her temples.

"Girl, go on and say what you got to say because I am tired of babysitting, him and you. I need to go get me some sleep."

"Well, then you're not going to like what I have to say. I don't want to get into it all, but I riled up some dangerous people earlier today. I'd like to have gotten myself shot in the process."

"That sounds like something you'd do. So what it got to do with me?"

"That's what I'm getting to. These guys know where I live, I think. I don't know how, but they do, I saw them parked in front of the house the other day. And they'll be looking for me after what happened, guaranteed."

"Which means you gonna tell me to go stay at my mama place, I already know. Honestly, I been considering it anyway, after last night."

She sighed and sank into her chair. "Girl, I can't live like this, crazy hours and constant drama, you not even pretending to tend to your life when you can hide from it in a case."

"I know, it's not fair," I said. "And I ask too much of you as it is, L."

She rolled her eyes and looked away.

"Hey, look at me," I added. She did. "I shouldn't have asked you to stay up here for me, I know that. And I know how important family is to you, how hard it has to be to understand my decision making at the moment. You're the best friend I've ever had, and I don't deserve you. I'm sorry, and I'm so grateful for what you've done. I know I'm always promising to make things up to you. I know it's not right. Go and stay at your mama's for now, and I'll be in touch later. We can meet over at the house and grab some of your stuff then but don't go over there without me. Please."

"Aight, I hear you. But you got to do one thing for me."

"Okay, shoot."

"You got to rein it in with the risky behavior. Look how much good it done your brother. You ain't careful, you be next."

L stood and walked away toward the exit before I could respond, always too smart to sit around and let anyone bullshit her if she didn't have to.

CHAPTER SEVENTEEN

BACK AT THE OFFICE, I changed into a spare set of clothing I kept on hand for covert situations, a nondescript long-sleeve grey blouse and loose, casual jeans. I sat down at my desk and dove into old-school investigative tactics by preparing to call the entire list of Carmen's contacts that Paul Wallace had provided.

Probably not the best strategy, considering kids don't use their phones that way anymore, but I didn't want to put too much in writing a text.

I dialed the first number on the list, then hung up when the name sent chills down my spine. Darlene Webb. John Webb's daughter. I'd wondered if the girls knew each other. I redialed the number, but it went to voicemail, so I left a message explaining who I was, ended the call, and saved the number. I was preparing to call the next number on the list when she called back.

"This is Riley," I answered.

"Yeah, hi, my name is Darlene Webb, I'm returning your call?"

"Yes Miss Webb, thank you for calling me back so quickly."

"Totally not a problem. Is there something you needed from me?"

I hesitated, wanting to measure my words. "Yes ma'am, I think maybe so. I'm trying to get in touch with a friend of yours, Carmen Wallace, but having some trouble. Would you have any idea where I might get in touch with her?"

She cleared her throat before speaking. "Who is this again?" she asked.

"My name's Riley Reeves. I'm a friend of her family. She told her folks last night she was going to be hanging out with you today, and they're having trouble reaching her." I hated to use a pretext but had been given strict orders by LeeAnne Wallace not to reveal what was going on to anyone, for fear of gossip.

"Oh, yeah, of course. She was with me earlier but not anymore. She might have gone home."

I had to give her credit for trying to cover for her friend, however transparently. I decided to level with her as much as I could.

"Listen, Darlene. I'm just gonna be honest with you, and I hope you'll do the same with me. I know she said she'd be with you, but we already know she's not. I'm a friend of her parents, and I'd like to get in touch with her to make sure everything is okay. Her parents aren't mad or anything like that."

She didn't say anything, so I continued. "I'm sure she's fine, it's just a precaution. But I could really use the truth from you now, not that I'm accusing you of anything but being a good friend and covering for her, as you should. When is the last time you did actually see her?"

"I… I saw her yesterday. She said…" I waited for her to finish the sentence, but she didn't, so I pressed on instead.

"She said what?"

"Just, like, I don't want to get her in trouble or anything. But she was trying to get me to come to Austin for a shopping trip with her. I thought it was weird because she usually goes to Dallas to shop with her mom, but I figured maybe she had some other stuff planned too since she's moving there pretty soon."

"Was she with anyone when you saw her?"

"No. She was going to meet her boyfriend, Don, after we visited. She doesn't really bring him around anyone. I know her parents don't approve of him. Does this have something to do with Don?"

"Maybe," I said. "What do you know about Don?"

"He's a bully, or so I've been told. I don't really get to do very much, my folks are always breathing down my neck. That's why Carmen was trying to get me to come along to Austin, to break away from their smothering and have some fun. I told her there was no way I could go, not even if I pulled out all the stops because they track my phone anyway. But she really wanted me to go, which is, like, kind of weird."

"Why is that weird?"

"We're not really all that close. I mean, we've hung out off and on for a long time, but we don't hang out much anymore. Yesterday she just sort of showed up at my house proposing this trip.

"That's why I called you back if I'm honest. I'm worried about her, she seemed really off. Are you worried that she ran off with Don or something?"

"Not necessarily. Her parents are more worried because they had a fight and she left. Does she go through this kind of thing with her parents a lot?"

"As I said, we don't really hang out much. She didn't used to back when we hung out more often, at Hubbard in middle school. Her mom and she have always been fairly close. When she got sick her mom practically had to be attached to her hip to care for her. She's always pried into every inch of everything Carmen does, too. She used to have a way of making Carmen's illness about her, if you know what I mean. Carmen used to get really upset about it. Does that make sense?"

"It does."

"The last few times I've hung out with her she's been kind of weird. Like trying to get me to come to hang out with her and Don and another guy. My parents would never allow that, of course. And as much as I sometimes don't care for their control, I'm not exactly rebellious, you know? She seems like she's involved in stuff I don't really want any part of, anyway. I think they're into drugs."

"What makes you say that?"

"Well… I mean, I saw her do a line of coke one time at a party. Carmen called me the next day and asked me not to say anything to anyone. She wasn't exactly friendly about it, either. I never brought it up to anyone again. I think her boyfriend sells drugs. He might even be using Carmen to sell them to people our age, though I can't base that on anything and no one would tell me either way."

"That's really good to know, thank you for telling me. Do you have any idea where I might find her?"

"I bet she went to Austin with Don instead of me since it sounds like she didn't go with her folks."

"Why do you say that?"

"Because I know Carmen that well, at least. She's never been a great liar. The way she handles lying is by mostly telling the truth and just changing the bad details."

"Well, thank you for being so straight with me," I said.

"You're welcome, is there anything else?" she replied.

"Just one thing. If she calls you or contacts you in any way, would you mind giving me a call?"

"Not at all. We're not close, but I don't want anything to happen to her."

"Me either. And can I give you a little advice, while we're on that subject?"

"Sure, I guess." She sounded unsure.

"If she does call, don't go and meet her anywhere. I have it on good word that Don does hang out with a rough crowd, and they're not the kind of people you want to be around." I wanted to say more to her than that but couldn't without risking my client's confidence.

I thanked Darlene for her time and promised to call and let her know when Carmen was okay. Of everything she'd told me, one thing rang undeniably true. Carmen was probably in Austin. But how to find her there?

I combed back through my file on Donovan Mills until I found the section of the Delvepoint report I'd run detailing all his related and cross-referenced potential contacts. After some digging, I found two addresses in Austin, one for a woman named Selma Grady off Slaughter Lane, and another for a Christine Mills off East 8th Street. Either of them could be old and outdated. Or completely irrelevant, which happened all the time in those reports.

Some more digging revealed that Christine Mills was Donovan's sister. I ran a report on her using that address as an identifier, and it gave me a different address in Austin, predicted to be her current. It wasn't much of a lead, but it would suffice if I couldn't dig up anything else.

I didn't want to go to Austin to look for her with Chip still in the hospital and Marty sitting in the morgue, waiting to be buried. But if push came to shove, I knew I would. It wouldn't do much for my souring relationship with Chip or with L, but I had a strong feeling now that whatever Carmen was doing in Austin, it had an illegal, if not sinister, tilt to it. How far her involvement went was hard to say, for now. But I needed to find her.

I checked Christine Mills' various social media accounts, attributing the correct one to her as best I could. They all appeared to be locked down. Donovan didn't have Facebook. Carmen's most recent post was dated two years ago, though she might be posting under more severe security settings in recent years. I figured her for a Snapchat user like most girls her age. She had a private Instagram as well. Having left her phone with her parents, I didn't find it likely she'd be giving herself away on social media anyway. That in itself suggested an intent I felt less and less comfortable with.

I decided it was time to stop by the Wallaces' home and give them an update. If they wanted me to head to Austin, I would need a portion of the five thousand upfront, having long exhausted the initial two thousand already.

Paul opened the door before I even got out of my vehicle.

"Miss Reeves, please tell me you've found something," he said. His face bore a look of genuine panic. Neither LeeAnne nor her car were anywhere around. Probably out running down her own hunches.

"I've got a very strong lead," I said, following him into the house. "It's not exact, but it will have to do."

"Well, we've got nothing, so you're ahead of us. I've tried everyone we know. Smith County Sheriffs are treating her as a runaway. They'll bring her back if they find her, but I don't get the impression they're putting all that much into it. What's the lead?"

I explained to him why I believed she was in Austin, leaving out Darlene's name even as it again brought up my darkest suspicions about her connection to Danny Simms, and how complicit Carmen might be in attempts to lure the girl to him. After I laid it all out, Paul folded his hands and sat with his elbows on his knees, almost as if in prayer.

"I think it's worth checking out," he said finally. "If she was here in town I feel like we'd have turned her up by now. And with you unable to find Donovan Mills too, there's a good chance that wherever they are, they're together. I guess you can see why I was so concerned with him now. My wife will barely speak to me on account of not telling her my secondary motivations for hiring you."

"I can," I began. "And I can see why she's upset, too. She'll cool down once Carmen is back home."

"Do you need more money for traveling to Austin?" he asked.

"I appreciate you bringing it up, I didn't want sound like it's my only concern. But it would be helpful to extend our retainer, yes sir."

"The money is not a problem, especially considering what you're walking away from to help us. In fact, I'll give you the full five now if you promise to bring her back safe."

"How about half?" I said, uncomfortable with taking the full amount in advance. "I don't want to make promises that I'm unable to keep. I can guarantee that I'll leave no stone unturned looking. I don't want to set you on edge, Mr. Wallace, but these people she's dealing with are dangerous, and they may have additional motives for targeting your daughter.

"They very nearly killed me earlier today. Granted, I was trespassing on Danny Simms' land, but still. He's a shoot-first-and-ask-questions-later kind of guy, just know that. When I bring Carmen back, we need to find a way to get her to separate from Mills, no matter what."

"We've already been trying everything to do that. What do you mean when you say additional motives for targeting our daughter?"

"It might be possible to get a restraining order on him, I don't know yet, and I'm not a judge. How well do you know John Webb?"

"He used to be our attorney, years ago. Carmen and his daughter Darlene are still friends. I know Darlene was the last person she called yesterday, too."

"You mentioned Mr. Webb was assaulted, and Darlene nearly kidnapped in the aftermath."

"I did."

"I don't believe in coincidences, and I think at a minimum these guys may have been trying to use Carmen to lure Darlene to Simms or his henchmen. Her parents keep a close eye on her, from what I've been able to find out, so they've had little luck, so far."

His face showed a flash of anger. "You don't actually think our Carmen knows about that and is helping them, do you?"

I sighed. "I don't know, Mr. Wallace. It seems unlikely, but all this being a coincidence seems even more unlikely."

He looked stunned. We stood there in silence, me being glad I hadn't had to say these things to his wife, and him coming to terms with the possibility that his innocent girl might have lost some of that innocence, or worse, shed it voluntarily.

"I'll let you know when I get to Austin, that's our best start, for now. I've got an address there where I might find her. I may not, too. But I won't sleep until I know where to look, at a minimum. If she calls, resist the urge to chastise her. Ask her to come home and talk about things, make like it's all your fault, whatever it takes to get her here. In my experience runaways are less likely to come home if you're hostile, and they respond better to admissions of guilt when they feel wronged."

"Understood," he said, still clearly struggling with the information I'd just dropped on him. "I can't make promises for LeeAnne, especially when she hears all this."

"I get it. Maybe give her the abridged version until we get Carmen home."

"All right, good idea," he said, patting his pockets. "Tell you what. Let me grab you your money. I'll have the rest waiting on you when you bring Carmen back."

I nodded and he marched off into the house. In our entire conversation, we'd never made it past the entry hall. A minute later he reemerged with the cash, as promised. I wondered if they had a Scrooge McDuck pool in the back or something, the way he handled cash.

"Be safe, and call us if you need anything," he said. "LeeAnne might be a pill, but she'll do whatever is in her power to get our daughter home, so you can count on her, too."

I thanked him and said I'd be in touch. He closed the door as I stepped back into the sunlight on the driveway. I put the AC on high, plugged my phone into the radio, and threw on a podcast for the four-hour drive down to Austin.

I drove south on highway 155 over Lake Palestine and into Coffee City. The liquor stores lining the highway had far less action now that Smith County had gone wet for beer and wine.

I took the loop around Palestine and found my way to highway 79. I took it southwest through rural towns like Oakwood, Jewett, and Buffalo, until gradually pine trees gave way to a prairie that would eventually become the Texas Hill Country. I listened to podcasts and admired the rural Texas beauty as I drove, hoping to make it to Austin before nightfall.

I stopped off in Hearne for gas and a Coke, then settled in for the last push to Austin. Had I known what was waiting for me when I arrived there, I might have been in less of a hurry.

CHAPTER EIGHTEEN

I ARRIVED AT CHRISTINE Mills' address around nightfall. I'd let several calls from L go to voicemail on the drive and had a stack of text messages to accompany them. I knew I should call her back, but my mind had gone into full obsession mode since Danny Simms had tried to shoot me. I wanted to get Carmen away from these assholes. Bad.

I made a lap up and down the surrounding streets but didn't see Donovan Mills' truck. Not knowing what else to do, I parked down the street in the direction of the main egress out of the neighborhood and waited. While I sat, I sent L a text saying I would meet her at the house tomorrow afternoon when she got off work. I didn't have the guts to read any of the texts she'd sent to me. I can face down a serial killer or run from gunfire but ask me to face someone I've let down and I go limp.

I left the car running as a reprieve from the heat and waited for hours, not having a better lead to go on. I kept the dash lights dimmed and dome lights turned off all the time in my vehicle anyway. I stuffed a t-shirt into the instrument panel to block the remaining light.

They could be staying in a hotel, be in Dallas, or Antarctica as far as I knew. I'd come down here on a hunch, and given that the house was my only lead, I resolved to sit on it. Had this been an insurance case I'd have been sent home by midnight with no evidence that the target was in the house.

So I fought exhaustion and passed the time by listening to more podcasts, then an old country station after that. By two thirty I could hardly keep my eyes open anymore and had lost the will to keep trying. I decided to climb in the back and take a nap before making the long drive home. I'd been impulsive in chasing down this lead. Sometimes it worked, sometimes you came up empty. Just as I moved to open the door a pair of headlights turned the corner behind me and crept up the street.

As the vehicle passed, my heart started pounding. It was Donovan Mills' truck. I checked the clock on my phone: 2:49 a.m. I hadn't slept in almost twenty-four hours and felt every inch of it.

I left the engine running and slipped out of the car while they parked a few hundred yards ahead, past Donovan's sister's house in the other direction. I stayed up close to the cars along the sidewalks and crept toward the truck, paused and leaned up close to a black Tahoe when Mill's passenger door opened.

Donovan Mills climbed out. He looked angry. I heard the driver's side door open and shut but couldn't see who got out from my angle.

And then Carmen came around the front of the truck as Mills stomped off toward the house without waiting for her. That put him between Carmen and me.

"Come on, Don, I'm sorry," Carmen said. "Really. I didn't mean anything by it."

Mills stopped and turned to face her. "Just shut the fuck up," he said. I could hear the alcohol in his voice. "I told your little ass not to embarrass me."

"I laughed at a joke, Don. I didn't realize it would upset you. Please, don't be like this. You know I didn't mean anything by it."

Mills took two big steps and grabbed a fist full of her beautiful brown hair. "How many times have I told you?" he said, raring his arm back as if to slap her. I moved in range and slipped the Taser from my waistband. He must have heard me coming because he turned to face me. I didn't give him time to do the right thing. I put the targeting laser on his torso and lit him up like Christmas.

His knees buckled, sprawling him out onto the concrete, dragging Carmen along by the hair. She screamed.

"You're okay," I said to her. If she recognized me in the dark, she didn't show it. I moved closer as she fell into the grass. Mills let go of her hair when the Taser shut off. Carmen ignored me and made a lame attempt to tend to Mills.

"He'll be okay, too," I told her.

She turned to face me. "What the fuck are you doing here?" she screamed. "You've got no business meddling in my life like this."

"I do very much have business with it, but that's not

the point. You can't just run away from home, Carmen. It's against the law." I gesture to Mills like a pile of dogshit on the sidewalk. "And he absolutely shouldn't be putting his hands on you, either."

Mills had started to come back around, so I lit him up again. Carmen stood straight up and barreled into me then, which I hadn't anticipated. We fell together off the sidewalk and out into the street. I hit my head on the concrete hard enough to see stars on impact. The Taser flew off into the dark somewhere, leaving me outnumbered and without a weapon.

Carmen climbed onto my chest and clawed for my eyes in the dark. I kept fumbling for her hands, gaining just enough control to keep her from gouging my eyes out.

"Stop," I said to Carmen. "I'm trying to help you."

She managed to dig her nails into my right cheek then.

"I don't need your help," she snarled. "You're just like my mother. I'm tired of everyone telling me how to live."

I reached and shoved the bottom of her chin up and back, managed to get her off me using her head as a primitive lever. At any moment I anticipated Mills rejoining the fight by stomping my head until it burst like a rotten piece of fruit. Carmen came up to her knees swinging. I scooted backward to avoid her flying fists. As I moved back something heavy crashed into the back of my skull and I slumped forward, an electric haze burning in the space between reality and sleep now. The second blow turned my world horizontal and put me out cold.

When I came to, swirling red-and-blue lights from the top of an Austin police cruiser danced in my peripherals, and the outline of an officer knelt just above me.

"She's awake," the shape said to another officer standing ten yards away. I tried to sit up, but he stopped me by placing a gentle hand on my shoulder. "Just take it easy, ma'am," he said. "I need you to stay where you are for now."

I did as instructed, rubbing my eyes to clear the blurriness from them. They cleared to a chaotic scene. Donovan Mills was pressed up against the hood of the car.

I found out later that a neighbor had heard our altercation and called the police. If a unit hadn't been in the area, I can't say for sure what might have happened to me. Mills, for his part, had tried to run at the sight of the police but hadn't made it far.

"Ma'am, can you tell me what happened?" the officer kneeling next to me asked.

"I'm a private investigator," I said. "I have my identification card in my wallet. I was hired by her parents." I gestured to Carmen, who was sitting on the curb. "She's only seventeen. I ran down a bunch of leads and found her here. My intention was to take her home, but when I came up behind them he was grabbing her by the hair and getting ready to smack her around, so I popped him with my Taser." I indicated the direction where I thought it might have gone. "I think it's over there somewhere in the grass. I lost it because the girl jumped on me."

"We already found it," the officer said. "And you're lucky this whole thing didn't turn out worse. You've got a nasty bump on the back of your head and you could easily have been shot. The fella you Tased had a loaded pistol in his vehicle."

"I feel the opposite of lucky," I said. "In fact, I feel it all over."

"Do you want to press charges on them?" the officer asked. "Either way the male's going downtown. The firearm is unregistered. Even if it wasn't, he's a convicted felon so he can't have it."

"No, sir. All I want is to take Carmen home to her parents. I can get them on the line if you want to speak with them to confirm."

He hesitated. "I'd better have her get them on the phone, to be sure. You're in no condition to drive, either way."

I told him I would be fine and handed over my P.I. license. He had me sit on the curb far away from Carmen while he called it in for verification. I watched as they questioned her, wondering what she might tell them. She stood up to protest as they put Mills in cuffs and dragged him into the back of a car. I locked eyes with him as they helped him into the back seat and he smiled a sinister smile at me.

I wanted nothing more to do with Donovan Mills. With the gun charge, he would be out of all our hair for a while, at least.

What I did want was to get Carmen to her parents, collect what they owed me, and concentrate on burying the dead. It was time to stop playing hero and start putting my family and friendships back together. Unfortunately, like most things in life, it didn't turn out to be that simple.

CHAPTER NINETEEN

MORE THAN ANYTHING, IT was seeing Marty's casket that drove reality home for me. I'd had a few tough days since bringing Carmen home. And an even tougher ride getting her there. The hospital in Austin had reluctantly released me after the confused doctor marveled for a bit about how I'd managed to avoid a concussion. In this moment, with Marty laid out in a casket at the front of the room, I understood how lucky I'd been.

Carmen had wailed and screamed and cursed the whole drive in a way I could only describe as aggressively bizarre, a mixture of teenage angst, fatalistic posturing, and outright disassociation. That we hadn't crashed was a small miracle. The experience had been intense enough to make me research her diagnosis after dropping her off, only to discover it was exactly these kinds of episodes that characterized the psychological parts of it. She spoke and behaved like a different person from the girl I'd first interviewed. I imagined her socialite mother had taken her out of school to avoid having others see her in that state and talk about it after.

But even that experience hadn't been as tough as this, crammed up in a tiny one-room church with a bunch of people who hated my guts and no doubt blamed my brother for Marty's death. Maybe me, too, for that matter.

Up to that point I'd managed to hide from it in my work. I hated the thought of Marty's lifeless body sitting in that chrome-and-black casket, the last vestiges of a man I'd known most of my life and loved for half of it.

I kept to the back of the room to avoid causing controversy with my presence. His family viewed our divorce as my abandoning him when he'd needed me most. It may even have been true for all I knew anymore. But most of all, I wanted to avoid Marty's sister, Anne, if I could.

But I never do manage to avoid trouble. I knew it the millisecond our eyes locked, her standing there primping permed black hair with a look on her face that said I'd crossed the last line she could handle by showing up at all.

Anne and I had once been more than family by marriage. We'd been friends, of sorts. When it comes to strong women, it takes one to know one. I knew Anne was every bit the force of nature that I'd ever been, and so did she.

Her emotions tended to get the best of her like mine, too, most of all her sense of outrage. She had a vindictive streak the size of Lake Palestine, and she knew how to use it. Especially on her home turf of Pine Grove Baptist

Church, where her father had been the pastor half her life.

In a way, Chip had been lucky the doctors wouldn't release him for the service. From the looks of the room, we might have ended up burying Chip alongside Marty if they had. The thought made me even less comfortable, worried they might take me in his stead.

When it came to my turn to pass by the casket, it was all I could do to put a hand on the lid and shed a few tears. I would have said something if words were something that came to me in such moments. In truth, death tended to render me speechless, if not totally spent.

Latonya had stayed away, not wanting to bring any trouble to the service. And though she said she understood why I had to go, I got the feeling she thought I was making it about myself somehow in doing so. She'd been staying away in general, really.

The first night after Austin I'd slept on the floor of my office. In the two nights since then, I'd alternated between a cot in my office and a chair in Chip's hospital room. I was afraid to stay at our house, where the NHB would surely be planning a visit sooner than later. Especially with Donovan Mills taking such a hard fall at my doing.

I'd never built up proper security in the house; it felt somehow wrong to alter a house that still felt like my parents' in all the ways that mattered. Cameras, alarms, and stronger doors would have felt like pushing my parents and the past a little bit farther away, so I'd always found reasons not to do it. I didn't want to lose them for good even as I knew they were already gone.

Besides, it wasn't like I could afford that kind of equipment at the moment.

As I made my way from the casket toward the door Anne appeared so suddenly that I figured she'd been tracking my presence since the moment she saw me. Her haggard brown eyes had bright red lines surrounding them as if she'd continued to cry well past the last teardrops. She cut me off with such precision that I almost fell trying not to bump into her.

"You've got some nerve showing up here," she said, waving a finger in my face I felt certain she'd rather poke into my chest.

"Anne, I'm sorry for your loss," I said.

"The only thing sorry is your worthless brother. He always needed Marty to circle the toilet bowl with him."

I could have pointed out that Marty was a grown man who made his own choices, but she deserved a better explanation than that.

"I don't know about any of that," I began, working hard for the right words. "But I do know that Marty was a decent man and he didn't deserve to die like this."

"He deserved better than you, than both of you," she snapped. "He deserved someone who would stick around for him, what he got was two people who only stick around for themselves, one of them not even that."

"Yeah, well, so you say. But I am sorry, Anne. It breaks my heart too. This isn't what I wanted for Marty either."

She snorted at that. "You all but shoved him in the hole," she replied. "And he still loved you anyway. That's why he left you as the beneficiary on his will."

That stopped me cold. "Do what?" I said.

"Don't act like you didn't know. You didn't deserve him back then, and you don't deserve him now. He didn't have much, but it ought to go to us, to people who loved him instead of throwing him to the wolves when the going got tough."

I felt tears and rage welling up inside me. It took every ounce of my self-control not to let them run wild. I felt a lot of things about Marty, but responsible for his choices was not one of them. Hell, I'd taken half of them on the chin, which was why I'd divorced him.

"I didn't know," I said. "And you can have it all back. I swear. Draw up whatever paperwork you want and I'll sign it."

She gave me a hard stare through those bloodshot, tired eyes. "Yeah? We'll see. I'm gonna call you on that in a couple of days. Right now I need to bury my brother and care for our family. I think I speak for all of them when I say you are not welcome at the gravesite, so don't even think about showing up."

With that she gave me her back and moved off into the crowd of people, her hips swaying defiantly below her professional-looking black dress. I tucked my chin and headed straight for the door before my emotions overwhelmed me completely. I wanted to both cry and shout in equal parts. It felt like everyone and everything I'd ever had in my life wanted nothing more to do with me, not even myself.

After the funeral, I went back to the office and tried to hide in my work again. Several insurance surveillance cases had come in while I'd been focused on Carmen. I ran the reports and started to sift through them to develop an investigative action plan, but focus eluded me.

As evening's darkness set in, I finally gave up trying. I got in the Pilot and drove around with my phone turned off for what ended up being the entire night, creeping down deserted blacktop country roads that wound into the countryside like pine tunnels through the darkness. Sometimes I listened to music, then I'd open the windows so that the acidic pine smell could bring back memories of better times, of nights spent driving those same roads with Marty in his truck, still under the spell of what I'd thought to be love at the time.

Age had made me realize it was infatuation, which faded to friendship over time. He'd been the first and only boy to ever look at me with desire, intuited how much I needed to feel visible to someone or something. I'm not very feminine, nor have I ever desired to be. But all girls want to feel pretty, and I'd never really come close to that.

And all of us, even absent, emotionally unavailable workaholics like me, need to feel desired, at least some of the time. Say what you wanted about the way Marty's life turned out, but he'd desired me.

Deep down I knew my absence had driven his addiction to new depths. I could not clear myself of some burden for his death. And Anne had been right about Chip, too. His presence back in town all but sealed Marty's fate. I wanted to think he felt the same sense of shame I felt just now, but so far he hadn't expressed it.

The drive felt cleansing, therapeutic even. Part of me wanted to just keep driving south toward the coast until I ran out of land, but some other part kept circling back as if East Texas had an inertia that wouldn't let me leave its pull. I'm not wired for escape, and the world has always seemed to know this about me. No matter how much I tried to hide, it always found me sooner or later.

No sooner did I pull back into town and turn my phone on than the voicemails started popping up on my phone screen.

One from L, another from the hospital, and five more from Paul Wallace. I sighed, not wanting to listen to any of them, but knowing I would listen to all of them anyway. I started with the one from the hospital, but it turned out to be Chip trying to guilt me into bringing him a bucket of Church's chicken.

"I been thinkin', and we need to talk," Latonya's message said. "Call me when you get this, I think the best thing for everyone be for me to move out the house."

The news that Latonya might have soured on our living arrangements brought up a burning in my throat, the same acid reflux that had plagued my mother for years. We both only got it when stress was overwhelming us, or when we'd spent so long ignoring the bad things in our lives that we'd run out of places to store them inside our bodies.

It didn't stop me from trying anyway. I told myself I'd call Latonya tomorrow and tried to reason with myself that she was moving out because of Chip.

A wiser part of me knew the whole truth, that she was sick and tired of worrying about me all the time, and disgusted with the way I'd handled Marty and Chip's accident, checking out and hiding once again behind the emotionless wall of the job.

I took a few deep breaths and decided to call Paul Wallace, get it over with. He'd paid me the rest of the five grand and assured me the case was over, but I'd had a feeling I would hear from him again.

No way Carmen would stop asserting her independence. And the condition I'd left her in was anything but stable. Like many girls I'd helped before her, I expected we'd be seeing each other again sooner than later.

But that's the thing about expectations: they almost never mirror the reality you actually get.

From the first syllable of Paul's initial voicemail, I knew that reality had arrived, and there would be no hiding from it. His voice sounded contorted and jumbled, so much so that I could barely understand anything in the first message, other than the word "gone."

I didn't bother with the rest of them, opting to call him back instead. The call went to voicemail and I hung up, relieved. My phone lit up with his call back five seconds later.

"Mr. Wallace, everything okay?" I answered. People moved around and shuffled in the background behind him. The sound of a car door shutting seemed to mute the noise out all at once.

"Miss Reeves, I've been frantically trying to reach you."

"I noticed," I said, measuring my words. "I'm sorry, I've been out of signal for a bi—"

"Carmen is…" his voice collapsed before he could finish the sentence. "She's gone," he finally managed.

I exhaled a slight breath. "Again?" I said.

"No, you don't understand," he replied. "She's… dead."

I gasped into the receiver before I could catch myself, took a deep breath, and tried to straighten my voice up as he sobbed audibly on the other end of the line.

"How?" I said, my voice shaking.

"It's, I, I don't know. LeeAnne found her unresponsive." He broke off into heavy, desperate sobs then, hollow noises heaving out of his chest like gunshots, the kind of sobs that make you worry the person will suffocate if they can't get air ASAP.

"Breathe, Mr. Wallace, you've got to breathe," I said, failing to find the right words for the second time that day. "Take some deep breaths, it will help."

"No, it won't," he stammered, his voice shrill and breathless now. He sucked in a deep, loud chest of air finally, then added, "Nothing will help it."

"Mr. Wallace, where are you?" I asked. "Are you at home? Tell me and I'll come straight there."

"Ye-Yes, at home, they've got us all outside. The police are here. One of them had to pry LeeAnne away from her. I didn't know who to call, LeeAnne had to be taken to the ambulance, she's half catatonic. Her sister is on the way from Nacogdoches. They won't let me talk to LeeAnne and my attorney is on vacation."

"I'm headed over there right now, I promise," I said. He replied something unintelligible and I hung up, already making the U-turn. In no way was I ready to see another parent who'd just lost their child, but some days are just like that in my work. Everyone I encounter professionally has either suffered a loss or anticipates suffering one in short order.

As I drove, something Carmen had said on the way back from Austin kept repeating in my head. In one of the few moments I'd been able to get her to communicate at all, I'd assured her that her mother loved her and wanted the best for her future, which Donovan Mills should not be a part of.

"She wants what's best for herself," Carmen replied, the look on her face as if all her emotion had evaporated, leaving behind a desolate landscape of pale skin and drained, sunken eyes. The anemic characteristic I'd noticed the first time I saw her seemed to have grown exponentially.

"You'll see what I mean someday."

I had an idea of what she meant. LeeAnne seemed to want to live through her, to be a part of everything in the girl's life. In a place like Tyler, where women were raised to find the richest or most prestigious husband and marry him as a happy life strategy, lots of mothers did the same. Maybe it was staring in the mirror day after day, year after year, watching the looks you'd been assured were your only advantage dim beneath creases that started from smiles and hardened under frowns over time. Or knowing that your husband's eyes hungered for a younger version of you, before family and children and putting his needs first drained the vital parts out of you.

Either way, many of them coped by focusing on their daughters, now old enough to repeat their same mistakes. I found it ironic—the mothers' interest never seemed to take the form of new choices. Instead, they reveled in whatever cheap thrill their daughters' experiences might rekindle from their own misguided and wild past, however short-lived. Their daughters became new ways to command attention as the years piled up and the days ran short.

I saw the lights from a half mile up the road, a cyclone of reds and blues from three or four vehicles, at least. As I turned into the driveway a young sheriff's deputy held out a hand to stop my progress. I rolled down my limo-tinted window and read his nametag, D. Bell.

"Deputy Bell," I said. "Riley Reeves. We spoke on the phone a few days ago." His eyes dropped some of the professional bravado as my words landed.

"Yes, ma'am, I remember. I'd recognize you from television anyway. Your hair is longer now."

"Very observant," I said, not knowing how else to reply to something like that. "Paul Wallace called me to come over. As you know, I've been working for them regarding Carmen."

"Yes, ma'am. We're keeping everyone outside of the house right now, but I'd imagine you can drive down there still, if you want."

"I don't think anyone wants to be down there right now," I said. "But it's my job. Any chance you can tell me what's going on?"

He sighed, took off his cowboy hat, and wiped the sweat off his forehead, then replaced it.

"I'm afraid not," he said. "And honestly, all I can tell you at the moment is Carmen didn't survive, which I'm sure you already either know or have figured out on account of the coroner is already down there. All I've been told is she may have died in her sleep. Maybe Paul will have more for you, but that's all I can say."

He waved me past, and I realized he was having trouble maintaining his composure. I nodded and drove down the road, happy to give him space. I hated losing control of my emotions in front of others, too. Paul was standing next to a few officers at the rear of one of the squad cars pulled up out front of the house. I parked next to an unmarked cruiser that was behind Carmen's 4Runner, the sight of which sent chills through my body.

As evidenced by the way I had kept my parents' house after their deaths, I'd always felt an odd reverence in the presence of a dead person's possessions. Life goes on, but seeing it go has always made me want to latch onto whatever might slow it down. Seeing her vehicle shook my soul.

I caught Paul's eye and he nodded but continued speaking with the officers, so I leaned on the hood of my Pilot and scanned the area.

Kaleb Parks and what looked to be an older woman, perhaps his mother, looked on from their front porch about a hundred yards away. The Wallace's house had no crime scene tape or anything else that might clue me in about what had happened inside. I didn't get the sense there was any sort of criminal investigation going on outside the home, but that didn't tell me much.

The low clouds and overcast sky felt closer than usual, like I could reach up and touch them, or jump too high and disappear forever in their fog. Paul shook hands with one of the detectives he'd been speaking with and made his way over to me. His eyes had the same black circles as Carmen's had the last time I saw her, his cheeks the same sunken, gaunt quality. I'd never realized how much the girl looked like him until right then.

"Miss Reeves, thank you for coming," he said, his voice all but a whisper.

"I'm so sorry, Paul," I said. I had to fight back tears at the sight of the poor, broken man.

He looked like he wanted to say something but couldn't get out the words.

"What can I do to help?" I asked, more to fill in space than solicit an answer.

"I-I'm not sure," he managed. "They gave LeeAnne a sedative and took her to the hospital to keep under observation for a while. I've never seen her like that. I-I'm sort of fading in and out right now. They've asked me to come down to the station for some more questions. The coroner is going to do an autopsy on, on…"

I nodded and put a hand on his shoulder. He looked at it like something otherworldly had appeared there, and after a second I took it back. I've never been good with physical affection, but this might have been the most awkward movement I'd ever experienced. I felt a deep need to comfort this man, who'd just lost his precious daughter, coupled with a deep sense of inadequacy for a task that has always plagued me.

The same inadequacy that always drove me to run as long and as far as I could from emotional situations in my own life. From Chip, from Marty, from everyone that mattered to me when they needed me the most, except my clients. Even now I could not comfort this stranger who had invested his money and the safety of his daughter in me. I'd failed him on an unimaginable level, and I felt that in the most vulnerable parts of myself.

It didn't matter what had happened to Carmen; it had been my job to keep her safe and I felt embarrassed to stand in front of her father now as the failure I'd become.

"Have you been in contact with your attorney?" I asked, realizing how odd and incriminating it sounded only after the words left my mouth.

To my surprise, he nodded. "LeeAnne did. As soon as we realized Carmen was gone she called him, then checked completely out of reality not two minutes after. I'm kind of amazed she still had the foresight. He's going to meet us at the station. My understanding is they're keeping LeeAnne for observation overnight, they're worried she's had some sort of psychotic breakdown."

"I don't know how to ask this with any tact, so I'm just going to say it," I began. "What happened, Mr. Wallace? Do you have any idea?"

"I—they—we... I know LeeAnne wouldn't want me to say this. But when we found Carmen her medicine bottle was empty on the bed next to her. She'd gotten sick on the floor at some point. It was so odd, the vomit had black specs all in it, like charcoal or something."

"I see," I said, searching my memory for what medication Carmen was on. "She took amitriptyline, right?" I finally managed.

"That's right," he said. "I'm sorry I brought you here and now I've got to cut you short, but the deputy over there is waiting to give me a ride down to the station, so

I need to get going.

"If you want to follow us there, maybe we can talk some more at some point. Right now I'm not really sure I'm still breathing, so no promises, you understand."

I nodded. "Again, I'm so, so sorry for your loss, Paul." His first name felt too informal, but if he found it such, his face did not register the disturbance. He turned and walked over to the waiting squad car, got into the passenger seat. I got back in the Pilot and backed my way to the road, gave a slight wave to Deputy Bell, and drove off toward the sheriff's office on Spring Avenue, where I figured they were taking him.

I had no idea what I could do to help, but maybe I had some information that the officers would find useful. I wanted to be there out of respect for Carmen. I wanted to help her in some way that was no longer possible, but I needed to try no matter the odds.

I tried to call Latonya as I drove, but the calls all went straight to voicemail. I felt too guilty to call Chip at the hospital, who wouldn't be much in the way of emotional support anyway. I realized a truth that had escaped me for a long, long time.

I had no one else to call.

L was the only friendship I'd maintained over the last fifteen years, and my parents were gone. Now that Marty was dead, Chip and L were the only people on earth I could turn to. Which realistically only left me with L, who seemed to have had enough of me at long last. The thought of losing her felt like another death creeping into my life. I couldn't imagine how to live in her absence.

I tried her one more time and then gave up. It must be how she felt all those times she had tried to call me with no answer. It made me realize I couldn't remember the last time we'd discussed what was going on in her life. Like the narcissist I'd become, we only ever talked about my problems.

When I bothered to pick up the phone at all. I didn't deserve a friend like L, and it looked like she might have finally figured it out after I'd known it for so, so long.

CHAPTER TWENTY

AT THE SHERIFF'S OFFICE, they had a few questions for me, as I expected. I answered them as best I could, told them what I knew about Carmen and her movements, and gave my general thoughts on her disposition. The investigating officer, Detective William Howell, was tight-lipped but friendly, overall.

"The mother is inconsolable," he confided in me. "Which I suppose should be expected. But she's calling it murder, and we just don't have anything pointing us in that direction yet. What do you think?"

His question took me by a bit of surprise. My experience with law enforcement had mostly been that they don't play well with private investigators. I wondered at the motivation behind such a question and tempered my response accordingly.

"It would be hard for me to say," I began. "I haven't seen the scene or any of the evidence. Carmen had troubles, but I also saw her mother throw around what appeared to be unfounded accusations surrounding the stalking behavior they were experiencing.

"She's very emotional and sometimes that doesn't lead to clear decision making. I can't say for sure. I will say what you already know. If I were you, I'd let the evidence lead me and only consider the context when I could not ignore it. It seems premature to come to any conclusion yet, especially without a cause of death."

He thought about that for a moment. "That's a damn good answer," he said, shaking his head. "You looking to make a career change? We could use that kind of discretion on our side. Might be we would have taken Carl Farlow a lot faster if you'd been on him in an official capacity."

The compliment was meant to make me smile. But my emotions had been hovering above empty for a few days, and all I could manage was a soft "thank you."

"If something sinister has happened to Carmen," I said, "I'd look into the boyfriend, Donovan Mills, and his bunch, first thing. It seemed clear to me they were using her for something. I've got my ideas on what, but I don't want to say just now. Mind if I ask a couple of questions of my own?"

"I don't mind, but I might not be able to answer them," he said. "Shoot and we'll see what you hit."

"Were there signs of forced entry?"

He hesitated. "No," he finally said. "Not that we can tell. But we're checking with the alarm company to see if the alarm was shut off or otherwise tampered with. Anything else?"

"I mean, yeah, I've got a bunch more. I reckon you won't be able to answer most of them yet. I would like to ask one more thing, and of course, you don't have to answer. Based on what you've seen so far, do you suspect foul play is a likelihood?"

He sat back at that question and ran a hand through his neatly parted salt-and-pepper hair. I figured I'd get a standard response about suspending judgment, just as I had given, but I got a question of my own instead.

"Miss Reeves, can I trust your discretion?" he asked.

"Discretion is my currency," I said. "So in my opinion you can, yes. However, I need to be clear. I'm not certain as to whether I'm still in the employ of the Wallace family or not. My loyalty has to be to them where discretion is concerned. Any information I believe will help them I will have to share."

He thought that over. I liked what I knew of him so far. He displayed a moderate temperament and at least appeared to think before he spoke. I got no sense of emotionality from him, and everything about his demeanor demonstrated what an awful situation he considered Carmen's death to be. After a moment of silence, he let out a big sigh.

"I reserve the right to change my answer, of course, but it looks for all intents and purposes like the girl might have taken her own life. It breaks my heart to say that to you. I've got a daughter around her age. She goes to school out in Bullard. If she died I'd wish I were dead with her. I can't say what I would do if she took her own life other than wish she'd taken mine instead. At a minimum, I'd have questions. At a maximum, I'd make any accusations I could put to words in order to will it into being something different. LeeAnne Wallace insists she was murdered.

"But like you said, we don't even know the cause of death, though there's plenty of evidence to suggest one. The girl was on medication for ongoing psychosis. Everything I've been made privy to says she was chafing at parental control, struggling under the weight of her illness, and entering a challenging, though exciting, new phase in life. When people are sick in that way, they don't always respond the way you or I would. On the outside, she might look like she's got everything to live for. But on the inside, she might feel like she's drowning. We will let the evidence tell the tale, but it's already beginning to tell it."

I found his words beautiful in a painful way. It made me wish more men and women in law enforcement spoke with that level of professional compassion.

He reminded me of my father.

Something I'd always struggled with about Marty was how different than my father he'd been, simultaneously more and less vulnerable in all the wrong ways. It made me wonder how my life might have been different had I married a man more like my father. My respect for Detective Howell grew exponentially in that intimate moment.

"Thank you for your candor," I said. "You seem like a good man, I'm glad you're in charge of the investigation. Frankly, I'm surprised the task of interviewing me fell to you, given you're the lead detective."

He gave a sheepish grin. "It didn't exactly fall," he said. "I wanted to meet you on account of the Farlow thing. It left a bad taste in the mouths of a lot of people in this department that someone from the private sector finally took him down. But not me. Your courage and tenacity impressed me. I can only imagine how thankful I'd be if someone took down my daughter's killer that way, no matter who it was. And listen, I'd like to be candid once more."

"Please, do," I said.

"I know you'll probably be looking into this matter on your own. I don't have a problem with it, but the official department policy will be to discourage it. I have to act within the bounds of professional ethics, but that said, if there's anything I can do for you, or if you have anything helpful to share with me, I would like for you and I to remain friendly. I get the impression that we can trust each other."

He handed me his business card, so I took out one of my own and returned the favor as I stood up.

"Likewise," I said. "And thank you for your time. If there's anything I can do to help without stepping out of place with my clients, I'm willing to do so." We shook hands. "If it were possible for me to see the autopsy when you get it, I'd like that. I can wait and get it from the family, assuming they want me to have it, but I'd expect LeeAnne Wallace is likely to send me packing once the dust settles. She's made it repeatedly clear she has little to no use for me."

"But that doesn't mean you're going to stop looking into the case, I take it."

I nodded. "I made a promise to keep that girl safe and I failed. The least I can do is see this through until I'm satisfied it wasn't the work of the predators she was hanging around, or anyone else."

He rubbed his chin as if thinking it over. "Again, no promises, you understand, but I'll share what I can."

"All I can ask for, I suppose. By the way, I know you're a homicide detective, but I'd love to sit down and tell you some stories about Donovan Mills, Danny Simms, and all the rest of the NHB when the time is right. I think major crimes might appreciate the heads up."

"I'd be happy to. At the least I can turn you over to the boys in major crimes and see where it goes. I know there's plenty of folks around who'd love to stick a fork in that bunch."

"Sounds good. Maybe I'll supply the fork, who knows?" I walked out of the room. I wanted to speak with Paul and LeeAnne Wallace, but they were tied up with questioning of their own and probably would be for the foreseeable future. Things might turn out better if I waited for some of their raw emotions to fade anyway, so I decided to sleep on it and give them a call in the morning. Until we had a cause of death, more questions might only muddy the water.

In the meantime, I decided that my best course of action for Carmen would be to head to the office and learn everything there was to know about acute intermittent porphyria and amitriptyline. Whatever had happened to Carmen, I had a hunch that her illness and her psychological state would be somewhere near the center of it, twisted up into the same knot. The autopsy would be a great asset, but I couldn't count on getting a copy.

I'd be lying if I didn't admit that my own psychology was hopelessly tied up in the case now, too. I'd failed Carmen, and now no one would ever fail her again. Whether the Wallaces intended to employ me further or not, I had every intention of getting to the bottom of the matter.

If nothing else, at least to try and put my conscience to rest. Not that I had much hope for that now.

CHAPTER TWENTY-ONE

I HADN'T EVEN MADE it all the way down the hall toward Chip's room before the head nurse on the floor approached me, an aging, plump woman with thin grey hair pulled back into a bun the size of a quarter on the back of her head and strict lips that looked like they only opened for food.

"Miss Reeves, is it?" she said, so quiet I almost asked her to repeat it before getting the gist of it.

"Yes?" I replied.

"I'm Caroll Flatrock, the head nurse in this ward."

"Nice to meet you," I said, even though it may or may not have been true, I wasn't sure. "I'd introduce myself, but it seems like you already know me."

"I recognized you from the night your brother was admitted. I'm sorry to disturb you, I hope I'm not intruding?"

"I don't think you are, but should I be worried?"

"No. I mean, maybe, but not about that. I did want to catch up before you went in to visit your brother, however."

I tensed up out of reflex. "Causing trouble, I assume?" I said.

"No... well, yes. I mean, sort of. Are you aware that your brother has, well, has some issues surrounding substance use?"

I frowned and clenched my fists. "About as aware as I am of my own nose sticking out in front of my face."

"I—well, I spoke with Dr. Breland, who's been overseeing him. We've had some issues with your brother's behavior on the ward. More specifically, he's been berating staff and demanding that someone bring him alcohol. He asked the night nurse for some mouthwash and drank half the bottle she brought him from the Walgreens down the street. She tried to stop him but he refused, said he'd ingested worse in prison. She wanted to have his stomach pumped on account of the ethanol, but I didn't think it would do much good. That said, he's in bad shape, and Dr. Breland has decided there's too much liability in continuing to provide him with pain medication and care."

I felt my shoulders sink. I knew Chip was bad off, but mouthwash felt like a new low. Family lore had it that our grandfather's brother had died on his mother Laverne's back porch from alcohol poisoning, having ingested too much mouthwash, which he'd broken in and found under the otherwise teetotaler's sink. Lore also had it that Laverne had never touched a drop, having been brutally beaten and neglected by her own alcoholic father.

The disease served as an intergenerational curse on our bloodline, one of the reasons I rarely drank.

"How did he react to that news?" I asked.

"He screamed until we had to have an officer come in and threaten to move him down to the county jail if he didn't compose himself. That seemed to do the trick, but he's taken to giving tongue lashings to anyone who enters the room now. I wanted to warn you because I expect he'll do it to you, too."

"I see. Thank you for letting me know," I said. I started to continue on toward Chip's room, prepared to rip into him, see how big of a chunk I could tear off.

"Miss Reeves?" she said again, her tone almost contrite at having to keep bothering me.

I stopped and turned back to her. "Yes ma'am," I said.

"I had one other issue to discuss with you."

"Okay," I said, bracing for what I could only be bad news.

"We feel that your brother is ready to be discharged. I have personally felt for a couple of days he might be exaggerating his symptoms to keep getting medicated. Is there somewhere for him to go after we discharge him?"

I'd known this was coming for a while, and I knew it was about more than just Chip's behavior. He didn't have insurance. I'd been amazed already at how long they'd let him stay, I suppose out of compassion for Marty's death.

"Of course. We have a family home, and last I checked he's still got a room."

She chewed her lip a bit, which meant there would be more to the story. "I see," she began. "What I meant was, is there someone to care for him? Your brother has sustained serious internal injuries. He's on a catheter, and he needs help changing the bags, as well as the dressings on his wounds."

She paused and looked up and down the hall before continuing. "You seem like a nice person, Miss Reeves, so I'm just going to be frank. Your brother will need to be checked up on by medical professionals, moving forward. But without insurance, our hospital won't be able to provide any follow-up treatment. Is there someone, a family doctor perhaps, who can provide care for him?"

I sighed and shook my head. "Our family saw Dr. Brown for most of our lives, but he died about ten years ago. And let's just say that Chip made a habit of milking anyone else dumb enough to care for him out of whatever drugs they were willing to prescribe. To my mind, there's not a doctor east of Dallas who would even let him in the front door now. At least, not one worth seeing. But I'll see what I can come up with, and I guess I'll have to be the one to care for him in the meantime."

That seemed to satisfy her. She forced a half smile, thanked me for my time, and said something about the paperwork that I paid little attention to, already dreading the coming encounter with Chip. The first of many, if he were as bad off as the doctor said. My big brother, always the victim, always the burden.

And that was only half the problem. I'd been avoiding the house altogether on account of my run-in with the NHB. With Chip getting discharged there would be no way to continue avoiding it. I felt like cursing myself for not installing better security at the house.

And it wasn't like I knew anything about medical care. A selfish part of me reached for my phone to dial L, who knew plenty, but I resisted the urge. The last thing she deserved was to take a bunch of shit from Chip while he recovered.

I told myself I'd reach out for advice and nothing more, making sure she stayed away from the house until I was sure the NHB wouldn't come calling. If I could ever be sure of that.

"How long do I have before you want to discharge him?" I asked.

She looked away, then back again. "We'll be discharging him at eight tomorrow morning. I'm sorry, I know how soon that is. I'd have to do it even sooner but Aretha, the night nurse, happens to be the only one who can handle him. I wish I could give you more warning, but I can't."

I understood, so I nodded and told her I'd be here to get him then. We still had my mother's electric wheelchair out in the shed behind the house, so as long as they could get him to the car, I'd handle him from there.

With that decided, I took a deep breath and headed to face fate. I paused outside the door, then walked in to deliver to my brother the news that he'd landed under my sole supervision after all, for better or worse. If he didn't like it, that made two of us.

CHAPTER TWENTY-TWO

I DROVE BACK TO my office and spent the rest of the night reading up on the symptoms, characteristics, and other details of acute intermittent porphyria. It appeared to be a genetic disease and to present in a wide variety of physical symptoms such as abdominal pain, vomiting, weakness, numbness, and other symptoms. It could also lead to psychological symptoms such as hallucinations, paranoia, confusion, depression, anxiety, and general psychosis. It appeared that Carmen's parents had been treating her psychological symptoms with amitriptyline.

It sounded awful, the kind of disorder that could destroy the quality of life, and lead to serious long-term health problems. Could Carmen have chosen to take her own life during a bout of psychosis brought on by her disorder? Maybe. It was also possible that the onset of symptoms could have simply caused her to stop breathing, or perhaps accidentally ingest too much medication while seeking relief. Without the autopsy, it would be impossible to even begin to tell.

For now, the best I could do was cross my fingers and hope to get my hands on the autopsy. I had a contact down at the coroner's office who owed me a favor, but I didn't want to put them in the position of jeopardizing their job.

Whatever the outcome, it would have to wait until the autopsy was complete. Which left me with few avenues to explore and even fewer places to go. I drove out to the house and even ended up driving up the driveway. Everything seemed normal. On the way back into town I finally made the decision to place a call I'd been struggling with whether to make or not.

I got the after-hours voicemail for John Webb's law office and left him a message saying I had some information about Danny Simms he needed to hear, and he should call me as soon as he was able.

I wasn't even back to the office yet when my phone lit up with a 903 number I didn't recognize. "Hello," I said into the receiver.

"Miss Reeves, this is John Webb, returning your call, ma'am. I hope it's not too late to call back? I assumed by the timing of your call it might not be."

"No sir, not at all. I'm surprised, though given I left the message on your office phone, I didn't expect to hear from you until tomorrow, if ever."

"I keep a close eye on the office voicemail, but I happened to be up there working on a case file by coincidence."

"Ok," I said. "I know you're busy, so I'll just get to the point. Your daughter has a friend, Carmen Wallace. Do you know her?"

"Vaguely. Her father is a former client, but I don't know much about what they've been up to in recent years. Why do you ask?"

"It's kind of a complicated thing, so please bear with me."

"I'll do my best."

I explained to him who I was, what my involvement with Carmen was, and Carmen's involvement with the NHB according to my investigation. I capped it off by telling him she'd passed away.

"Did Simms kill her?" he asked almost before I finished.

"No," I began. "Or, well, I don't know, at least not yet. But her death isn't what I wanted to tell you about."

"I see," he said. "Then what did you want to say?"

I hesitated, knowing that my words would amount to a betrayal of a client whom I'd already failed enough. But I was worried about more death, too. One father had already lost his daughter. I did not intend to see another lose his, too.

"I spoke to your daughter as part of my investigation. Some of the things she told me, combined with other information I already had, have led me to believe Simms' cousin, Donovan Mills, might have been using Carmen to try and lure your daughter to Simms."

The line stayed silent for a full minute. I could almost feel the gears turning in his head, working back through the precautions that had become part of his daily life, wondering where his daughter was in that exact moment, and if she was safe.

"Damn," he said. "I've been worried about something like that. What makes you think so?"

"Mills and Carmen ran off to Austin a few days before her death. I found evidence that Carmen had tried to get your daughter to tag along, and that she hadn't told her the whole story. I'm not sure if Carmen understood she was being used, but I doubt it. She was a sweet girl, but maybe a little naïve. I've got my suspicions that Mills targeted her specifically to try and exploit her relationship with your daughter. As you know, retribution is kind of a thing for his cousin, Simms."

He seemed to measure his words a long time before responding. "Okay then," he finally said, "I appreciate you telling me this. I feel bad for saying it, but it makes me feel safer knowing the girl is dead."

"I understand. If it were my daughter, I might feel the same. But the reason I'm calling is I want you to be aware that if they did it once, they might do it again. For sure it seems to me like they're determined to get at you, whether through your daughter or by other means. I guess what I'm saying is, you might want to go on full alert again for a while. I don't imagine he will stay free forever, but in the meantime, well, you know…"

"I do. We already are, trust me. And again, thank you. Is there anything else I need to know?"

"Not really. But if you need anything from me, or want further information, please don't hesitate to call."

"I sure will. Take care, Miss Reeves, have a good night, I know you're putting yourself in a risky position by making this call, and I'll keep it to myself."

"Thank you," I said, then hung up with guilt already starting to set in. I told myself I'd done the right thing, that betraying Carmen's confidentiality didn't matter now that she was gone, but I knew the truth. I felt it in my bones that she'd consciously tried to lure the girl, and that she'd known exactly what would happen after. Had she not attacked me in Austin, I might have thought different. If I kept that to myself only for the Webb family to experience tragedy, I wasn't sure I could live with it.

I didn't blame Carmen for her actions. She was young, confused, and afraid. And given the company she kept, it was no wonder she had a difficult time discerning friend from foe. And I was still her friend, even now. Sometimes being a good friend means setting limitations for the people you care about.

I decided to try and finally get some sleep. I arranged my blanket on the fold-up cot I kept in the office storeroom, laid down, and shut off the lamp on the desk. But once the quiet set in, I couldn't get my mind to calm. I still hadn't heard from L and felt too much shame to call her again. I didn't want her around the house, even if Chip and I had less of a choice, given the circumstances.

And the thought of taking my half-invalid brother, who had for all intents and purposes cheated death, into more potential danger didn't sit well with me. I turned it over and over in my mind but could only come to one conclusion. I needed to eliminate the danger if I could. I was done hiding from whatever the NHB had in store for me. Let them come.

The time had come to drag the M&P Shield back out of the nightstand and stick it in my waistband again. The time had also come to get to the bottom of what happened to Carmen Wallace. Even if the death turned out to be suicide, it didn't absolve Donovan Mills, Danny Simms, or any of his other sociopath underlings for the influence they'd exerted over her.

They'd used a lonely, sick, and naïve girl in hopes of luring Darlene Webb into God knows what kind of horror. The stress of Carmen's relationship with Mills had no doubt taken a heavy toll on her already shaky mental state.

My racing mind was all the proof I needed that I wouldn't be getting any sleep that night. How long had it been since I'd slept? Two days? More? It would have to wait, either way. Once my mind clicked into obsession mode, the only way out was to go through.

I clicked the light on and made a few notes on the yellow legal pad I kept there. I needed to price out a security system for the house, dig out my mother's old Hoveround chair for Chip, sweep the house for hidden alcohol, and once I had Chip settled, spend some time talking with the Wallaces to see where things stood.

At five a.m. I was still up and sitting at my desk trying to work out the details of how to proceed.

I devolved into the kind of mindless web surfing that seems to be consuming the world more every day. I've never had any sort of social media, but I've used it quite often to snoop. Work had long ago taught me about the deep level of exposure an online presence can provide.

The morning's weather forecast showed a tornado watch all day and into the night. It was peak tornado time in Texas, after all. At some level, it might be easier if all my problems were to be hoovered up at 250 miles per hour and dumped somewhere south of Nacogdoches to rot.

Hell, make it Houston. Or drop us all kicking and screaming into the Gulf of Mexico, let the water wash our sins away.

I shook off the thought. I'd long ago learned to be careful what you wish for. The things you say and think determine who you become, one word and decision at a time. Problems are only solved when you solve them yourself. Any other approach brings a new set of troubles to replace the old.

Memories of Carl Farlow with a bloody knife in hand and dead eyes darker than new moons filled my mind. Far from a man at that moment, he'd become a pure monster, a predator harvesting human blood like barrels of oil out of the Gulf's surging floodwaters. I'd been the only thing standing between him and more death, and I'd stopped him.

I could almost feel the M&P Shield click in my hands again, as it had that night. I thanked God for that small mechanical malfunction, the only thing separating my fate from Farlow's. I'd discovered something sinister inside myself that night, a murderer I'd spent my whole life believing could not exist. It terrified me to realize that murderer was never far from taking control of everything, had never been far from it.

Now fate required me to strap the pistol back into my waistband and face another set of monsters. I had my doubts about whether I was ready to resume the responsibility. I could hear my father's grizzled voice as he painstakingly recited the first rule of gun safety to my brothers and me:

"Never point your weapon at anything you don't intend to destroy."

I'd intended to destroy Carl Farlow. And I might try to kill the next man whose victim fetish put him in my crosshairs. The thought both terrified and exhilarated me. It made me realize that we're all capable of grotesque evil if put under the right circumstance.

I didn't want to be evil. My mother would have simply said, "Then don't." In her world, things had always been that black and white. Good guys and bad. Right decisions and wrong.

My world had never been so simple, and it never would. I did my best to navigate the complications.

And still, somewhere in the back of my mind, my greatest critic spoke a truth I couldn't shake: Soon enough, I might run out of people to fail, and where would I be then?

CHAPTER TWENTY-THREE

GREY DAYLIGHT FOUND ME on the road headed out to my house, windshield wipers beating a rhythm against the rain to match the chorus of thoughts circling my mind.

As I drove I dialed L's number, knowing she was an early riser, like me. I got her voicemail, again. Swallowing my pride, finally, I left her a message. "Hey L, I know I'm a jerk. And a piss-poor excuse for a best friend. But I love you and I'm sorry and I want to make it up to you. I'm headed out to the house to check on it and pick up a few things. Chip is coming home from the hospital later today. If you want to come home, I think it's safe, now that Carmen is gone. Which is my way of saying, please come home, it's not the same without you."

I disconnected the call thinking how strange that feeling was, that my childhood home could not feel right without my best friend living there, too. I'd been a detective for ten years, but the greatest mysteries for me always happened in my personal life.

I'd never been good about understanding when something became the new "norm" for me. Not when Marty's drinking was out of control, not when my father drifted off into his own mind never to return, and not when Chip had been in prison, probably looking forward to visits from his bossy sister who never showed up.

In every personal relationship I'd ever had, it had been a problem, this complacency. Now it left me with a deep fear that those around me, living and deceased, never knew how much they meant to me. Maybe never would.

So even on that morning, with charcoal clouds balled up like fists in the sky, and the slanting rain with the faintest tint of yellow-green, I had no concept of what normal looked like. Much less what constituted an adequate level of risk, anymore.

The house looked undisturbed, beyond the usual puddles and pools in the pastures, as I rolled over wet caliche rock and down the driveway. I raised the garage door before I crossed over the second cattle guard. I backed the Pilot up and left it facing the road in case I needed to make a quick escape, then headed through the garage into the house to retrieve a pistol I was no longer sure I could handle the responsibility of carrying.

Inside, the stink was overpowering. I traced the smell to rotting food in the garbage can, pulled the bag, and dropped it in the garage, for now.

It didn't look like L or anyone else had been back to the house since the night of the accident. I slid into my bedroom under a silence so still it made my ears ring. I'd become so accustomed to adrenaline that it barely registered beyond a feeling of heightened awareness, yet another norm I'd failed to identify. I opened the nightstand drawer to retrieve the pistol only to discover it was gone.

Panic set in and put my head on a swivel. I had that creepy feeling you get when you know you're alone but feel someone or something watching you. I held my breath, but the room around me remained still. Finally, I remembered I'd stored it in the biometric gun safe beneath the bed, afraid to even have it within reach anymore.

I got down on my knees and slid the small black safe out from under the bed, then used my index finger to open the lock. The pistol's grip felt as cold as snow and almost as suffocating. Then the world flashed white and dropped me into a hole that never seemed to bottom out.

When my eyes opened again the white they saw was from the popcorn ceiling above my bed. I tried to rub my forehead but discovered my hands had been tied behind my back. My shoulders and biceps ached from lying that way for who knows how long. The room smelled like copper and urine, which explained the wet sensation I felt both in my hair and my jeans. I had no concept of how long I might have been out, only that I had been out, and anything might have happened in that gap without my consent.

Reality set in as I remembered where I was, and why. I heard voices talking in the next room but couldn't identify them. Panic hit me all at once and I began thrashing against my restraints. One of the voices must have heard the commotion because footsteps approached across the wood floor.

The door swung open and in an instant, all the pressure went out of the room. Our eyes met and Danny "Danimal" Simms flashed me an evil grin as if to say I told you we'd end up here sooner or later.

I tried to speak only to realize I'd been gagged.

I tried to use my tongue to push what felt like a bandana out, but it was tied so tight the skin at corners of my mouth started to split from the friction.

"See, I knew you been following me," Simms said. "And now I caught you."

I struggled to make sense of the statement. Why would I have been following him to my own house?

"You thirsty?" he asked, gesturing to a Dr. Pepper bottle on the nightstand.

Not knowing what else to say and wanting to get the gag off my mouth, I nodded.

"I figured. Here, I'll help you out."

I twitched a little as he approached the bed. He stroked my cheek with the back of his rough hand, then used it to palm my head to the side. He produced a serrated Case knife with his other hand, flipped the blade out, and casually brushed it along my neckline. "I was you I wouldn't move," he said. I expected the knife to plunge into my throat at any moment. I prayed to God or whatever made the universe go around to stay the blade, but help didn't come, just as I'd known it wouldn't. The knife sliced through the bandana's fabric with ease. Simms pulled the fabric away and I took a deep breath through my mouth. In all the panic I hadn't realized how little air I was getting, unable to breathe well through my nose due to face-planting my bicycle into a mailbox as a little girl.

I gasped, came very close to hyperventilating, then regained control of my emotions. I needed to use my head if I wanted to survive. And worse, my greater fear was starting to become what might happen instead of death. I focused on my breathing, relaxed my muscles as best I could before I spoke.

"Thanks," I said, my voice raspy and hollow.

"Don't speak too soon," he said, smiling as he swung his knee over my torso and mounted me like a horse.

He smelled like Axe body spray and the metallic odor mechanics and electricians carry home from their work. The way he positioned his weight made it hard for me to take a deep breath. "Now, how about that drink?" he said.

I watched from the corner of my eye as he picked up the Dr. Pepper bottle, unscrewed the cap, and dug in to clear his throat as deep as possible before dropping a long, sticky string of spit into the bottle.

"Don't act like I ain't never did nothing for you," Simms said.

I clamped my mouth shut and tried to turn my head to the side. He pressed the serrated blade to my throat, the knife's teeth digging into my skin. Warm blood trickled down my nape.

"Two choices, babygirl," he said. "You open your mouth or I open your throat. It don't make a whole lot of difference to me which one. We be waiting here for someone but it might make a better impression to see you all bled out when they come."

When I didn't move he let the knife's blade dig in a little deeper. The teeth sank deeper into my skin. If he cut much deeper he'd puncture my windpipe and I'd drown on my own blood. I had no choice.

I steeled myself against the disgusting sensation and opened my mouth.

The syrupy mixture of soda and spit fizzed as it hit my mouth. He poured it so heavy that it went straight down my throat. I choked and coughed and retched. Simms laughed and kept pouring. I was starting to worry I'd made the wrong decision and would rather have drowned on my own blood than his spit when he tipped the bottle back upright.

"Now, swallow," he said.

I moved to spit and he shook his head. "Swallow that, or you'll be swallowing something else, trust me."

I swallowed and applied every bit of self-control I've ever developed to keep from puking it right back up, fearing what he might do if I vomited on his expensive embroidered jeans and velour Sean Jean sweatshirt. Finally, I lost control, turned my head, and projectile vomited on the nightstand. Simms stood up off me on the other side of the bed and broke out in genuine laughter.

"Yo, that shit is fucked up," another voice said from beyond Simms, which I believed belonged to Evans.

Simms didn't respond. Instead, he prepared to repeat the process with another mouth full of spit into the bottle. I opened my mouth voluntarily this time, immediately started choking again as the liquid fizzed in my throat.

I coughed and choked to the brink of unconsciousness. With every heave, I felt blood spurting out of the wounds on my head and neck.

"Yo, look at her eyes bugging out," Simms quipped. I tried to focus my sight, but everything had a haze on it from the heaving. For a moment I forgot how I came to that place, or what had happened. I could only have told you my name two out of five times if you asked. I saw outlines of shapes, held together as fragments of reality in my consciousness.

"All right, enough fucking around, time to do a little business. That sound good to you, detective?"

It took a moment for me to realize he expected an answer.

"Yes," I managed.

"Yes," Evans mimicked.

They both cackled some more about that. Their laughter stirred up the fury inside me, but I kept a lid on it. I needed to buy some time, recover my wits from the blow to the head and avoid drowning on a cocktail of Dr. Pepper and psycho saliva.

If I was going to survive I'd have to harvest my emotion as raw energy. I'd have to be strategic about every move, or risk tumbling off the planet.

"I know that was you out at my farm the other day snooping around," Simms said. "Second time we seen you out there, too. Now my cousin locked up, probably gonna do some time over that bitch you was chasing. Even still I was gonna let that shit go, leave you alone. Bad for business. But we just keep running into each other, and I'm starting to feel like you want my attention."

I tried to make sense of what he was saying. They had come looking for me, not the other way around. Now they had me, and the best plan I could come up with was to stall until I could come up with something better.

"Okay, I'm going to tell you the absolute truth," I began, trying to calm myself in hopes it would slow the blood flow out of my wounds and bring some stability to my vision.

"I sure would, I was you," Simms said. "The answers you give gon bring consequences, I promise you that. Me and TJ, we be down to do some seriously fucked up gangster shit if we gotta, and I promise you'll tell the truth then. I'd come to Jesus first time out the gate on this, you feel me?"

I nodded as best I could, tried to look defeated. "I do. Really," I said. "I get the impression there might be some misunderstanding between us. Maybe we can clear it up before things get out of hand."

Evans burst out laughing. "Yo, he just about cut your throat and half drowned your ass with loogies and Dr. Pepper and now you worried 'bout shit getting out of hand? You got a little gangsta in you, I give you that." Evans doubled over but stopped laughing when he looked up to see Simms staring a hole through him.

"Lady got good instincts," Simms said. "I be just getting started with the out-of-hand shit. Now tell me, detective, why you fucking with me?"

I took the deepest breath I could and began. "The best answer is, I'm not. Not really," I said. "Our paths keep crossing because of the girl, Carmen Wallace. I followed her to your farm and anywhere else we've met. Her parents hired me because I'm good at helping troubled girls. They were worried about some stalking incidents involving Carmen. I didn't even have bad intentions for your cousin on what happened down in Austin. I was asked to find the girl and bring her home by her parents, and when I tried to do that, we had a scuffle, which I got the better of."

"That ain't the way I heard the story," Simms said. "I heard Carmen knocked your little ass out. Yo problem is you think you tough, but you ain't. Now you in here bullshitting, tryna act tough, but you got straight merked by a teenage girl."

My sight had focused back enough to glare at him, which I knew was a mistake but couldn't help. A better strategy would be to let him keep underestimating me, so I tried to settle into the role again. He kept grinning after I looked away, but something had changed in his eyes just before that.

In a split-second, he had his hand wrapped around my throat, crushing the windpipe and causing the cuts to tear deeper. I felt lightheaded almost immediately. Still, I resisted the urge to fight back, knowing he wanted information or entertainment, and not necessarily in that order. He would have to stop squeezing to get the first, and my silence would deprive him of the second.

What I didn't count on is that he would choke me all the way unconscious. As the lights faded I started struggling out of instinct, providing the entertainment he'd been seeking. Our eyes met for a half second and then he seemed to get sucked down a dark tunnel away from me, replaced by nothing but blackness.

I came to with a feeling of being trapped beneath the surface of my face, as if gradually sliding back into my body. Evans was laughing again when I opened my eyes. This time it must not have bothered Simms because he made no move to correct him.

"Yo, do it again," Evans said.

Simms locked his hand around my throat again and squeezed. This time I thrashed from the first touch, afraid to go back to that desolate headspace. He sat on my chest again and put his weight on me to keep me still. The darkness seemed to stretch on forever. I had the sensation of spinning, which eventually spun upward and thrust me back into consciousness. I heard a terrible gurgling sound, then realized it was coming from my own throat. The thought of drowning on my own blood was much worse than the alternative I'd considered earlier. I gagged, coughed, and turned my head to the side just enough to vomit what felt more like phlegm than bile.

And behind all of it, I heard both men's laughter. It had an undercurrent of superficial joy, the cackling of men as incapable of actual happiness as they were of any other emotion. Men like these only ever experienced rage, first as the receiver, then eventually as the owner. I hated them both at that moment. I hated whatever men and women had helped to create them, and whoever had failed to protect them.

Most of all, I hated myself for not being able to save Carmen Wallace from their destructive inertia. Men like these destroyed things because they could. They couldn't conceive of any relationship other than the parasitic kind. No telling what kind of mind games they'd played with her during the time she'd been entangled with them. And no telling what kind of games they had in store for me if I didn't figure a way out of this soon.

"Aight," Simms said, wiping my blood off his hand onto a sweater on my dresser. "Now that we through acting tough, how 'bout you tell me who you really working for?"

I wanted to shake my head, but the movement sent electric waves up my neck and another flow of blood down it.

"I'm telling you the truth, that's the best I can do," I said.

He shook his head as if I'd given a wrong answer again. I'd already learned the rules of the game. Wrong answers earned punishment. I prepared myself for another trip into my subconscious, but he made no move to choke me again.

"If that's the truth, then why you here now, following us?

I exhaled a large breath and sucked in a fresh one just in case.

"I didn't follow you here," I said. "This is my house. You came here looking for me."

Simms shook his head, but something resembling doubt registered on his face. "Bullshit," he said. "We here looking for someone, but it ain't you. Ain't that little girl, either, though she might be next."

"I doubt that," I said failing again to choose wise words. I studied his face as best I could without looking him in the eyes, which he seemed to take as a challenge.

"That right?" he said, leaning toward me. "Cause I be

happy to remind you."

"No need," I said, working to choose better words now. "What I mean is, Carmen Wallace is dead."

That gave him pause. "No shit?" he said.

"None at all."

"Damn. It must be my lucky day then. Especially with you showing up like a gift."

His words came into context all at once. No good investigator believes in coincidence, and yet it appeared that the NHB and I had landed in a coincidence neither of us would find easy to believe.

And worse, even if they believed the coincidence, I knew right away it would only make things worse. The truth seemed so obvious now that I could hardly believe I hadn't figured it out sooner. Though, of course, I'd had no information to go on. They were here for Chip, not for me. And if I had to guess, they'd run Marty's truck off the road, which would explain the damage I'd seen on Simms' Jeep.

"I think I know where we're misunderstanding each other," I said, my eyes tracking Simms as he walked around the room, opened a few drawers, and fumbled with the small tin of jewelry I kept on the dresser.

"I'm listening," he said. "For now. Best get to telling the real story before I think of something better you can do with your mouth." He turned his head toward Evans as if proud of his own rape joke.

The thought made me shiver. I'm not a sexual woman. I've never been, not really. The only man I'd ever been intimate with had been laid to rest that week, and part of me intended to keep it that way. I made up my mind right then to bite anything that came near my mouth, consequences be damned. Some things were worse than death, and I knew in my heart my pride would not survive such an experience.

My mother had always said pride was my greatest flaw. Pride and anger. I felt a mixture of both, which could get me killed. I choked them down into the bottom of my being, tried to sound calm when I spoke.

"You're here for my brother, not me," I said. His ears perked up like a dog's, and I knew I had both their attention then.

"Yeah? And who's that?"

"Charlie Reeves. You probably know him as Chip."

Simms and Evans exchanged a look that told me I was right. I pretended not to notice. Simms set down my jewelry box and moved back to the bedside. He put his left hand on my right thigh and ran the knife up my left leg toward my private region. The contact sent hot sparks through my nerves, like touching a door with a fire hidden behind it. I forced myself not to revile from it, not wanting to give him any more reason to hurt me, at least not yet.

"Brother, huh?" He traced a circle with the knife on my leg. "Sounds like bullshit to me."

I nodded. "I figured it would. You remember a couple nights ago when I came and got Carmen from your cousin's place?"

"Hell yeah, I remember."

"Well, then you also remember that I told you then I'd seen you outside my house, which you denied. You want, I can go to the window in the dining room and point out right where your Jeep stopped out there. Crazy as it sounds, we've got ourselves one hell of a coincidence here."

Simms clicked his tongue. "Could be. Or maybe the girl was just a cover for you to come after us for your brother. Me, I don't believe in coincidences. I think maybe you planned all this shit, and now you stuck cause we gonna fuck you AND your brother up. Which means it's time to stop playing around and find his bitch ass." He shifted his eyes to Evans. "Bring me them clippers from the bag."

Evans grinned and left the room, returned a few seconds later with a canvas backpack that sagged at the bottom as if it had something heavy in it. Simms took it and reached inside, came back with a set of pruning shears.

"Roll her on her side," he directed. Evans forced me on my side while Simms cut whatever had been used to restrain my hands. "Get her arm."

I didn't know what was coming but couldn't imagine it would be good for my health. As soon as the arm came loose, I yanked it away and swung for the fences, catching Evans with a glancing blow on the chin that ricocheted like a BB shot at a brick wall. His eyes went black with rage. Instead of attempting to get control of my arm now, he reared back and slammed his fist into my nose so hard that lightning flashed and blood squirted out like lava from a volcano. I had no time to react before he hit me four more times, just as hard.

I felt something collapse in my right cheek as the lights went dim for a moment. I tried to open my eyes and discovered I couldn't open my right one. I tried to reach for it out of instinct and felt two rough hands trap my arm. I had blood in both eyes, blood in my mouth, blood in my stomach. I struggled to push through it. I could just make out Evans holding my arm while Simms held what looked to be the pruning shears to my hand.

"Try that bullshit again and I let TJ beat you to death next time," he said. I felt my hands clench into fists, my natural response to danger. "Make her open that hand," Simms said to Evans like a doctor performing surgery. I tried to resist, but everything felt heavy and wet and sticky.

For a moment I couldn't remember where I was, again, what day it was, or what it meant to be a human being. My body had lapsed into survival mode, had very little left to give in the way of physical resistance. Evans forced a thumb into my palm and wrenched my fingers as if to either straighten them or break them off entirely. I broke in that second, could no longer muster the will to keep fighting. The world spun circles around me. It felt like I'd stepped off the planet and could only watch as it spun further and further out into space.

I wanted to pray, but no words would come. I wanted to scream, but no sound would come.

I wanted my father, but he'd been dead for years. And Benjamin, gone years before him. Poor Marty. Poor Carmen. Lord have mercy on anyone unlucky enough to have me land in their orbit. I brought death to everything around me except myself, and now I longed for it in some dark corner of my being. Craved it, even. I realized I no longer feared it. A small consolation, at least.

Simms took the pinkie finger on my right hand and

placed it between the blades of the shears. "You move, I chop them all. You don't, just one. You give bad answers, I chop. You don't tell me what I want to hear... I chop. Get it?"

I couldn't talk so I nodded that I understood. He squeezed the shears until I expected them to puncture the bone at any moment. I prayed in my heart for a quick and painless end, then threw it on top of a pile of unanswered prayers and accepted that God had abandoned us all.

"Now," Simms said. "Where's your bitch-ass brother?"

I tried to answer, but what came out sounded inhuman, like a foreign language predicated on gurgles and grunts. My inner voice screamed he was at the hospital, but my mouth refused to form the words. Warm tears streamed down the sides of my face.

"Aight, have it your way," Simms said. As the blade seared off the tip of my finger the sound of a siren pierced through the window, masking my agonized scream.

I would have laughed like a lunatic were such things still within my control. It felt like the whole finger was still there, but I could see part of it sitting on the floor. The siren outside the window had taken Simms and Evans' undivided attention then.

The sound was too deep and too slow for police sirens. It sounded familiar, but where had I heard it before?

A memory flashed through my head, of me and Chip and Benjamin, huddled in the bathtub of the Jack-and-Jill bathroom that connected our room, a flimsy twin mattress pulled over our heads.

It was a tornado siren, and the storm had to be close. I slowed my breathing to control the bleeding in my finger and neck. It was right about then that the windows started to vibrate and shake.

CHAPTER TWENTY-FOUR

THE WIND OUTSIDE HOWLED behind the siren's moaning. I wondered if I'd crossed over into a dream or found the centrifuge steps up into the afterlife. As my vision drifted in and out of focus I could see Simms and Evans staring at each other. Simms set down the shears to look out the window, which made his eyes go wide.

"Holy shit, dog," he said, "I think there's a straight-up tornado out there. And close."

In time to his words, the house began to shake. A rumbling like a train barreling down tracks filled the room.

With Simms and Evans distracted, I gathered my wits and the last of my strength. My hands were no longer tied, though I made sure not to draw attention to the fact.

"Yo, you remember what to do in a tornado?" Evans asked.

"Not really. Get under the desk or some shit, that's what we did at school."

The roaring grew louder.

The look on Simms' face was more confusion than fear. Evans walked out of the room as if looking for somewhere to go. Simms turned his back on me and opened the door to the bathroom, stuck his head inside. As soon as he did, I ripped myself up from the bed and sprinted for the door. As I hit the doorway, I met Evans coming in the other direction. He reached out for me, but too late. I slammed my forehead into the bridge of his nose. The crunch it made would have been satisfying under other circumstances, but all I felt was terror. Somewhere across the house, a window shattered.

Evans dropped to the floor as I burst out through the common area into the living room. The windows on the back of the house blew out like a shotgun blast, spraying glass all around me. I closed my eyes and ran into the kitchen out of memory. Benjamin and Chip and I had played a game as kids to see who could get across the house blindfolded the fastest. I'd always won, having a better sense of space than the boys. Back then my life hadn't depended on it, though.

Everything shook and roared and groaned. I was no longer worried about Evans or Simms. I was no longer worried about anything. Instinct took the wheel. I made my way out through the garage, was almost to the car when I came to understand I didn't have my keys. I tried not to look toward the sound, might have been saved by the blood in my eyes from falling into a paralyzing panic. I could hear it, and I could make out the shape, but had I seen the cyclone swirling fifty yards away I might have just sat down and let it take me.

Instead, I ran barefoot up the caliche rock road. The rocks tore into my feet like razors. I fell and got up, fell again, got up again.

In that moment I no longer felt separate from the things around me, just another pebble tossed around by the storm with all the others. I pounded my feet into the jagged rocks as I ran, just as Ben and I had run up that same road all those mornings as kids, back when the world seemed like a beautiful place that never took anything away from you.

I ran until a new sound invaded my ears. A car horn. The last thing I remember seeing was Latonya's round, terrified face clamoring out of the driver's side door of her car. The last thing I felt was her sturdy arms scooping me up and dragging me down into the ditch next to the elevated road, her weight landing hard on top of me as the world roared and churned all around us.

CHAPTER TWENTY-FIVE

THE NEXT THING I remember was a suffocating, heavy silence. Then the sudden sound of crickets. I sat up and rubbed my eyes, discovered that the right one had swollen shut. It took what felt like several minutes to bring my good eye into focus.

When it did, a stabbing panic came keyed in with it. L's motionless body was facedown a few feet from me in the ditch, which had several inches of water in the bottom. Her head was turned just enough to the side to keep her mouth and nose out of the collected water. A deep red gash traversed her normally smooth, ebony forehead just above her right eye. I sprang to my feet, then collapsed again as my right knee buckled. Pain pulsed up my leg straight into my brain. Something akin to the sound of metal grinding tore through my consciousness.

The throbbing pain in my head seemed to reset my nervous system all at once, brought back not only the memory of where we were but also the pain of my previous tortuous injuries with it.

I dragged myself through the mud like a soldier crawling in a foxhole, braced myself as well as I could on my knees, and checked L's pulse. It was strong, and I thanked a God I did not believe in.

"L," I said. "LATONYA. Can you hear me?"

I gave her a gentle shake. The look on her face said she might be sleeping, maybe even having a pleasant dream. She didn't move. I wanted to shake her again but decided against it, in case she'd injured either her neck or back.

As I contemplated what to do her eyes popped open, and the look on her face shifted from serene to terrified.

"L," I shouted. "Are you okay?"

Her eyes lost and then regained focus. She seemed to be getting her bearings, the same as I'd done. She started to sit up on her haunches, so I put my hand on her chest to ease her back down. She swatted it away without even looking at it.

"Girl, chill. I'm all right." She nodded as if to convince us both, then added, "That was absolutely the craziest shit that has ever happened to me."

This time I nodded. "Yes," I said, though maybe the same was no longer true for me. We stared at each other for a long time then, the way only two people with deep knowledge and understanding of each other can. She looked like she might laugh, or cry, or maybe couldn't decide.

As I studied her my eyes lost focus, and honed in instead on something beyond her.

The house.

The entire roof had been peeled off like the pull-top on the beer cans my father had drunk when I was a little girl, and it was ejected into the pasture. The brick structure itself seemed mostly intact, though all the windows no longer had any glass.

Behind us the highway had been bisected by the tornado's path. It had torn through the trees and cut across the back pasture straight to the house like a dually truck swerving to hit a squirrel.

That the structure had only lost its roof and windows was a small miracle. I was just getting ready to thank that God I didn't believe in when I noticed the smoke just behind the house, where the back porch would be. My first thought was the gas line for the grill.

The second was that Simms and Evans were still inside. I had no reason to believe they'd survived, but the structure had, so it was possible.

I tried to stand and had the same response as before from my knee.

"Girl, is you crazy?" L said. "Stay down, Ima find my phone and call for help."

I pointed over her shoulder. "The house is on fire," I said. "I think the gas line might ignite. We need to shut it off before it explodes."

L's eyes grew big and displayed a sense of disbelief I'd never seen in them before. "Riley, has you lost your mind? If that gas line catch it gon blow the house to high heaven, and us with it."

I knew she was right, but I also knew my friend well enough to know how to get her to help me anyway. I hated myself for the way I was about to manipulate her even as I knew I was going to do it anyway.

"There are men inside the house," I said.

"What?" she said, looking at me like I'd knocked every screw in my head loose.

"Two men from the case I was working, they were lying in wait for me when I got here." I paused, then corrected myself. "Or, not for me, actually, for Chip. It's a long story. They're the ones I was worried might come, the reason I had you stay away. They attacked me but I escaped and they're inside now. They could be alive."

A sadness washed over her face now, then something akin to a mixture of anger and determination.

"We cain't go in there. This the lowest you done ever sank, Riley," she said, standing up. "I don't know if I'm more disgusted that you don't really want to save those men, or that you just manipulating me so you can save the house."

"We can do both," I said, justifying it more to myself than to her. "If we turn off the gas before it catches, we can get inside and drag them to safety, then wait for help."

L just sighed, gave me the disgusted look again. "Like I said, lowest. We need to call for help."

"L PLEASE," I said, desperate now. "Half the county is calling for help right now, they'll never come in time to save them. Call help while we walk, but we need to get them out of the house NOW."

Her face went blank then. She used her right wrist to

wipe a stream of blood from her cheek, then looked at it almost in disbelief.

"Okay," she finally said. "But this the biggest line you ever crossed with me, I want you to know that now."

I nodded, having known it before I even asked.

"Let's go, then." She helped me to my feet and together we limped across the pasture, stumbling several times over debris and into imperfections in the pasture's surface. It seemed to take hours but could only have been minutes.

By the time we reached the house, I could see the flames coming from the area where the kitchen used to be. A small explosion rocked the house and we both dropped to the concrete. More flames rose from the kitchen area, and I knew we had very little time.

"We need to hurry," I said to L. I led her—or maybe she led me—to the main gas shutoff, near the back of the garage. I let L set me down while she turned the lever to shut the line off.

When it was done, she scooped me back up.

"Okay, we can go, now." I was satisfied now that some part of the house had a chance of surviving the flames. I started to pull in the direction we'd come from when L lifted me off my feet and tossed me over her shoulder.

"What the hell, L?" I said.

"You think it end just like that?" she said. "Like I'm just gon let you manipulate my compassion to get what you want and then leave them men in there to die like you really intended?"

I scrambled in my head for how to dissuade her from what I knew there was no stopping now.

"They tortured me, L," I said.

She looked away.

"LOOK AT MY FACE," I snapped, louder than I'd intended. "LOOK AT MY FINGER. It's not from the storm, it's from one of those psychopaths in there beating the living shit out of me. If they're alive and able, they'll try to kill us. If not, the world is better off without them."

She shook her head as if I'd failed her yet again. "It don't matter. You said we was gon save 'em, and now we gonna. You might not do what you say, but I do." There was not a hint of anger left in her voice as she continued. "We leave them in there after we come all the way over here just to save your idea of a home and we have nothing left. Yo folks raise you better than that, same as mine." She gestured to the house, then pointed a finger in my face. "We leave them there out of spite we might as well pick up where they left off, because we be torturing ourselves for the rest of our lives. At least I will."

She was right.

I knew it, and so did she. And yet the stubborn, vengeful part of me would not let it go. I hated these men. I wanted them to die a horrible death, had never cared for their well-being, only used them to manipulate the only person in the world who I could truly trust.

In that moment I knew that evil, the same evil that had tried to murder a neutralized Carl Farlow, the same evil I had stopped trusting with the responsibility of carrying a weapon, still existed inside me, waiting for the chance to manifest itself on anyone I deemed worthy.

To destroy.

I thought of a line I'd once read in a book my father

had given to me, though I could not recall it exactly. Something about the line between good and evil running through the heart of every man. It had always stuck with me, in part because I often wondered which side of the line I spent most of my time on.

I did know I landed on the wrong side of the fence and cattle guard, where L set me down and turned without a word to go into the house alone.

"L, wait!" I yelled, a little dizzy now, unsure if I was stuck in one of the nightmares that often kept me from sleep. I called again and she just kept walking. As she reached the garage I felt around me on the ground for something to use as a crutch. I found it in the form of a fence slat, realized that a portion of the fence had been blown away like leaves off a tree. I gripped the slat and jammed it into the ground, managed to get to my feet, and started a slow limp across the driveway into the house. Or what was left of it. As I entered, parts of the ceiling had simply collapsed, others been ripped away by the storm. I made my way among the debris through the hallway into what remained of the kitchen. I drew back at the heat coming off the burning cabinets, called out for L, but got no response. "L!" I called again.

The hairs on the back of my neck stood straight up, the same as they had just before the storm blew out the windows.

As I moved toward the living room my makeshift crutch set on something moveable and slid out all at once, dumping me to my knees. I cried out in unreal pain as my right knee hit, felt the cap move off to the side and knew I'd really done something awful and irreversible to it. I took a deep breath to calm myself and started choking on the acrid black smoke surrounding me. I considered giving up, just lying there and letting myself suffocate.

My instincts were having none of it. As I fumbled to regain the crutch my hand touched something warm and made of steel: the handle of a butcher knife.

I gripped it in my left hand and used the crutch to work to my feet in stages, my leg unable to support so much as a pound of weight. I moved again, even slower than before, into the fiery hell in front of me.

I felt the urge to call for L again and suppressed it. What remained of the furniture in the living room looked like someone had picked the house up and shook it.

I felt woozy again and had to stop, thought I might pass out from the smoke if I didn't get out of there soon.

He hit me all at once, his full weight slamming into my back and sliding down to my knees. I felt another pop inside my right leg and screamed, somehow managed to flatten the knife to my body so that I did not land on the blade. Then he was on top of me, his weight pressing my body flat onto my hand and the knife, pinning it.

"This where you gon die, bitch," Danny Simms growled into my ear. "Just like your friend."

Was he saying he'd already killed L? Anger sparked in my chest, caught fire in my veins. I forgot my leg, forgot the house, forgot Marty and Chip and everything that had happened, and focused on the knife. Clarity and purpose washed over me.

I was going to die here, that seemed to be true. BUT SO WAS HE.

I slammed my head into his face as hard as I could. The impact sent stars shooting through my field of vision.

Simms moaned and attempted to wrap his arm around my neck. I felt his weight come off me for a split-second. I rolled as best I could to my right, over the knife and onto my shoulder, finally freeing my right arm. Shock registered on his face when he saw the knife, then I buried it in his collar bone.

He pulled back as if to get away, but it was too late. I let go of the knife and left it in him as he pulled away. He tried to get to his feet, stumbled, and sat straight back onto his butt. He seemed to be trying to turn his head to look at the hilt but had apparently lost that motion from the damage.

I looked away as the blood poured out of him in a thick maroon stream.

"L!" I called out, then coughed and choked and had trouble even getting another full breath.

"L!" I managed one more time.

No response. I sat back and prepared to go unconscious, not seeing any other way out.

That's when I heard it.

"Riley?" L's voice said, louder than a whisper, but too strained to be full volume.

"I'm here," I said.

I heard shuffling and a dragging sound, then L's shape appeared from around the couch on her hands and knees.

"Are you okay?" I managed.

"I think so," she said. "That motherfucker snuck up on me and choked me unconscious. Can you stand?"

"No," I said. She didn't look like she could stand either. Until she did. Her big, strong legs wobbled, then caught, and in a few steps, she was above me, lifting me by the arm. I did my best to use my good leg to stand. My right leg flopped around at the knee now.

"Front door, behind me," I said, though she was two steps ahead of me and already dragging me under the armpits toward it.

I pushed with my left foot as best I could. She set me down to get the door open, then did her best to move my father's ancient NordicTrack out of the way so it would open. The rush of cool air would have felt great except it seemed to have a backdraft effect on the flames behind us. L grunted like a powerlifter, forced the door the rest of the way open, and snatched me up by my collar with one hand, pulling me out onto the porch, then into the yard. She stopped at the former fence line when she could go no further and dropped to her knees beside me. We sat there like that for a long time, choking and coughing and retching from the smoke and blood.

As we lay there, half dead, I reached out and took L's hand. She didn't pull it away, nor did she squeeze mine back. We sat there like that, silent, watching history burn away until the sound of a different kind of siren carried down to us from the highway.

CHAPTER TWENTY-SIX

THINGS HAPPENED FAST AFTER that. L and I were loaded into an ambulance. A neighbor had seen the house go down and called emergency services. At some point, they separated us and shot me up with something that put me in a daze.

Sometime the next day I woke up calling for L. A nurse, the same one who had approached me about Chip, came and calmed me down, assured me she was okay but that the police didn't want us having contact until they'd had a chance to speak to us both individually. As if on cue, Detective Howell replaced her in the room.

"They told me you were awake," he said as a greeting. "That is one hell of a mess out there at your place, Miss Reeves."

I tried to sit up and groaned.

"Don't sit up on my behalf," he said. "But I would like to get your account of what happened if you're up to it."

I'd been fading in and out of confusion since waking up an hour earlier. Still woozy from the drugs and nervous about seeing Latonya, I just started talking. I told him about the NHB, and Carmen, my theory that Simms and Evans had run Marty off the road, and why. I even told him about the illegal things like trespassing and assault I'd done while searching for Carmen. He nodded at each point to show he was listening, but his face showed nothing of what it made him think or feel. When I finished he sat back and considered it all for a long time.

"So?" I finally said. He hadn't used a recorder or taken any notes, which I wasn't sure how to take.

"So," he said, the contemplative look still on his face.

"So what do you think?" I finally asked again.

He sighed, folded his hands together and leaned forward with his elbows on his knees.

"I think the next time you tell that story you leave out all the trespassing and assault and just point out they came looking for Chip, found you instead. Clear cut case of self-defense. We already pulled a warrant for Simms' place and raided it. I'll make sure they take a look at the Jeep and see if we can connect it to the accident with your brother. Won't matter for Simms, but I'm not sure if you heard that they found Evans alive about a hundred yards from the house."

"How's that?" I said, a hint of disbelief in my voice.

"Must have gotten sucked up in the tornado and dropped on his head in the ditch. They're telling me he's paralyzed from the waist down but will survive. Not sure if it'll be permanent, but a man can hope."

I smiled in spite of my pain, again recognizing a kindred soul in Bill Howell. I lost the smile just as quick when I remembered what that said of the evil in my heart. I wondered if he struggled with it too. Bill Howell didn't come off as a man who struggled with much. I didn't ask.

We talked for a while longer and he told me he'd take an official statement from me in a day or two when I was on my feet, and to get the right version straight. When he left, I buzzed the nurse and begged her to either roll me into L's room or her into mine.

"Miss Johnson has already been discharged this morning," the nurse said. "I suppose she'll come by when she's ready, but she needs rest the same as you. I can bring your brother if you would like? He's been asking to see you."

I thanked her but declined, said I was too tired for him just yet. She nodded like she was too tired for him too, walked out of the room. I pressed the pump on my morphine drip and was back asleep in minutes.

CHAPTER TWENTY-SEVEN

TWO WEEKS LATER, MY homeowner's insurance had Chip and I set up in a Residence Inn south of town, off Broadway. Chip had been taking the opportunity to seek out the right combination of his medication and whatever alcohol he could get his hands on. We had barely discussed the house's destruction, but I already knew that rebuilding was out of the question. He would take his half of the structural replacement cost and fall down a bottle, most likely. That meant we would most likely just end up selling the land. It surprised me to realize the thought didn't hurt the way I would have expected. It seemed as though everything in my life had changed, but maybe I had needed the change.

Within a few more days, my pain pills had started to disappear. I would hardly take them, in spite of the surgeries on my knee and my pinky finger. I was finally able to get around on crutches a little, and Chip, though out of traction, used a wheelchair. I hadn't been to the office and had not worked at all since Carmen's death.

Which made it all that much harder to swallow that I hadn't heard from L since the day of the attack. Over slow, long hours alone I began to see more and more all the ways I had been a terrible friend. I could not imagine why she, or anyone else, would want me in their life. She hadn't answered any of my calls and wasn't staying with her parents, at least according to her mother, Bernice, who seemed anxious to get me off the phone when I called.

It appeared I'd finally destroyed our relationship for good, and I didn't even blame her. I'd put our lives in danger out of a selfish need to try and save my childhood home, which had burned to the ground anyway. Now I couldn't drive, which meant I couldn't work, and I had no prospects even if I'd been able.

That is until I got a phone call from Detective Howell telling me to check my front porch for some files he suspected could have found their way there.

"Told you I'd help if I could," he said. "The official department line is this file is closed, ruled a suicide. I'm sure you've seen LeeAnne Wallace all over the news screaming about murder, but no one is taking that seriously."

"I haven't seen, actually," I said. "But I've heard about it. I don't really watch a lot of TV."

I didn't mention that I'd been dealing with grief and guilt about Carmen so intense I could barely sleep, or that his mere mention of the case had awoken the obsession inside me again.

"I hear you," Howell said. "And by the way, this is all off the record, but if I was you, I'd take a good, close look at her medical history. It's in the alleged file, too. I'll never admit it came from me if someone catches you with it, so be careful."

My ears perked up at that. "Anything special I should be looking for?" I asked.

"I really couldn't say," he said.

"You mean won't say," I corrected.

"Maybe. Interesting pattern of treatment in there, though. Been to nearly every doctor on the planet, but not a single one of them is local to Smith County, and they never stayed with the same doctor or hospital for more than six months."

I wasn't sure exactly what he might be getting at, and it seemed out of an abundance of CYA he wasn't going to say it. I promised to take a thorough look, hung up, and spent the next sixteen straight hours looking at the file. As I went, I made a list of what I felt to be oddities, both in the autopsy and Carmen's medical records. Then I hobbled my way down to the front office, where I used an archaic fax machine to fax the records, and my concerns, to a former medical examiner I sometimes consulted on files, Dr. Quan Chu, in Nacogdoches. I used PayPal to send him payment for looking at it, then sat back into the quiet, monotonous nothing to wait.

I spent the next two days going stir crazy, feeling a mixture of aching regret and powerful relief that I had not died. I'd failed my client in every way. In the end, I'd failed even to figure out who had been harassing her.

Which is how I ended up sitting across the back seat of an Uber to keep my leg straight while they drove me to my office, where I retrieved my full file on Carmen.

That night I walked back through every single detail of the harassment. The more I turned it over, the more amateurish it felt. I had to agree with Deputy Bell, it had a childish, nonthreatening element to it. I couldn't see Simms and his psychotic bunch bothering with it, nor did I have any reason to think any of Carmen's scant peers might have been involved.

I was still turning it over in my head on no sleep the next morning when Dr. Chu's examination of Carmen's medical file popped up in my email. Before I could download his report, he rang my phone.

"Hey Quan," I answered.

"Riley, how are you holding up?" he asked.

"I've been better. What do you have for me?" I blurted out, far too anxious to consider making small talk.

"Right to the point," he said. "I get it."

"What did you think of the abnormalities I found?" I asked, cutting him off. I was grasping at straws, trying to make sense of the chaos.

"I mean, it's definitely weird that they went to so many different hospitals," he said. "But a lot of people think they know better than their doctors. That's the impression I get of the mother from the physician's notes about her."

"Yeah, she's a bundle of fun," I said. "But what does it mean?"

"I couldn't say. We're used to seeing addicts adopt this kind of care pattern. 'Doctor shopping,' as it's called. But it doesn't look like she was taking addictive or psychoactive drugs, other than the amitriptyline. Honestly, that's not the bizarre part anyway."

"Oh"?" I said.

"Oh is right. She had abnormal levels of lead in her system, according to the autopsy. Maybe the medical examiner didn't know what to make of it since it isn't the cause of death, but if I'm her doctor, I'm wanting to know how it got there."

"I see," I said. "Do you think it had anything to do with what happened to her?"

"I mean, I don't see a direct link. But I will tell you something you may not realize."

"Please do, this is all way out of my wheelhouse."

"Lead poisoning can have similar symptoms to those of acute intermittent porphyria. Given its presence and some other abnormalities in her diagnosis, I don't trust the diagnosis at all. It looks to me like her exposure to lead over time is the cause of her symptoms. In that sense, she may be better off dead.

"Had it continued she was in for some really painful experiences and terrible death. Not that this one could have been pleasant."

I didn't know what to say to that. I tried to fit it into my immediate understanding of the case but couldn't. I thanked Quan for his time and dug back into the file from the beginning. Except this time I decided to focus on her diagnosis and all those related items. I wasn't sure what I expected to find but figured it could be a potential path to new information.

Sometime around midnight, fearing I'd hit bedrock on this hole, I threw up a desperation shot and began Googling her medications and supplements.

One of them, a Chinese herbal supplement called Herbal Mood, had been banned from import to the United States for several years. I found the reason shocking—Herbal Mood had been discovered to be tainted with lead, one of a host of supplements with this same problem.

I checked back through the hospital records and discovered that a doctor had brought this to LeeAnne's attention at some point, but the file didn't say what her response was, and Carmen never saw that doctor again after.

A theory began to form in my mind, though the thought of it made me sick to my stomach. I decided to follow up with the Wallaces, share with them what Dr. Chu had helped me find, and see what they thought. Or, rather, how they reacted.

I contacted Paul Wallace and got permission to stop by and share with them the new information, which I purposely didn't elaborate on.

We agreed on six p.m. so I showed up at five-thirty to catch them off guard. The Uber driver, an older man driving for fun in his retirement, was nice enough to help me to the door and wait until they let me inside before he left.

"I was so sorry to hear about the attack," Paul said. "It's been hard for us accepting that Carmen was tied up with people like that."

"They MURDERED her," LeeAnne broke in. "Those savages murdered my baby and you did nothing to stop them. I knew we should have hired a man, but no one would listen to me. Now she's dead and her blood is on both of your hands." Her eyes stabbed into me and then Paul, then back into me as she spoke. I took a deep breath, tried to write it off as a mother's grief, but could not.

If my theory was true, I owed her nothing but ire. I decided to get to it.

"Don't speak too soon, Mrs. Wallace," I said, "I've been doing more digging, and I think I came up with something you'll both want to see."

Paul looked hopeful, his wife doubtful. Before either could say anything, I continued.

"Is Carmen's room still the same as it was before she died, by chance?" I asked.

"I—Yes, it is," Paul said. "Why do you ask?"

"I have a theory, but I need to see something in her room to confirm it. Only, as you can see, I can't get up the stairs."

"What is it you want to see?" LeeAnne demanded.

"A few things, actually. But, first things first." I shifted my focus to Paul. I needed him to retrieve the item because it would give me some idea of how much he knew. "Paul, could you bring down Carmen's basket of pill bottles and supplements, please?" I said. I tried to sound like it wasn't a big deal.

LeeAnne stood up as if to stop him. "What's this about?" she demanded. "I personally oversaw every single medication Carmen took. I can answer any questions without the bottles."

"That's good," I said, "because I'm afraid I'm much less knowledgeable than you about them. Why don't you and I chat while Paul runs and grabs them. I need someone who knows what they're talking about to fill me in."

LeeAnne nodded, an odd look of pride and desperation smeared across her mascara-stained cheeks. Paul went up the stairs to get the bottles.

"Now I demand you stop beating around the goddamn bush and tell me what all this has to do with Carmen's death," LeeAnne hissed as her husband rounded the corner at the top of the stairs.

"Working on it," I said. "So Carmen mentioned she takes a lot of supplements in addition to her medication, in order to stave off side effects."

LeeAnne rolled her eyes. "They're for more than that. Because of her condition she had a lot of deficiencies. I spent hundreds of hours researching her every need. The damn doctors ought to have been asking me how to help her after a few years, because they were all but useless, every single one of them. I am... I mean, I was, her mother. No one loved her more than me." Tears began to pour out of her eyes, flowing down the mascara lines as if they were channels cut into her cheeks. She reached for a Kleenex on the table as Paul came back down the stairs with a basket of pill bottles in his hands. At the sight of him, she broke into a hysterical sort of sobbing that seemed genuine but still struck me as odd, almost as if it were for his benefit somehow.

Paul handed me the basket and sat down to comfort his wife, who all but collapsed into his arms. I sifted through the basket until I found the bottle in question. I held it up for them to see, watching their faces for a reaction. Paul looked puzzled, but his wife's face hardened at the sight of it.

She started to say something but I cut her off. "LeeAnne and I were just talking about how much research she did finding medicines and supplements for Carmen," I said.

He cradled his wife and said, "Of course. I told you before, no one has done more or given up more for Carmen than LeeAnne. She spent years finding the exact combination of supplements to help Carmen."

As I spoke I paused upon recognizing several other labels in the basket, all of which had been known to contain elevated levels of lead contamination. I knew then that my theory was right, and I hated LeeAnne Wallace for it.

I tried to quell the anger welling up inside of me by taking a deep breath but could not. Finally, I went on, but my voice had taken a hard tone of its own by then.

"It seems to me you have that backward, Paul," I said. "The way I've come to understand it, no one did more for LeeAnne than Carmen." I let it hang in the air. It didn't hang long, shot down by a gasp and a hiss from LeeAnne.

"How DARE you," she screeched. She tried to come at me off the couch but her husband restrained her. "Let me go, you son of a bitch," she screamed at him. She gnashed her teeth and tried to bite him, but he wouldn't release her. "I think it's time for you to go, Miss Reeves," he said. "It's starting to seem like LeeAnne was right, hiring you was a mistake."

"I'll be happy to go," I told him. "But don't you want to know what I uncovered first?"

He looked sick, and I hated treating him that way. His reactions had all been genuine as far as I could tell, which left me certain he had not known what was happening, or why. I decided to fill him in while I still could.

"This stuff," I began, holding up the bottle of Herbal Mood, "this highly researched, provided with love, supplement your wife has been giving your daughter for years, has been banned in the U.S. since 2011.

"You see, it contains elevated levels of lead, which can be dangerous. In fact, looking over this basket, I see at least two other bottles banned for the same reason."

Paul took that in, then shrugged. "LeeAnne wasn't about to let the cronies and crooks up at the FDA tell us how to care for our daughter. If she was giving them to Carmen, she had a good reason"

I nodded. "I'm sure we agree on that," I said with as much compassion as I could muster. "Except its import wasn't banned because it was experimental, or because it didn't meet some nominal FDA guidelines. It was banned because it has dangerous levels of lead in it. If you Google it, hundreds of articles on the subject appear immediately. In fact, they're the top results. Which is why your daughter's autopsy showed she had dangerous levels of lead in her system."

LeeAnne began struggling to get up again, and Paul had to shift his weight on top of her to keep her down. She'd stopped ranting and was now resorting to snarls and kicks. It took three more minutes before he could get her still so I could continue.

"I don't understand," he finally said, breathing hard from the struggle.

"I know you don't. But I do. I know who was stalking your daughter, and I know why. But most important of all, I know who killed her."

LeeAnne's eyes went wide and still and almost catatonic. Paul sat up, suddenly beyond interested in what I might say next.

"Who?" he said when I didn't continue right away. "For the love of God, tell me who killed my daughter."

I took a deep breath and sent the words out into space, words that could never be taken back.

"Your wife killed her." LeeAnne was catatonic, appearing to have checked out of reality altogether, either as a defense mechanism or as an act.

"That's impossible," he said. "Are you suggesting LeeAnne forced Carmen to take an overdose of pills? What the hell is wrong with you?"

"I'm suggesting she might as well have," I said. "And nothing's wrong with me. I can't say the same for your wife, though." I stared at LeeAnne's glazed over eyes as I spoke, daring her to try to stop me, to look at me, to do anything, but she didn't move.

I continued. "Your wife knew what those pills would do to your daughter before she ever ordered the first bottle. Because she wanted it. She said so herself, she was a voracious researcher when it came to Carmen. Your daughter wasn't sick, it was your wife who was sick, poisoning her daughter so she could harvest sympathy at church, at home, everywhere she went. Playing the worn down, obsessive mother willing to go to any lengths to fix a child she was the one breaking in the first place. It's called Munchausen's by proxy. LeeAnne's condition, not Carmen's. Carmen's only fatal condition was trusting a mother who was hurting her out of a combination of narcissistic jealousy and a sick need for attention."

Paul's face looked shocked, then horrified. Anger filled the room when he spoke.

"That's absurd. You're out of your goddamned mind, coming into my house and throwing accusations around that way. I'll ruin you in this town, do you understand me?" He shook a finger at me as he spoke. "I am going to destroy you, guaranteed. I might even find a way to bring you up on fraud charges for the way you've handled our case."

I shrugged and worked my way to my feet, my leg throbbing as I moved. "Believe what you want. I can prove it, or near enough to bring about an investigation, maybe have your daughter's body exhumed, whatever it takes.

"I have no doubt that with more investigation I can prove your wife was climbing out her window to knock on Carmen's, putting notes on her car, painting the windows. That's why you could never catch the perpetrator, they were never on the ground in the first place. The game cameras were disappearing because she knew where they were, and how to approach them unseen. The boogie man doesn't live next door, he sleeps under your roof."

The room went silent when I finished my rant, LeeAnne still catatonic, Paul unable to move, the unmistakable look of realization on his face. Maybe he'd suspected that all along, or maybe it was news to him. He must have at least been coming to understand why LeeAnne had been so against hiring me. He let go of her and stood up. She seemed to snap back into reality all at once as he did.

"Paul, please," she squealed through more tears. "It's not true. Of course, you could never believe this kind of nonsense. Tell her we'll sue her into bankruptcy. Or get a restraining order."

Her husband turned his back on her, unable to look at her now. I moved into position and made LeeAnne look at me then. "Look at me, LeeAnne, because this is the last time you and I are ever going to speak," I said. "I want you to understand something." I paused, staring into her eyes and trying to convey my rage when what I wanted to do was beat her to death.

"Carmen took her own life to get away from you," I said. "She died because she decided that no future was better than a future under your thumb, and you were never going to let her go. She obviously knew you were poisoning her and trying to scare her into staying here. She had stopped taking the pills, that's why her symptoms abated. I should have figured this out sooner, but there it is.

"Now, I'm leaving. I'm going to turn this over to the sheriff's office, see what they can do. It won't be much, because Carmen is dead, and you weren't physically involved in her suicide. But you and I will always know the truth, won't we? That you killed your daughter, consumed her to fill your own inadequacy a piece at a time until she didn't know who she was, or where she could go to get away from it. From you. The day you die you'll know it's true, and may God forgive you then, because I never will."

I crutched my way out the door into the night without another word, leaving them alone together to sort out their differences. An Uber arrived five minutes later, and I cried the whole ride back to my hotel. The driver never said a word, maybe knowing there's nothing you can say to a person feeling like that.

EPILOGUE

I STEPPED OUT OF my office to load the last box of files into the back of my Pilot and found Latonya leaning against the bumper, a purple suitcase next to her feet.

I felt the electric warmth of love radiating out from my heart. L cracked half a smile, then suppressed it. I noticed the new scar on her forehead and that made me look away. I had a few new scars of my own.

I'd been off crutches for about a week, was probably pushing the limits of recovery, but that's always been who I am, for better or worse.

I set the box down and turned to lock the door to my office for what might be the last time. I put the key in a lockbox the realtor attached to the outside, then picked the box back up. As I did, the cardboard brushed against my healing pinky finger, reminding me of how much I had lost, and how much of myself I still had left to find. Latonya was still standing in the same position when I turned back toward the car.

"So you just gon play it cool, huh?" she said as I approached.

"Who's playing it cool?" I replied, knowing I was but not wanting to concede the point.

"That really all you got to say?"

I set the box down next to the car and faced her. "No, of course not," I said. She cut me off.

"Girl, don't even start. You know I just be messing with you. Don't anybody need one of them sad-ass excuses for an apology you be handing out twice a year like they a gift. Now get over here." She reached out and pulled me in slow, accounting for the brace still on my knee.

We hugged for a long time, and I started to cry. Which, of course, made me angry. As much as I'd learned in recent months, I still hated to show weakness in front of others.

When we let go of the hug, Latonya was crying too. "I'll show you how to really do it," she said. "Girl, I'm so sorry for ignoring you like I been. I was mad you almost got us both killed. I'd have helped them men if you'd meant what you said. Not because they deserved help, but because you needed to do it. I finally come to realize you can't help this obsession with yo work, just like I can't help that I love you like I do."

I wiped away some tears. "I love you too, L," I said. "And I'm so, so sorry. For everything. I know how hard this has been on you, and it's all my fault."

"Forget it. We done with it now. You want to make it better, tell me where we goin'?"

"What do you mean, *we*?"

"Where do *we* be going? You all packed, I'm all packed, I know we going somewhere."

"Dallas," I said, smiling again. "For now. At least I am."

"I feel like you ain't listening to me," L said. "I been thinking. Without me, you probably would have died out there in that storm."

"True," I said.

"Right. And, you still planning on doing all this secret agent P.I. stuff, right?"

"I am."

She nodded. "Then it's settled. I don't want you to die, but you seem determined to die anyway. So I ain't got no other choice."

"Other choice than what?"

"Than to become yo' partner, go where you go, and make sure you don't die out here tryna save the world."

L was my best friend, and the only person I knew as stubborn as I was. We belonged together, I knew it in my heart.

"I see," I finally said through the tears. "It seems like I have no other choice then."

"About what?"

"About selling you half of my business. I've got a price in mind, and I think it's fair."

L gave me her skeptical face.

"Girl, just say what the hell you gon say already, this suspense always be killing me, we gon have to work on that."

"You got a dollar?" I asked.

"Of course, why?" She pulled a mess of crumpled bills

out of the front of her capri-style blue jeans.

"Great. Let me have it, please," I said.

She handed a folded dollar bill to me.

"Congratulations, you're now a fifty percent owner of the Riley and L Detective Agency. I look forward to working with you, *partner*."

L's laugh was one of the loudest I'd ever heard from her. We hugged again, cried some more, and then she helped me load the last of our stuff into the back of the Pilot. If we left soon, we might even beat the traffic coming into Dallas.

ABOUT THE AUTHOR

Michael Pool is the author of thrilling crime, mystery, and detective novels. Michael's stories are crafted from real-life experiences, many from his full-time work as a private investigator.

Michael lives and writes in Denver, Colorado, where he investigates real mysteries by day, practices martial arts by night, and roams the countryside in his trusty home away from home, *Vancy Pants*. Find him online at www.michaelpool.net.

ABOUT P.I. TALES

P.I. Tales chronicles modern detectives investigating the modern world with all its technological, sociological, and psychological obscurities. The crimes are the same as ever, it's only the details surrounding them that have changed.

Our goal is to pay homage to the great detectives of the "Golden Age" while adding to that tradition a new generation of modern (and maybe even future) detectives investigating the contemporary world.

P.I.s are the ultimate unsung heroes. Down these mean streets they must go with no legal authority, no official resources, and no one to rely on but themselves (and a few databases, or maybe the pistol in their pocket).

The greatest private detectives balance the scales of justice without bowing to authority or losing themselves in the process. They play by their own rules and make their own luck. Most of all, they follow a moral code exclusively their own...

P.I. Tales is the home of the modern P.I. mystery. We are proud to present to you a new generation of classic detectives. Our goal is to entertain and enlighten with each tale we tell. We dare you to stop turning the pages.

To keep up to speed on our latest investigations, get early access to the next Riley Reeves mystery, as well as receive special offers and exclusive content, log onto www.pitales.com.

If you enjoyed *Throwing Off Sparks*, please take the time to support us by reviewing it on Amazon, Barnes & Noble, Goodreads, or wherever you get your books.

Reviews are crucial to spreading the word about our books.

Thank you for reading!

Printed in Great Britain
by Amazon